The
Rug Merchant

The Rug Merchant

A Novel

Meg Mullins

Viking

VIKING
Published by the Penguin Group
Penguin Group (USA) Inc., 375 Hudson Street, New York, New York 10014, U.S.A. •
Penguin Group (Canada), 90 Eglinton Avenue East, Suite 700, Toronto, Ontario,
Canada M4P 2Y3 (a division of Pearson Penguin Canada Inc.) • Penguin Books Ltd,
80 Strand, London WC2R 0RL, England • Penguin Ireland, 25 St. Stephen's Green,
Dublin 2, Ireland (a division of Penguin Books Ltd) • Penguin Books Australia Ltd,
250 Camberwell Road, Camberwell, Victoria 3124, Australia (a division of Pearson
Australia Group Pty Ltd) • Penguin Books India Pvt Ltd, 11 Community Centre,
Panchsheel Park, New Delhi – 110 017, India • Penguin Group (NZ), Cnr Airborne
and Rosedale Roads, Albany, Auckland 1310, New Zealand (a division of Pearson
New Zealand Ltd) • Penguin Books (South Africa) (Pty) Ltd, 24 Sturdee Avenue,
Rosebank, Johannesburg 2196, South Africa

Penguin Books Ltd, Registered Offices: 80 Strand, London WC2R 0RL, England
First published in 2006 by Viking Penguin, a member of Penguin Group (USA) Inc.

1 3 5 7 9 10 8 6 4 2

Copyright © Meg Mullins, 2006

Photo of Moustasha Kashan Carpet (Persian) courtesy of Art Resource, NY.

PUBLISHER'S NOTE: This is a work of fiction. Names, characters, places, and
incidents either are the product of the author's imagination or are used fictitiously,
and any resemblance to actual persons, living or dead, business establishments,
events, or locales is entirely coincidental.

LIBRARY OF CONGRESS CATALOGING IN PUBLICATION DATA
Mullins, Meg.
The rug merchant / Meg Mullins.
p. cm.
ISBN 0-670-03481-9
1. Immigrants—Fiction. 2. Iranian Americans—Fiction. 3. Women college
students—Fiction. 4. Rug and carpet industry—Fiction. I. Title.
PS3613.U454R84 2006
813'.6—dc22   2005042405

Printed in the United States of America
Designed by Nancy Resnick

for Brad, from the beginning . . .

The
Rug Merchant

One

Ushman Khan doesn't like tourists. It is June, though, and tourist season in New York, and, as he double-parks his van outside Mrs. Roberts's apartment building, they are everywhere. Dressed in T-shirts and sandals, fancy cameras dangling from their necks, they run for awnings and bus stops as a hard rain begins to fall. Watching the chaos, Ushman smiles. He holds a newspaper over his head and, nearly dry, makes his way through the crowd.

Mrs. Roberts's maid comes to the door, letting Ushman into the cool, dark apartment. The girl is young and squat and motions for Ushman to follow her into the den. He has been here before and walks silently through the expansive apartment. In nearly every room there is a rug from his small showroom on Madison Avenue. They are comforting to him, each one reminding him of his wife. She is still in Tabriz, where she selects and commissions hand-knotted wool and silk carpets and woven kilim from the women in the bazaar and private workshops. Every month she ships two or three rugs to Ushman with a note that reads, *Sell, Sell, Sell, Your Wife, Farak.*

Last year, when Mrs. Roberts and her husband moved across the park, she commissioned Ushman to cover all the floors in the new apartment. The job enabled Ushman to absorb the increase in the rent for his shop and nearly double his inventory, but he never liked being in Mrs. Roberts's apartment, with its high, echoing ceilings and drafty, perfumed air. And she had not been easy to please. Ushman must have hauled two dozen rugs into and out of the apartment after Mrs. Roberts had lived with them for a few days only to find their colors too muted, too bright, or just wrong. On these occasions, she seemed perversely pleased, as if she enjoyed finding flaws. And then, when Ushman rolled out the rug that was eventually to stay, Mrs. Roberts would appear in the doorway grimacing. Ushman, sweating and impatient, would ask, "Not this one, either?"

She'd bite her bottom lip and place both hands on her hips. Then, as she turned away, she'd say, without looking back, "It's perfect. It stays."

After he'd finished the project, Mrs. Roberts still kept in touch. Often, she would come by the shop with a friend of hers, winking at Ushman as the other woman knelt to admire an expensive silk. Or she would call, asking about a rug's origin or care or something else that Ushman knew was on the appraisal documents he'd given her. This persistence made him anxious, made him think that maybe she would try to say he had cheated her or been dishonest. So, when Mrs. Roberts called this morning and asked him to come to the apartment right away, Ushman felt nothing but dread.

He waits for her in the den watching the rain fall in a dark haze over the park. It is an unusually cold day for late June and Ushman shivers, even in long sleeves. From a bedroom off the den, Mrs. Roberts appears just as Ushman is looking at his watch.

"You have somewhere to be," she says, more of a statement than a question.

"Yes, hello. An appointment." Then, with a gesture he learned from his father, Ushman raises his eyebrows and extends his arms toward her as if he were displaying a precious object. "But what may I do for you?"

Mrs. Roberts looks past him, out the window. "It's a terrible day to be working, Ushman," she says.

Ushman lowers his eyes, fiddles with the keys in his pocket. "You're right, a terrible day," he says.

Mrs. Roberts looks down at her feet. "I have grown a distaste for this rug," she says, walking across the center of it. "I want another."

Ushman smiles, tries hard to hide his irritation. "It's been over three months, Mrs. Roberts. The trial period is finished. You own the rug now."

"Oh, for goodness' sakes, I know that. I don't want a refund, Ushman. This one will go to my niece, I think." She turns to look at the closed door from which she came, listens for a moment, and then turns back to Ushman. "But," she says, pacing the length of the rug, "I wanted to remind you of the space so you could pick out an appropriate few and show them to me."

Ushman nods, but cannot contain his disapproval. The royal blue and red silk from Karaja truly belongs in the room. As any good rug should, it makes the room appear bigger, warmer, more textured. But, most importantly, it gives the room weight.

"This rug, though, in this room, I have never seen a more perfect match . . ." he begins.

Mrs. Roberts waves her hand at Ushman, signaling for quiet.

She turns her head again toward the closed bedroom door. Ushman hears it just as she does—a dull thud, followed by a thin, scared voice calling for help. Mrs. Roberts places her hand on her chest, as if she were trying to keep something in place. Ushman watches her jog awkwardly to the door, pull it open wide, and kneel next to a figure who is lying, nearly motionless, on the floor by the bed. He must have fallen out, Ushman thinks and is startled by this part of Mrs. Roberts's life. He had always known of Mr. Roberts's existence, but not of his condition. He had assumed that her husband was simply uninterested in domestic issues like rugs. Mrs. Roberts lifts her husband's head into her lap, but he is still calling for help, his voice full of panic.

"I'm here, I'm here," she says, and in one motion rings a small brass bell by the nightstand, turns on the oxygen compressor, and positions the mask over the man's nose and mouth. The young maid comes running through the den, past Ushman, and kneels next to Mrs. Roberts.

Ushman watches the two women as they try to negotiate the man back into bed. Not sure if he should look away in respect for their privacy or eagerly volunteer to help, Ushman approaches quietly. Standing in the doorway, he sees that the man is white-haired, pale, wearing navy silk pajamas that are wrinkled and twisted around his long, thin frame.

"I think we need his help," the maid says, gesturing toward Ushman.

Mrs. Roberts looks up at Ushman, her face flushed and tense. Ushman steps forward.

"Please, then," she acquiesces, moving away from the man's head. "My husband," she says, absently watching Ushman slide his arms beneath the man's armpits and lift him back onto the bed, the maid holding his feet.

"Who's this?" Mr. Roberts says, pulling the oxygen mask away for a moment.

Mrs. Roberts strokes the hair away from his temples. "This is the rug merchant, sweetheart," she says quietly.

Mr. Roberts looks at Ushman, his thick white eyebrows raised in comprehension. "Ushman," he says, closing his eyes, a brief smile crossing his lips.

"That's right. Ushman is going to find us another beautiful rug, sweetheart," she says, carefully pronouncing her words. There is little about Mrs. Roberts or her life that Ushman understands.

Mrs. Roberts stands, showing Ushman out of the room. She is composed again and all business. "Until tomorrow, then," she says, smoothing her hair into place. Ushman nods and closes the door.

The rain passes momentarily, but the afternoon remains cold and dark. Ushman drives through the park, feeling as though he's seen something he shouldn't have. He had been grateful for Mrs. Roberts's formality, ushering him out quickly, the look in her eyes assuring him that she would not want to speak of this again, that he should not have been witness to any of it. Ushman thinks of her husband's body, so small and weightless in his arms, and shudders realizing what he had been trusted with, if only for a moment.

Witnessing the interaction between Mrs. Roberts and her

husband reminds Ushman of his last days in Tabriz, before he came to America. He would stand and watch, through the ajar bedroom door, hoping to catch a glimpse of Farak's hands as she bathed his mother. Silently stroking a washcloth up and down a limp leg, Farak would not acknowledge Ushman, even if she saw him. She would simply squeeze the dirty water out the open window and start on the other leg.

Ushman could not see his mother's face, and should not have even seen her feet, bare and twisted. But as Farak worked her hands over his mother's body, conceding gracefully to her sharp demands, Ushman kept watching, hoping for a look of clemency from Farak as she scrubbed and wiped.

He merges into traffic on the Queensboro Bridge, not having felt so alone since his first days in America. He was living with his cousin in Howard Beach, across the expressway from Kennedy Airport. The roar of jets startled him at first—picture frames and ashtrays buzzed against tabletops like the beginnings of an earthquake. On the small balcony the three rugs Farak had sent him were wrapped and huddled like refugees and Ushman had wondered if coming to America was the right thing. He missed Farak and worried that he would not be successful.

Each day had been the same and each day he cringed to think of Farak seeing him this way: riding the A train, passing out business cards that read *carpet merchant* under his name, passengers mistaking him for a beggar and offering him change. Then one day he sold the first kilim to an Italian man for five thousand dollars. He counted the hundreds over and over and wished he could take Farak to the big department store on Fifth Avenue and let her pick out a dress or some jewelry. He begged Farak to come then, to bring his invalid mother with her and move into the small apartment he'd found in Flatbush. But she told him she would not come until it was a better life than in Tabriz, where the money he sent them bought fresh vegetables, black-market stockings, and all his mother's medications. Then last year, when he'd done the job for Mrs. Roberts and could promise Farak a two-bedroom apartment in Manhattan, she'd told him she still wasn't sure that America was the place for her. Ushman was beginning to understand, though, that it was not the country, but Ushman himself with whom she wasn't sure she belonged.

Yesterday Ushman delivered a privately owned carpet to his shop for inspection, and has decided to buy it for twelve thousand dollars. In his shop, Ushman knows, he can sell the rug for nearly twenty. The owner, a retired military man, lives in Jackson Heights. He told Ushman he brought the rug back from Germany. Ushman has a cashier's check in his satchel and the rug in the back of his van. With private owners, Ushman does not bargain. If the man will not accept the twelve thousand, he will give him back his rug and drive away.

As he turns the corner onto the man's block, Ushman notices a single ambulance, its lights flashing brightly against the dullness of the day. Approaching the house, he sees a stretcher being carried out of the same front door from which Ushman took the kilim yesterday. There is a figure on the stretcher, but it is covered by a thick white sheet. Ushman parks the van across the street and watches the paramedics load the stretcher, turn off the flashing lights, and drive away.

There is a young man standing in the yard next door, smoking a cigarette. Ushman gets out of his van and asks the man what has happened.

"Heart attack. Quick and brutal," he says, snapping his fingers loudly, "like that."

"I'm so very sorry," Ushman says, backing away.

The young man shrugs, stamps out his cigarette. "Didn't know the dude," he says, and turns to go inside.

Ushman sits in his van with both the money and the rug, his feet tingling. He cannot believe this turn of events, his good fortune. The man lived alone, probably has children living in another state who are just now being lifted by the gentle roar of a jet, and whose last concern will be a rug of which even their father didn't realize the value.

Impulsively, he drives away, back across the Queensboro Bridge, remembering the makeshift stretchers that his neighbors had made out of the kilim, and how, that day two and a half years ago, he found Farak, still crouched, afraid to move, and bloodied when he finally rode back into Tabriz. Feeling as though it were that day again, and as though now he might be able to change that day's events, he drives even faster.

Farak had had her fifth miscarriage early that morning, just before the earthquake. When the house began to shudder Farak knelt in the bathroom doorway, already weeping, and watched the roof crumble on either side of her. Ushman's mother was in bed still, and her spine was crushed beneath the weight of the dirt roof.

Ushman had been in Karaja, a small mountain village near Tabriz that has no road access, where he ran another small workshop. He had two Karaja rugs tethered to his saddlebags and was descending the mountain when the camel stopped and sat down.

Hours later, when Ushman found his damaged house and saw Farak so bloody, he was afraid that she had been badly hurt. She was crying, though, and he knew that was a good sign. But as he held her to him, dragging her out of the rubble, he understood that beneath her whimpers, she was saying, *The baby, the baby.*

Kneeling in front of a loom for all of her childhood, at the demands of Ushman's father, had misshaped Farak's pelvis so badly that doctors told her a baby's skull would be crushed if she attempted a vaginal childbirth. Farak had accepted this fact, but so far she had not even been able to carry a fetus past the first trimester. Though the doctors could offer no medical explanation for this, Farak insisted it must have the same cause as her misshapen pelvis.

More than thirty-five thousand people were killed in the earthquake, and Ushman wanted to blame the miscarriage on it as well.

"No," Farak said as they stood over his mother's hospital bed, "it happened before the earthquake."

"We will try again," Ushman said, placing his hand on Farak's back.

"It's no good, Ushman. I will lose the baby each time. Don't make me lose another one to prove it to you," Farak said, and lowered her head.

Ushman spent the week before they brought his mother home from the hospital rebuilding his own roof. Both of Ushman's workshops were destroyed and four of his weavers were dead. There was no electricity, so Ushman spent the evenings lying in bed, hoping Farak would understand that the miscarriage was his sorrow, too. But she would come in late from speaking with neighbor women in the courtyard, and take

Ushman's cigarette from between his fingers, grinding it into the dirt floor without a word.

After the earthquake, Ushman decided to try his hand as a merchant, something his father had always planned. It would be costly for him to rebuild his workshops, and he knew the merchants sold the rugs in Tehran and Kashan for twice what they paid Ushman. Farak suggested America. "They are rich there, you can sell the kilim for four times what we get here."

They were finishing a dinner of lentil stew. Ushman looked up from his bowl. "I cannot go to America alone. I have responsibilities here."

"Your mother is my responsibility. You can go and I will send you the carpets each month."

"You will get cheated," Ushman said and lifted the bowl to his face, pouring the remaining lentil broth down his throat.

"I will buy from the women, they will not cheat me."

"And when my mother dies you will come?" Ushman asked under his breath.

"Don't talk of that," Farak said and cleared away their bowls. She entered his name in a lottery and Ushman won the ultimate jackpot: a green card. Three months later, Ushman was sleeping on a mat in his cousin's apartment in Queens.

Last year in a letter from his mother, Ushman learned of the Turkish tailor from Tehran who had come to the house. His mother told Ushman that the tailor had visited Tabriz three times that fall, and that each time she could hear him and Farak talking in the dim courtyard while her own neck cramped up, long overdue for her nightly massage. Ushman wished his mother would die.

Two

His store is nothing more than a desk, a chair, and a small stack of rugs. Its size, Ushman reasons, is secondary to its location. He has sunk most of his profits into maintaining this address and the expensive advertisements he places in select periodicals and Playbills. Ushman sets the stolen rug down near his desk, still unable to believe the afternoon's events. He unrolls the rug, though, and is startled by its beauty. It is a Kashan Ardabil Shrine design carpet, semi-antique, probably made in the late 1960s. Ushman notices that the first two stanzas of Shiraz's *ghazel* that were woven into the border of the original Ardabil Shrine carpet in 1539 are typed in English on a sheet of stationery and stitched to the back. Ushman reads over the verses, remembering having to learn them in grade school.

When he examined the rug last night, he knew immediately that it was authentic and had only checked the fibers to verify its age and condition. Now, in the daylight of his shop, the rug's golden red tones are brilliant. He does not regret his decision. In its weave, he sees the marketplace of Tabriz, the early days of his marriage, the easy way in which Farak would lay their dinner dishes, light a candle, steep his tea, all while holding his gaze across the room. Anyway, he tells himself, the Ardabil rug would have been sold for a fraction of its value at some early morning estate sale where it could never mean as much to the buyer as it does to Ushman. The rug had been meant for him.

Excited and lonely, he cannot help himself from placing the call to Tabriz, though he knows it will wake her.

"Farak?" he says to the sleepy distant voice that picks up. *"Az emri ka sobh bekhair."*

"It is dark here, not morning."

"Forgive me."

"Ushman, what has happened to you?"

He instinctively changes the story a little. "I got an Ardabil carpet for free today. I was going to give him twelve thousand for it, but . . . he left town, Farak. A twenty-thousand-dollar carpet, he leaves it behind." When she is silent, Ushman adds, "With me."

"Nothing is for free, Ushman."

"How is my mother?" Ushman replies.

"Like a sack of bones," Farak says. "If you sell the Shrine rug, perhaps you will then have enough money to pay a nurse." He has not expected this. Ushman is afraid his mother is right, that Farak has a lover in Tehran who will never make her touch another kilim as long as she lives.

"I can provide her with a nurse. Then you will be free to come. Yes?" Perhaps it is only her duty that keeps her in Tabriz, caring for Ushman's invalid mother.

Her silence is an insult.

"I am not American," she finally says, a familiar refrain.

Well, then, Ushman reasons, it is also her duty to love him, and he holds on to this thought. Quickly, he invents other ways he could spend the money.

"I could use a bigger shop," Ushman says, and Farak doesn't reply. "Or perhaps I could come for a visit, like a vacation."

"Since when is Tabriz a vacation spot, Ushman? Come if you have to, not for the scenery."

He does not know what to say, but is glad that he cannot see her eyes, which, even on the morning he left Tabriz for his long journey to America, had been full of blame. She had allowed him to lift her veil and place one kiss on her dry lips before she covered her face again. It was their only act of marital intimacy since the earthquake, as she was still in mourning for the lost baby.

Ushman had hoped for children. He had expected them. But he did not need them if he had Farak. When she spoke of feeling incomplete, he was insulted and baffled.

Though he understood why she held him and his family's workshops responsible, he did not agree. The rugs had been good to Ushman and his family. Even after the revolution, when his family lost much of their wealth, his father had been able to rebuild their rug trade. The rugs had brought Farak to him the first time, and he was sure that the Ardabil would bring her back again.

She had been a weaver in Ushman's father's workshop in Tabriz from the time she was seven years old. Her small hands maneuvered the thread expertly: spinning and dyeing wool in the evening and weaving every day. When Ushman was thirteen he accompanied his father into the workshop to inspect the women's progress. Farak was squatting over the loom, her veil hanging low over her forehead, tying the tight little knots that Ushman's father and the merchants from Tehran raved about.

Outside one day soon after, Ushman spotted Farak sketching a design in the dirt. He approached, and told her she had lovely technique, the highest compliment Ushman had ever heard his father give to a woman. She was humbled by his attention and lowered her eyes in respect. His big feet, the toes clumsily hanging over the edge of each leather sandal, must have moved her and she dared to let a smile spread across her face before returning to her work.

Years later, after his father's death, Ushman married Farak and took over the workshops. She did not weave again.

Unsure what to do, Ushman rolls the Ardabil rug back up and places it in a corner. If he sells the rug for what it's worth, he could afford to pay a nurse for the rest of his mother's life. He can almost afford it now. But the only reason for a nurse, he realizes, is to set Farak free, and Ushman, although he has not seen her for nearly three years, cannot imagine that.

He never should have told Farak about the rug, Ushman thinks. He must be more careful of his urges.

The next morning, summer is back and the air is thick with humidity. The hot months are always slow, but Ushman has not even read the headlines of his morning paper before someone rings at the door. It is Mrs. Roberts, dressed in white linen. She waves at Ushman through the glass door and he buzzes her in. He did not expect her until later; she has never come before noon.

She greets him as if she has not seen him in weeks. He bows, relieved that they are back on familiar territory. She looks around his shop, then to the window. He turns and follows her gaze across the street to a man and woman arguing over a taxicab.

"I must confess," she finally says, removing a compact from her handbag, "I'm a terrible voyeur. We live so high that people on the street become nothing more than movement. But here, you're so close to the street, it's really quite mesmerizing, isn't it?"

Mrs. Roberts looks at Ushman with strangely bright eyes. It makes him suspicious, this look. He watches as she drags the thick powder across her nose. There is something terribly ugly about her face, Ushman thinks, something wide and shameful. He has never liked the looks of American women. He thinks of Farak: her delicate face, strong hands, and the small feet that crossed the floor of their bedroom at night in hushed strides.

Abruptly, Mrs. Roberts closes her compact, turns away from the window, and looks around her at the few rugs hanging and the stack just behind her. Then Ushman sees her eyes rest on the Ardabil rug, rolled tightly in the corner. "So," she says with her face already in a firmly established smile, "is this the one you've found for me?"

He is not prepared for this, has not yet decided just what he will do with the rug. But he understands there is no way to deny her. She smiles insistently. Ushman pulls the rug into the middle of the room, then gives it a kick and watches as it unrolls. It has one large medallion in the center surrounded by a sea of delicate flowers. The threads are warm shades of red and gold.

Mrs. Roberts's smile fades into some sort of astonishment. Ushman is proud of the rug's effect.

"It is a replica of one of the Ardabil Shrine rugs, woven in the sixteenth century. The original is in the Victoria and Albert Museum in London."

"It's the most wonderful-looking thing I've ever seen," Mrs. Roberts says, kneeling to touch the rug. Ushman kneels next to her, pleased that she appreciates the rug's value. Whatever anxiety Ushman has around Mrs. Roberts, she also makes him feel proud of his shop, his rugs. He wishes that Farak could see the way Mrs. Roberts looks at the rug, at him. Perhaps such an important woman's esteem would change the way Farak felt about Ushman and the rugs.

As Mrs. Roberts extends a hand to touch the Ardabil, Ushman notices the skin, wrinkled and spotted, her fingers beginning to bend under the force of swollen knuckles. He looks at her face, smooth and covered in a heavy layer of makeup, which, instead of giving her a more youthful appearance, Ushman thinks, makes her look raw and somehow vulnerable.

"What's this?" she asks, looking at the small yellowed paper stitched to the back side.

"It was woven into the original," Ushman says quietly.

She reads aloud, *"Except for your threshold, there is no refuge in this world for me; except for this door, there is no shelter for my head. When the enemy's sword is drawn, I throw down my shield in flight because I have no weapon except weeping and sighing."* She looks at Ushman. "It takes your breath away, doesn't it?"

"They are nice verses," Ushman says, and stands. "We studied them as children, but I was never very good in school."

"What is the price?" Mrs. Roberts suddenly asks, standing next to him, her eyes wide with desire.

Ushman panics. She is close to him, her lipstick melting into the wrinkles around her mouth, a hint of staleness creeping into her minty breath.

Impulsively, Ushman names his price, "Thirty thousand."

Mrs. Roberts's face relaxes into a frown, but she doesn't flinch. She has never questioned Ushman's fairness. "Fine," she says, disappointed. Then, with a pleading in her voice, she asks, "Why do you make it so easy for me, Ushman?"

"What do you mean?" he says, astonished that she has agreed to such a high figure.

"You always find the perfect rug. This one, it's like nothing I could have imagined."

"You are a good customer," Ushman says, turning his gold signet ring around and around. He is elated at the thought of so much money. He cannot believe that such wealth will not change Farak's mind. "I can see you love the rug," he says, feeling as though he is finally in control of his fortune.

Mrs. Roberts's face is quiet, though, even stern, and Ushman thinks maybe she's changed her mind. He tempers his own emotion, afraid of betraying himself. She looks at him hard.

"I thought that maybe it wouldn't even be for sale," she says quietly, turning away from Ushman and the rug. He intuits that something has happened, and he's sure that it must be his fault, but Ushman just stands looking at the ridges of her shoulder blades move beneath her tunic as she shifts in distress. Though her eyes are clear and dry when she turns to face him again, Ushman begins to understand that wanting is its own luxury.

And suddenly Ushman is sure of what Mrs. Roberts is asking him to do. He feels generous, standing over the rug, the sun making his shop warm and bright. "You're right," Ushman begins, watching her face for a response, "it is special to my

family." She raises her eyebrows, alert, encouraging. "I'll have
to check with my wife, you know," he continues. "Give me a
few days."

Mrs. Roberts seems quite pleased with this revelation, and
her eyes fix on the rug with what Ushman recognizes as longing. They stand in silence for a moment and then, with the arti-
ficial formality that occurs between two people aware of a lie,
Ushman and Mrs. Roberts say their goodbyes.

The next evening, Ushman sits in his bedroom with the window
open listening to his downstairs neighbor practice the clarinet.
He is drinking coffee. At midnight, he will call Farak as he does
each month. It will be morning there, his mother barking out
requests from her bed. Ushman has no nostalgia for his mother.
He knows that each time Farak lays her hands on the old
woman's greasy skin, massaging a stiff neck or arm, Farak's dis-
dain for him hardens. If his mother hadn't been crippled, he
might have brought Farak to America with him and let the
fresh flowers and hot dogs on street corners lull her into for-
giveness. It would be easier to love him here, where the rum-
blings outside are merely planes and trucks and where doctors
work miracles every day. She could watch the talk shows on
TV and see that there are men much worse than he. And they
could sit together in the shop on the rugs from their past and
dream about the people on the street they wished they were,
but would not know how to be.

Ushman still believes in that dream. He did not come to
America to lose his wife, he came to make a better life for both

of them. He knows that after he plays her game, Mrs. Roberts will give him thirty thousand for the rug, and with that money Ushman can give Farak what she wants.

In the dark, Ushman feels close to her and sure of himself. When it is time, he places the call. He can hear the radio in the background as Farak answers.

"Ushman," she says, *"hal-e to khub e?"*

"I'm well. How are you?"

"Your mother has a bit of a cold, but she is fine. She is sleeping now."

"What are you listening to?"

"The Beatles. Semah loaned me the tape."

"I could send you some tapes. Elvis, too."

"That would be nice. What happened with the Ardabil rug, Ushman?"

"Oh. One of my customers is very interested and she will even pay more than the rug is worth. She's a little crazy, Farak."

"Crazier than you and me?"

"She's very rich. She can have anything she wants."

"To be crazy like that, Ushman. Oh, if only we were crazy like that."

Ushman listens to Farak's lazy voice, the tinny *yeah, yeah, yeah* of the Beatles in the background. He thinks of Mrs. Roberts and how she had been able to make him understand that she wanted to lose sleep over the rug, to worry that she might not be able to have it for her own. He wants to tell Farak that they can be crazy like that; that they will be rich and crazy together in America. But something stops him. Ushman longs to see Farak — her face, her hands, her eyes. If he could see her, maybe he could understand her, too. Finally, in a hesitant voice, he asks what he's never before dared, what he realizes he's never known. "What is it that you want, Farak?"

The line is silent except for the music and Farak's quiet breathing. "It's not that easy, Ushman. Things just happen, no matter what you want."

"Tell me what's happened, then," Ushman says, his heart racing.

The music clicks off and Farak's voice quivers. "I'm carrying a baby again, Ushman."

Ushman listens to the little sobs she tries to muffle. "The Turk's?" he finally asks.

She doesn't say anything.

"You will lose it like the rest," Ushman spits into the phone. He can hear a small whine of pain and then there is quiet.

"Farak?" Ushman says, looking out his window, wondering why he ever left Tabriz.

She breathes heavily into the phone, but does not respond. "There's your mother calling," Farak says finally, her voice weak. "I've got to get her pills, Ushman."

He calls her name again, but she hangs up.

Ushman's chest heaves in anger. He stands up, as if movement will calm the burning in his stomach where her words have nested. He stomps his feet and shakes his head, fighting back tears until he is worn out and the cries of a child next door startle him into silence.

He gets to the shop before the morning has really gotten started. Bicycles whir through the streets unhindered and dogs

pee on the corner of every mailbox and newsstand as their owners follow sleepily in sneakers and sweatpants. The Ardabil rug
is in the center of the shop, its brilliant red and gold threads
taunting Ushman.

In the quiet of night, when the breeze still blew hot through
the window and Ushman's body was limp on the bed, he realized that the rug had tested him. How far, it had asked, would
he go for Farak? He had been thinking of nothing but her and
of the earthquake as he drove back into the city, the dead man's
rug in the back of his van. He'd thought the rug was a stroke of
luck. That's why he had played Mrs. Roberts's game and that's
why he had called Farak to tell her of his find, and that's why
he'd had the nerve to ask her what he never had before. And
that stupid lucky feeling makes him a bigger fool now than
ever.

Looking at the rug, he thinks of the dead man whose face he
cannot even remember. He thinks of the thousands of knots,
the fingers that tied them, fingers like Farak's that have stroked
the skin of another man. He rolls up the rug, heaves it onto his
shoulder, and stands on the avenue, waiting.

He knows their schedule and the truck pulls up just as he's
beginning to break a sweat. The streets are still empty, but
they're at the end of their route and the truck is nearly full. He
places the rug on top of the six trash bags and watches as the
sanitation worker stops to inspect the rug.

"It's trash," Ushman says, "terrible stains. Worthless, really."

Wiping his brow, the man looks at Ushman, then at the rug
again.

"Please," Ushman says, and raises his voice to a tone of urgency, "just take it."

The worker shrugs. "Whatever, guy," he says, and throws the

Ardabil up and into the compactor. Ushman stands listening to the motor and he imagines the rug, crushed between eggshells and dirty diapers, its proud design soiled by other people's filth.

As he's sure she would, Mrs. Roberts shows up before noon, inquiring about the rug.

Ushman notices that she is bright, hopeful that the rug may continue to be out of her reach for a little longer. It makes Ushman angry, that to want something she can't have is an indulgence, a fantasy he was willing to humor. He no longer feels generous or kind and so he turns to her with a somber face and says, "It's gone. You cannot covet it or pretend to covet it any longer."

"Oh," she says, shocked by his tone. "Well, I certainly didn't mean to offend you." She stands her ground and makes no move to leave.

"I am not playing," Ushman says. "It's really gone. So go try to find something else in this city that you can't have."

Mrs. Roberts smiles stiffly at Ushman. He remembers that she is older than her face looks; he remembers that her husband is at home, dying, and yet she's here, with him.

Having been up all night is beginning to make his head buzz, his knees feel loose. He sits down on the small stack of rugs, stretches his arms out the way his father taught him, and pleads, "What do you want?"

She doesn't answer but steps out of her shoes, walks across the room, and sits next to him. Exhausted, he lies down, turning his back to her. Without speaking, Mrs. Roberts moves her body close to Ushman, careful not to touch him. She lies there next to him, the way a wife would, in silence. Ushman closes his eyes. He thinks of the window on the other side of the room, and of the people who, seeing the two of them there, like lovers on the small pile of rugs, are undoubtedly longing to trade places.

Three

Suddenly, more than a month later, on a hot July evening when it seems as if darkness will never come, Ushman finds himself in the short-term parking garage of Kennedy Airport. It was a mistake, this destination. He was last aware of driving as he crossed the Triborough Bridge into Queens. Then, in what seemed like the blink of an eye, he noticed the signs announcing airlines. It gave him a jolt of adrenaline, uncertain for a moment if indeed he was to be traveling tonight, but certain that he did not have with him any of the necessary documents. Once he realized, however, that he had no travel plans, Ushman tried in vain to change his course. He meant only to go home, slip off his shoes, and lie prone on his living room floor. As had become his custom, he would lie this way, waiting for something to change. Visualizing some chemical or biological change inside of him that will remove the constant weight in his chest that requires so much effort to support. Or, if this weight cannot be lifted, he sometimes thinks he would rather acquiesce to it. Simply allow it to flatten each artery and vessel in his chest so that there is nothing left.

But each day has been the same as the rest. Nothing has changed. Except, perhaps, the fetus inside of Farak, which, when she told him of her pregnancy, was already four months along. Further than she'd ever carried one of his babies. And each day it continues to grow, it becomes more viable. As he lay there on his own Tabriz carpet night after night, watching the sky move from red to black, Ushman would find his mind wandering, from the condition of his own heart to the condition of that baby's. It would be simple, and painless, he's certain, for such a small, immature heart to stop. How many times had it happened before? Each of his own children's hearts had stopped. Perhaps before any had even really begun. He and Farak never heard a heartbeat. Never sat in a clinic with a little machine broadcasting that indication of life. But even though it's begun, this new baby's heart, this Turk's heart, beating a manic little beat, it is still vulnerable. So as he has waited for his own heart to slow and stop, Ushman has waited also for the baby in Farak's womb and its tiny brand-new heart to quit. Sometimes when he wishes for this, he cannot sleep. Lying on his side, on top of the sheets, he stares at the phone, waiting for the news.

Tonight, though, Ushman will not lie on the floor of his Flushing apartment and watch the sky's color fade away. Instead, he is sitting in his van, with the window cracked, listening to the whir of luggage wheels all around him as they are dragged, en masse, across the concrete. The noise is unsettling. Like the hum of insects. It makes Ushman feel anxious, as though his own immobility is foolish.

Tentatively, he shuts off the engine and rolls up his window. He has no suitcase, but he lifts his leather satchel from the seat beside him. Feigning a purposeful stride, Ushman follows the people around him into the airport.

Inside, the air is frigid. Ushman follows the concourse around to a line for security. Without a boarding pass, Ushman will not be allowed through. Realizing this, he steps aside, and watches as the ticketed passengers place their jewelry, wallets, and belts on the conveyor belt. He can't help but wonder about their destinations and the purpose of their travels.

Gradually, he notices that there are other people without boarding passes gathering around him. Some with arms crossed defiantly across their chests, others biting their lips or wiping away tears or simply looking down at their feet. Ushman watches them and realizes that this is the last place for good-byes. He is standing amid the grief of those who have been left behind.

It is not a place in which Ushman wants to linger.

Instead, he descends an escalator and stands near the baggage claim. Here, he recognizes the reunions. Couples, families, friends. So relieved, just as he had been, to see a familiar face. Even if it was only his cousin, Ahmad. And his breath had smelled like rotten figs and he refused to take Ushman directly to his apartment, but insisted upon stopping at his mosque—just another ugly brick building—for prayers. Even then, Ushman had been pleased to be with Ahmad. He felt less a stranger, less alone, less troubled simply because he had found Ahmad's eyes. Searching the crowd, a pair of eyes had picked out Ushman. They had made him welcome, made it known that his arrival had been anticipated. Ushman was grateful for that.

As he watches the passengers become reacquainted with their companions, Ushman leans against the wall. He sinks into an elaborate daydream in which it is he who is waiting for a plane. He who fanatically checks the arrival time. He whose eyes scan the crowd, expecting and finally finding Farak's eyes. Her deep green eyes and thinly arched eyebrows. They could embrace. There are no *komitehs* here. And he could offer her his arm and walk, with the weight and warmth of her hand on his elbow, to this very carousel. She might lean her head on his shoulder as they saved their words for later, for the moment when they travel together in Ushman's van through the streets of Queens. But now, the sound of the carousel turning and the jingle of his keys in his pocket—keys to the apartment in which there is an empty top drawer awaiting the day when she will deposit the contents of her suitcases into it—are the most benign, comforting sounds in the world.

For the first time all summer, Ushman feels relaxed. He breathes deeply into the bottom of his ribs. Eventually, he takes a seat in the vinyl chairs at the perimeter of the baggage claim area. As couple after couple are reunited and stand watching the bags, nuzzling and waiting, Ushman sees only his face and Farak's.

But there is one couple whose reunion is not without trouble. Their interaction is noticeably different. As they descend the escalator, their urgency is nearly contagious. Ushman resists his instinct to stand in order to observe them more actively. He can see that the woman is Asian with dyed platinum hair. She is wearing sneakers and a T-shirt that allows her huge pregnant belly to be exposed. Ushman has never seen this sight, and he averts his eyes to the floor. Her partner is Asian, too. He is speaking quickly to her, guiding her with his hand. They step off the escalator and quickly settle the woman in a chair right next to Ushman. She sits on the edge of the chair, holding her belly and moaning. Closing her eyes, she arches her head back. Ushman looks at her once again and notices how pale her skin appears. The man walks away from her for a moment to check the carousel. Ushman's breathing becomes shallow once again. He senses something imminently dramatic that he does not want to be a part of. As he stands, the woman's eyes open and she screams. She is looking right at Ushman and he hears, but does not look to see, something like water dripping from her chair onto the floor.

She calls out for her partner. He hears her and turns to see what Ushman assumes must be a small puddle forming just below the woman's chair.

This young Asian man yells at Ushman, but Ushman does not understand what he's saying. Ushman holds out his hands, as if to indicate he had no involvement in what had happened. The man keeps gesturing and yelling, pointing at Ushman's waist. Finally, Ushman realizes what is needed. He reaches for his cell phone, which is clipped to his belt, and dials 911.

As he does so, a guard from nearby approaches as other travelers begin to crowd around, watching the woman rock back and forth in her chair. The guard is trying to communicate with her partner. He points to Ushman, who is telling the operator that there's a woman about to have a baby at Kennedy Airport near Baggage Claim Four.

Ushman hangs up his phone and nods to the guard. "I've just rung for an ambulance."

The guard acknowledges him and then turns to the crowd, asking if anybody is a doctor. Ushman backs away from the still-moaning woman. Her partner is pushing the hair off her face and speaking to her quickly. As Ushman walks away from the crowd, he hears a woman say to her friend in a disparaging tone of voice, "I guess she made it just in time to have an American baby."

He stares at his feet as he passes them. Then, looking back, he can see that the guard has found a doctor in the crowd who has his hands on the woman's belly, telling her to wait. Don't push. Not yet, he tells her. Hold on.

Ushman begins sweating. He suddenly realizes his own stupidity.

It may not be over yet.

He's given up too soon.

In a panic, Ushman leaves the baggage claim area just as he hears a siren approach. He finds his way back to the parking garage, barely able to resist running. The sun has set and Ushman drives quickly in the dark.

His apartment is dark and quiet. He is in such a hurry, Ushman walks into the living room, neglecting to remove his shoes, as is his usual custom. Crossing the large, thin kilim he has stretched across the floor, Ushman is in the bedroom, the phone in his hand, before he realizes his keys are still pressed into his palm, making deep creases that pulse with pain. Hopeful and breathless, he listens to the hollow ring of the overseas connection. She answers.

"Oh, Farak," he says, relieved to hear her groggy voice.

"Ushman? What is it? Are you hurt?"

"No. Not at all. I have been stupid, Farak. Forgive me. I should have thought of this before."

"Thought of what, Ushman? You are not stupid. I know you're a good man."

"You can come, Farak. It doesn't matter about the baby. I will care for it as my own. There is no shame here. We can raise it together. It will not matter. It will be an American baby."

There is no reply.

"Farak? Are you there? Can you hear me?"

"Yes. Oh, dear, Ushman. America has made you very generous." She is crying. Ushman's heart is eager.

"And lonely, Farak. So lonely."

"But you have your wealth. And your freedom. There are possibilities for you there, Ushman."

"And for you, too. For the baby. No *hejab*. No *komiteh*. In January there is a whole new millennium. A new life for us. Think of it, Farak."

She breathes heavily into the phone. He waits for her to say something more.

"Ushman, I have petitioned for a divorce."

"But it doesn't matter. We can change all that. I was angry, Farak. What I said. You know that."

"It doesn't matter what you said. I'm doing this because it's what I want. Not because I'm angry with you."

"I don't understand."

"I want a divorce, Ushman. We are moving to Istanbul. To have the baby. To start over."

"But my mother . . ."

"I haven't told her anything yet. She will be taken care of, Ushman. There is a nice place. I have a friend there, she will get you a good rate —"

"Shut up. Shut up, Farak. This is not a negotiation. I want you here. With the baby. That is all."

"It won't happen, Ushman. The divorce has been granted."

"On what grounds?" Ushman had, for once, been grateful to the Islamic regime, for its mandates and prohibitions. He assumed these laws would prevent Farak from ever truly leaving him.

There is a long pause. Ushman repeats his question, hardly able to contain his anger. "On what grounds?"

"Desertion," she says finally.

Ushman squeezes the quilt beneath him into a fist. "You are a liar."

"There is too much pain between us, Ushman."

"Because you have put it there," he says, and hangs up the phone.

Sitting on his bed, both hands squeezing the bedcover with all his might, Ushman looks down at his feet. He lets go of the quilt and wipes at his eyes, his hands quivering. One at a time, he pulls the sandals from his feet and hurls them across the room, where they smack the wall before falling to the floor. Each shoe leaves behind a smudge of black on the wall, like soot left over from a fire.

It is still dark, but technically a new day has begun. Ushman has watched the clock move past midnight. He is unable to sleep. Finally, he gives up on trying. After dressing himself in yesterday's clothes, he leaves the apartment. Walking without a purpose, Ushman notices the number of lights on in the buildings around his own. So many people awake at three in the morning surprises him. He remembers the way people in Tabriz would stay up to watch a soccer game on TV. Even if it was not a championship game. If Iran was playing somewhere in Europe or Latin America and it was being broadcast via satellite, the whole city would be awake, watching. Ushman looks at the lighted windows and yearns to be let in. Even if there is no soccer match on TV. Just to sit around a table with people in the middle of the night, their camaraderie heightened by the absurdity of the hour.

Ushman sees the bodega on the corner is open. He decides this will be his destination and feels his pocket to be sure he's brought his wallet.

In the bodega, he chooses an orange soda from the cooler. There is one other person in the store. An old Hasid reading the labels on soup cans. Ushman pays for his soda and stands outside under the streetlight.

He drinks the soda and listens to the sound of heels clicking on the sidewalk somewhere behind him. As they get louder, Ushman turns and looks.

She is pale all over like the moon. Only her bright red lips give her face any contrast at all. Her hair, just like the woman's in the airport, is bleached white so that it blends almost exactly with her skin. When Ushman sees her up close, he recognizes the slight curve of her eyes as Asian. For a moment he is disoriented. Is it the same woman from the airport? But no, she is not pregnant, she is thin and alone. He cannot remember if what happened in the airport had been a dream, or perhaps if this, now, is a dream.

"Hey, dark boy," she speaks to him in a hard, choppy accent. "I'm cheap tonight. I got discount for you. Let me show you." She touches Ushman's arm with her short fingers. She is standing in the bright beam of the streetlight, her shadow stretching long behind her on the sidewalk. Her touch shocks him so it is as if he were four stories up and looking down on the intersection of their bodies. Time slows and he feels each finger's individual weight. It is the first time he has been touched in

America. The first time anybody has touched him since Farak's final dutiful kiss nearly three years ago. The back of Ushman's neck tingles.

"You lonely. I know. I see your eyes," the woman continues, but Ushman concentrates on the hum of faraway traffic that is suddenly echoing inside his head. "Let me give you company. Make you feel so good."

Ushman looks at her face. He allows himself to look carefully. She is not attractive. Around her eyes she's drawn thick black lines, but her lashes are short and unadorned. Her skin, though pale, is pockmarked. The tank top she is wearing reveals the slope of her bosom and the skin there is similarly blemished.

Since coming to America, he struggles to avoid looking at scantily dressed girls, afraid that his eyes will betray his filthy thoughts. He is still shocked, sometimes, to see so much female skin and hair, and he cannot help but think of naked, lustful things. Though Ushman was nineteen at the time of the revolution and resisted the Ayatollah's regime, he finds himself missing the *hejab* that every woman in Iran is required to wear. The long robes and head coverings succeed in hiding not only a woman's skin and hair but also a man's lust. Not destroying it, but hiding it from himself. Preventing him from seeing the parts of a woman that arouse, distract, tempt.

In Tabriz, when Ushman passed a woman in the bazaar or on the street, he may have had unclean thoughts about her, about the almost imperceptible rise of her chest beneath her manteau, or the strands of hair just visible around her ears, but he was not confronted with intimate stretches of skin from which it is nearly impossible to conceal his desire. In America, with women displaying their most sacred curves, a man is exposed also. As his eyes absorb each naked stretch of skin, so can his own longing be observed. Ushman prefers to keep his desire anonymous.

He also cannot imagine how it is that American men bear to have their wives or girlfriends ride the subway and go into shops while their figures are all but revealed. The thought of Farak walking through public places in a short skirt and bare-backed blouse is almost more troubling than the thought of her in bed with the tailor. At least the tailor is only one man. Not an entire city. He is just two eyes, two hands, two lips, and one dirty cock. Ushman reminds himself of this every sleep-less night, when the image of his wife with another man has kept him awake. And then, turning on the TV, he would watch American wives and daughters and girlfriends parade them-selves, nearly naked, in front of huge audiences. They would speak of their sexual desires and their numerous affairs and their bastard children and Ushman wept thinking of the men who must watch their women shame them so.

Tonight, he tells himself, as he looks at the eyebrows this prostitute has drawn above her eyes, I will not watch the TV. Tonight, I will be who Farak has told me I am. A bachelor once again.

Ushman does not acknowledge her offer with a reply. In-stead, he turns his face away, imagining her to be someone she is not. Someone whose face is shy and smooth; whose voice is hushed. He takes another long sip of his soda. His anger has grown all night and suddenly it is a mound of pressure in his groin. He wants to be rid of this.

As he throws the empty soda can into a wastebasket on the corner, Ushman nods his head in a subtle acceptance of her of-fer. He walks toward his building without looking back. Her shoes alert him that she has understood. Clicking behind him down the long block, she stays a few paces behind, like a dutiful puppy.

Ushman does not want to be seen riding the elevator with her. Beneath the awning, he says to her, "Wait here. I'll buzz you in. Apartment 10A."

He rides alone up to his floor. The hallway is quiet. His key in the lock echoes quietly. Inside, he does not turn on any lights. He does not want her to see his things. Instead, he waits by his door until she knocks. He leads her into the kitchen, where he flicks on the oven light.

"Here," he says, and pushes down on her shoulders.

"Not so fast. I get money first. Twenty dollar for a blow."

Ushman feels for his wallet and gives her a crisp bill. He wants her to hurry up, afraid that he might lose his nerve. She puts the twenty up under her skirt and unzips him. He leans back against the counter and closes his eyes. Though not a very religious man, he cannot help but move his lips to form the silent phrase, *Forgive me, Allah.*

He will remember nothing of her except her pale hair and skin and how the orange light from the oven has turned her golden. The warmth of her mouth is exactly as he'd imagined it would be, and the tingling in his neck that her touch had evoked continues down his spine and the backs of his legs, into his toes. He is electric in the small, dim kitchen. The buzzing takes over his eyes and ears and fingers until, at last, he comes.

She stands and spits into his kitchen sink. Then she smiles. He can see the big space between her crooked front teeth.

"Please go, now," he says, thinking of the mosques all around New York City with worshippers inside, praising Allah, the only God. There are no longer any sacred rituals for Ushman.

"Don't be so sad. You like to feel good, right?" she says as she passes Ushman and stands in the foyer.

"Goodnight," Ushman says, and she shrugs. Then she opens the door and is gone.

Ushman turns out the stove light. Now the only patch of light comes through the window, from the dawn. In this dim light, he runs the water in the sink to be rid of the evidence of their exchange.

He makes his way to the bedroom and lies on the bed. Exhausted, he closes his eyes. Still he sees Farak. But, mercifully, the tailor is gone. There is only his wife, walking through his mind as if in a motion picture. Coming from the bazaar with figs and a new saucepan. Laughing with her cousin as the two chased down a neighbor's toddler who'd run off with his mother's shoes. Reaching out for Ushman when he came through the front door after having been gone all day. These images coax him to sleep and continue to soothe him as dreams.

The noise of the morning's traffic awakens him. He hears the horns and the delivery trucks, a backhoe reversing, a siren. And then, with his eyes still closed, he hears the sounds of English being spoken. The elevator rumbles through its shaft and its doors creak open somewhere above him. And Ushman remembers where he is, that the proximity of Farak has been a dream, and that he ushered a prostitute into his kitchen the night before. He stands and panics as he thinks of AIDS and herpes and syphilis. And then he spends the morning in the shower, where the tears on his face become indiscernible from the shower's spray.

four

For weeks, Ushman returns to the baggage claim area at Kennedy Airport, to watch and dream. And then he returns home. In the middle of the night, after he's tossed and turned across the orange bedspread, making it rumpled and hot, he walks out into the darkness. He walks deliberately to the corner bodega and stands once again beneath the streetlight, looking up into the windows of the surrounding buildings. He waits, fingering the twenty-dollar bill in his pocket. Through a thunderstorm and a drug bust and a full moon, he waits. But she does not come.

Despairingly, Ushman thinks his life could go on forever like this.

And then, one evening, as he parks his van in the short-term parking garage, he makes a decision to try something new. He stands in a long line at the Air France counter. The passengers around him push their heavy bags forward. Ushman listens to them worry about the time, about the length of the line, about whether they reserved an aisle or window seat. He waits patiently, with the resigned attitude of a man without a schedule.

When he finally reaches the counter, Ushman buys a round-trip ticket for that evening's flight to Paris. It is expensive. He would not normally be so reckless with his money. But it is refundable. And Ushman intends to return the ticket this evening, before he or anybody else has boarded the flight.

He has actually spent the fourteen hundred dollars for a very subtle change of scenery. He wants to be on the inside. He wants to be out of the crowds of people waiting, left behind. The ticket buys him a pass through security. It allows him to walk through the metal detectors and sit in the vinyl chairs that surround each gate, watching the faces of the people as they disembark. And when he's seen two planes unload their passengers, he walks around the terminal, stopping to finger the plastic Statues of Liberty and the yellow metal taxicabs for sale in the souvenir shop. He feels triumphant in his new surroundings. The ticket has masked his voyeurism. He no longer feels so desperate or pathetic. After all, he does have a ticket to Paris in his pocket.

He walks the length of the terminal, watching the sky go auburn beyond the taxiing aircraft. Finally, he leaves the gate area, slowly passing back through security, lingering just where he used to mingle with the other nonpassengers. Ushman leans against a wall, watching the faces around him.

It is nearly nine o'clock and raining now, steadily. Reluctantly, Ushman knows he should return his ticket and go home. But he is inexplicably transfixed by a girl sitting near the window in an adjacent seating area. She said goodbye to her parents, in their raincoats and sensible shoes, as they passed through security fifteen minutes ago. And she has been sitting there, looking out the window, ever since. She has her back toward Ushman. Her hair is pulled away from her face. It is pale blond, like a child's. And her neck, just below her hairline, seems to extend for an unnatural length. Beyond her, the lights of jumbo jets taxiing in and out are blurred through the thick, rain-splattered windows. Ushman can see the girl's face only in its reflection in these windows. It is this blur of her face that has grabbed his attention.

He can see his own reflection as well, but it is familiar to him. His deep brown eyes, thick black eyebrows, and hair are unremarkable. He wears a crisp blue shirt tucked into dark jeans. There is a small black umbrella cradled under his arm. His shirtsleeves are rolled up one cuff and his forearms are exposed just above the wrist.

Because of the rain and the blurriness of her reflection, Ushman cannot be sure upon what her eyes are fixed. First he believes she is looking out, past the window at the arriving and departing planes. So he studies her without inhibition, this pale hair and long neck. But then he senses that her eyes are not looking beyond the glass, but at it. At him.

He panics, and looks away. This whole time, he wonders, was she studying him as well? Was she aware of his stare?

As he glances back at her reflection, he becomes assured that she had, indeed, been looking at him because of the delicate blush creeping across her cheeks and to the backs of her ears. Ushman smiles. Her blush deepens. She, too, smiles and looks away.

Ushman crosses his arms across his chest and looks away, petrified. Is this American life? he wonders. This flirtation with a young girl occurring so easily, so unintentionally, so unnoticed? Is it so simple to connect with a stranger?

As he thinks of the prostitute in his neighborhood who has abandoned him, Ushman reminds himself that nothing in his life is simple. He does not relate with people easily. Besides, all she'd done was smile, really. She is clearly not a prostitute. He cannot buy her attention; he must earn it. Looking down at his sandals and his long, dark toes, Ushman realizes that she will want nothing to do with him. In America, he is not a man. He is a curiosity, an oddity, a foreigner.

He takes the ticket from his pocket and turns away from the window, ready to return it and go back to his life. His lousy sham of a life.

As Ushman begins to walk away, he senses that she is watching him. He remembers the long curve of her neck. Stepping out of the flow of people, Ushman turns his head back to see her one last time and she is gone. No longer sitting in the vinyl chair, she is standing by the window now, her face hidden.

Damn it, Ushman says to himself, do something. Be somebody new. Be somebody who doesn't shrug and walk away. Be an American.

Placing the ticket back in his pocket, Ushman crosses the concourse and picks up the bag she has left in the chair behind her, where she was sitting.

"Excuse me, miss," he says, standing just behind her shoulder, with her bag in his hand.

She gasps and grabs the bag from him. He steps back, full of regret. "I didn't mean to alarm you," he says. "I apologize. They say it all the time—do not leave your things unattended—but I think they mean it." Ushman puts his hands in his pockets and begins to walk away.

"Wait," she says, putting her hand gently, and briefly, on his shoulder. She smells like citrus. "I'm sorry," she says, her voice more relaxed in its inflection than other New Yorkers'. "I've been sitting here so long, I think I forgot I was in an airport. I wasn't scared. I mean, of you. Or whatever." She rolls her eyes, remarking on her own awkwardness. "Anyway, thanks. You know, for my bag." The girl is suddenly out of breath, as if she's been running for miles. She places one hand on the crest of her forehead. Her face is flushed. Ushman notices the silver earrings in her ears. They are little new moons.

"You're welcome," he says, and turns to look out the window. "Sometimes I, too, forget where I am." Ushman does not know why he has volunteered this information. It sounds like an embarrassing admission. But she does not smirk. In fact, she does not say anything, but he can feel her eyes studying him. Looking at his clothes, his hair, the whiskers that have already sprouted since this morning. He is standing close to this girl, so close that she can assess each imperfection in his skin. He should move away. Remove himself from this scrutiny. But now it is he who has forgotten where he is. He is in shock, he cannot believe he has spoken to her, that she has touched him, that her face, when not blurry, is still very beautiful.

And the way she is looking at him makes him feel alive. He has not felt this kind of attention, perhaps, ever. She is unafraid to look at him, unafraid of the effect of her gaze on him. Even as he turns to look at her, she lets her eyes remain on him, on the place beneath his Adam's apple. The place where a tuft of black hair is poking out from beneath his undershirt. Then, slyly, she looks at his eyes, so that for a moment, they see each other. For a moment, she is not at all shy, and then she lowers her eyelids, their thick black lashes closing slowly, and a hint of blush colors her ears and the tops of her cheeks.

Ushman, too, averts his eyes. But he continues to look at her reflection next to him in the window, studying the composition of her face. Her skin is bright and clean, but unadorned. She has eyes that are a shade grayer than blue and the fine blond hairs around her ears and forehead are curled up, turning her hairline fuzzy. He decides that it is the simplicity of her appearance that is so lovely.

Ushman notices that her eyes are looking down, watching the tarmac and the men in rain gear directing planes. He realizes that they have not spoken for a few moments and this silence is dismantling Ushman's confidence. He does not want to turn and walk away from her, but he does not know how else to proceed. Suddenly she lifts a finger and places it on the window, pointing down at the tarmac. "What could they be thinking about as they stand there, so wet and cold?"

Ushman shrugs, cocks his head.

"I mean, they must have things on their minds. About their lives. Like all of us do, all the time. Just because you're working—even if your job is on the tarmac—doesn't mean you forget the rest of your life." Her eyes move sideways, to gauge Ushman's reaction. She is not asking him a question, there is no hesitation in her voice, but the way her eyes look to him for a response, Ushman understands that she is trying to understand something of life. She has the hungry look in her eye of youth and its desire to acquire and perfect her knowledge about the world and the people in it.

Ushman turns his face so that he catches her glance. She seems to know that she's been found out. That she is looking for some acknowledgment from Ushman that this observation of hers is smart and true. That she deserves entry into the adult world. She looks down again. "It's just strange to me that this guy is down there, guiding tons of deafening steel around, and he's, maybe, wondering why his kid has a punk haircut." She has changed her tone. It is light and confident and conveys nothing personal.

"I am not familiar with this kind of haircut. But I agree that people are never totally separated from their deepest concerns."

She cocks her head a little to see his face. Again, their eyes connect. "Airport small talk, huh?" she says, beaming, as though she is satisfied with herself. "The stuff great novels are made of." When she smiles, her top lip disappears and her nose wrinkles. Ushman knows what she must have looked like as a child.

"Yes," Ushman says, smiling just for the sake of seeing her smile. "In the airport." He is dumbstruck.

Finally, he forces himself to say something more, so as not to lose her. "Do you drink coffee?" he asks, his breath making a cloud on the window in front of him.

"Yeah. Yeah, I do," she says, as though this answer surprises her.

Ushman turns away from the window and looks at her straight on. "There's a place, just down the corridor. Can you take the time?"

She nods. "I'm not traveling. I was just saying goodbye to my parents."

Without any sarcasm, he says, "Very nice."

"You know them, too?" she says, a devilish smile crossing her lips.

Ushman shakes his head, only understanding her humor a moment later as she follows him through the wide concourse to a small, generic cafeteria. She carries her bag over her shoulder and walks with her head down, glancing at Ushman only as they turn a corner or are jostled by hurried travelers. Ushman moves with a swiftness that suggests he knows the place well, though he's only seen it this evening. He takes a mug for each of them from a tray next to the dispenser. "Cream and sugar?"

"Please," she says, smiling as she looks around the dining room. There is a scattering of two-person tables and a food line offering croissants, sandwiches, and slices of prime rib under a heat lamp. She follows him to a table by the window. He pulls out the chair for her and waits for her to sit down. She doesn't right away. She looks at him, as though she wants to say something. Ushman takes his hands off her chair. Is this wrong, perhaps? Has he frightened her again? He raises his eyebrows.

"Is there something . . . ?" he begins to ask.

"Your accent is . . ." She seems to be searching for a word. "Nice," she says. "I didn't realize that you would have an accent, is all." Then she sits and Ushman sits down across from her. She extends her hand across the table.

"My name is Stella."

"I'm Ushman," he says, and puts his hand in hers. It is just as he thought it might be. The fingers smooth and long and cool. His own hand is thick with calluses, his palm warm, his grip firm. He lets go first. Stella takes a sip of coffee. She smiles. "It's good. How did you know about this place? Do you travel a lot?"

"No. I haven't traveled in almost three years. What about yourself?"

"I moved here in August. But I flew into LaGuardia."

"How do you like New York?" he asks, genuinely curious.

She nods as she takes a drink. "It's cool. Like everybody says. So many people, so many things to do. But it gets hectic. I guess, maybe, I will love it more once I feel totally settled. Do you live here?"

"Yes. I guess I do. In Queens, actually. It still surprises me."

"That you live here?"

He nods and takes a sip of coffee. "I am Iranian. I never imagined living anywhere else. Certainly not America."

"So what happened?" She looks at him intently.

"It's a long story. A sad story," he says, and smiles.

"I like sad stories." Stella smiles slyly.

Ushman waves his finger at her. "Oh, no. You should change your taste. It is not good to have a thirst for sadness."

"Why not?" Her voice is suddenly strong, confrontational.

Ushman hesitates. "You are young . . ." he begins. She rolls her eyes. "What is it?" he asks.

"Not cool. I don't like condescension. If you're going to lecture me . . . at least be original."

Ushman is ashamed and awed. Her confidence is startling and attractive. He hangs his head and looks into his coffee. Then it occurs to him that he may not agree. "Sometimes the truth is not original at all."

Stella squints her eyes, as if she is reading something in the distance. Then, slowly, her face relaxes into a grin. "Okay. You got me there. Continue."

Ushman smiles, too, again, simply as a response to hers. "I only meant that often it is true of youth that you do not think you will ever have your own sadness. But you will. This is without doubt. And then you will regret that you ever enjoyed the sadness of others."

Stella leans forward, as if she might reach out to touch him. "Let me blow your theory about youth. I already have my own sadness." She says this quietly, as if it is a secret. But her eyes are bold. She wants him to ask. She wants him to know about her.

"I don't believe you. You are beautiful, American, and probably a good student."

Stella shrugs at the compliment. "It's my birthday. Today. Actually"—she looks at her watch—"an hour and a half ago. And I spent it watching strangers. Other people. You."

Ushman's face does not change. "Yes. Okay. Spending your birthday watching a man like me. Very sad." He smiles.

Stella shakes her head. "No, I didn't mean . . ." she starts, and then just blushes.

"It's okay. I'm a foreigner. I imagine I am quite often the victim of people-watchers."

Stella furrows her brow, then shakes her head. "That's not why I was watching you," she says, unafraid to look at him.

Ushman swallows. "Then why?" he asks, casually, as if it might not matter to him.

"I don't know." Stella bites her bottom lip. Then, leaning back in her chair, she folds her hands in her lap. "Your arms, actually. I liked the way your arms looked." She cocks her head, waiting for his response.

For a moment, Ushman goes blank. She has startled him with this admission. He thinks of Farak and her empathy for his big feet, which, as a child, always hung off the front of his sandals. He wiggles his toes under the table. Stella cannot see this. She only sees his fingers wipe over his eyelids, as if he were erasing something there.

"Oh, I'm sorry. I think this city has gotten to me. I didn't mean to be so . . . frank. It's not like . . . whatever," Stella says, but doesn't finish her sentence.

Ushman first thinks she has said Farak, his wife's name. "Please, don't apologize. But frank? I don't think I understand the meaning of this word."

"Oh. Okay. It's like blunt. Or brazen, you know?"

"Yes, I know brazen. Frank. That's funny." Ushman smiles.

"Hilarious," she says, biting her lip again.

There is a long silence. "I know somebody in Iran called Farak. I thought, when you said frank, that you were saying her name, Farak."

"Oh," Stella says. Her eyes are wide. Then, furrowing her brow, she says, "Why would I say her name?"

"You know," Ushman says, ignoring her question, "I'm not sure how these things go."

"What do you mean? 'These things'?" Stella leans into the table so that the edge of it is touching her chest. Ushman is struck by her physicality, the way she is so animated. He wonders if other people express themselves like this, with their bodies moving in conjunction with their speech, punctuating their thoughts. Perhaps it is an American quality he has just never noticed before. But its effect is one of contagious energy. She is so unmistakably alive, it feels as though his own vitality is magnified by hers. He begins to notice the way his own hands move when he talks, the placement of his body in the chair, the slight variations of his posture.

Ushman leans forward, emulating her position. "Does it sound terrible to say that I'd like to be your friend?"

"My friend?" she says. Stella smiles. "Do you know that's an American euphemism to use when you're trying to drop somebody? To get rid of them, romantically speaking."

"To call them a friend?"

"Yeah. It's sort of a reflection of how rotten the whole

romantic thing is here. How flimsy it can be. For 'the youth,' "
she says, smiling wickedly. "I'm disillusioned—can you tell?"

Ushman is utterly charmed by Stella. He did not anticipate
someone so young being so at ease with herself.

"The English I learned as a schoolboy in Iran was not totally
comprehensive."

Stella furrows her brow. "Your English is perfect. Better
than most of the people I went to high school with."

"But I do not understand all the cultural implications of the
words I choose."

"Neither do my parents. Or any of their friends. They're still
trying to figure out when cool means put on a sweater, and
when it means it's all good, you're swank."

Ushman raises his eyebrows. "Swank?"

"If we're going to be friends, I can fill you in."

"I could tell you my long sad story, but then you might feel
obliged. I'd like you as a friend without pity."

"Is Farak a friend?" Stella asks, while wrapping her hands
around her coffee cup.

He looks at her. "Farak?" He pauses, slides his coffee cup
away, toward the middle of the table. "She is my wife."

"Oh. Okay," Stella says, laughing in defeat. She nods, and
says under her breath, "Happy birthday, Stella."

Ushman ignores her sarcasm. "And she sent me here, to
America, three years ago, after a terrible earthquake, when we
lost many precious things." Ushman pauses, but does not look
away. "I haven't seen her since, but will receive word, someday
soon, that she has had a baby." He waits, to let this information
be understood. "And, because I often don't know what else to
do with myself, I come here and wait, like I have tonight. I
stand right where I have imagined so many times to have stood

so that my wife would come to me. Would walk off a plane and find her place by my side. But she never did. And she never will. And though I miss many things about my country, I will not go back because to do so would only leave the most important thing still missing. To go home only to have that one thing gone. . . . I don't think I could." Ushman continues to look at Stella's face. They are both quiet for a moment. Then Ushman clears his throat. "That," he says, twirling his ring around and around, "is my sad story."

Stella does not avert her eyes from his. Her demeanor is calm and composed. It is as if she is not yet distrustful of others' pain. She is not yet afraid that her proximity to Ushman's misfortunes may burden her with some responsibility to him. This innocence is why, perhaps, Ushman has told her, in the middle of a crowded airport, what he has told no other American since he has come here.

And because her innocence is combined with a bold sense of self, Ushman does not feel guilty about sharing his sorrow with her. Instead, he feels relief. And, oddly, more likable. Stella has heard that of which he is most ashamed, and yet there is no pity or judgment on her face. She has only gotten prettier.

They sit together in silence. Then Stella takes her last swallow of coffee and spreads her fingers out on the tabletop.

"I just turned nineteen," Stella says. Suddenly Ushman feels quite old and foolish, knowing that she is half his age. But he listens attentively as she continues. "My parents gave me a pink fleece jacket."

Ushman's expression does not change.

"The buttons are little pastel animals. A zebra, a hippo, a crocodile." She pretends to hold them between her index finger and thumb.

Still his expression does not change.

"It's sweet," she says, smiling too widely. "For a five-year-old." Her face goes sour, for effect. "For me, it's horrible."

Ushman smiles. And as he watches Stella shake her head, mocking her own self-pity, he begins to chuckle.

"If you saw it on me, then you'd really be laughing," Stella says. "But you should not enjoy the sadness of others."

Ushman bows his head to her, acknowledging her use of his own words.

"Especially that of a friend," Stella says, smiling.

"It is true. I'm sorry you didn't receive a birthday gift that pleased you."

"It was good coffee," Stella says. "That pleased me."

"And I, also. Maybe, there will be another time when I can buy you a coffee. My shop is in Manhattan."

"Yeah, I'd like that. What kind of shop?"

"Persian carpets. Kilim. From Iran, mostly." Ushman reaches into his wallet and produces a business card for Stella. He passes it to her. It is thick and substantial. The script is embossed in black. Stella slides it into the inside pocket of her leather jacket.

Ushman does not ask for her number. He does not walk too close to her as they pass through the terminal together, toward the airport exit. Momentarily, Ushman thinks of the ticket in his pocket. The money he has forfeited. He knows that when he finds his way back to his own car, alone once again, and puts his hands on the wheel to drive himself home, he will wish for that money back.

But for now, he directs her to the taxi stand and happily stands next to her, silently waiting, until she is at the front of the line.

"Happy birthday," he finally says as she turns toward him for some kind of goodbye.

"Thank you," Stella says, "and for the coffee, too." Ushman nods and then steps away from her and stands on the curb, watching as she tells the driver her destination. Stella does not wave. She simply looks at him with wide-open eyes, eyes that again have the look of someone searching for something of significance. Ushman raises his hand in a stiff, formal gesture and watches the cab turn the corner.

five

It is not unusual for Ushman to eat breakfast on Saturday mornings at the small coffee shop a few blocks away from his shop. They serve American fare. Ushman likes the roasted chicken with rice, green beans, and a roll. He also likes that he can have this at ten A.M. Though the rest of the patrons usually order eggs or pancakes or toast, Ushman loves the buttery rice and salty green beans. The waitress is always the same—a Greek woman, busty and graying, but still quick on her feet. She greets Ushman each time with the same phrase. "Come in, come in. Sit down. You're a long way from home," she says without inflection. Ushman watches her face carefully, because he would like to understand the sentiment behind these words. But she never conveys any emotion with her voice or her face. He might think this phrase was her standard greeting, but she never says the same thing to any other customer, no matter how foreign they appear.

The chicken is so good and the coffee shop is so convenient, Ushman does not let this habit of hers bother him. They also serve a wonderful coconut cream pie, which the Greek woman brings to him, without fail, as soon as he's finished his entrée. With black coffee, it is one of Ushman's favorite American treats.

He doesn't open his own shop until noon on Saturday, so he sometimes lingers with a second cup of coffee and watches the pedestrians pass by as the sidewalk becomes more and more crowded.

Today is a beautiful fall morning. The sun is warm in the patches where it falls between buildings, but the air is cool and thin with the approaching winter. It has been nearly a week since Ushman met Stella at Kennedy. He has heard nothing from her, but he is still anxious each time he checks his messages, hoping that she may have called. It is a juvenile distraction, an adrenaline rush Ushman could not have expected he would ever receive from a young blond American girl. But it is exactly the unforeseen nature of his arousal that has captured Ushman's imagination.

Because of a school friend's favor, Ushman and Farak had one of the first black market satellite dishes in Tabriz. For the first few months, they would host gatherings every Sunday evening for the neighbors. Together, they'd watch movies like *Grease* and *Top Gun*.

Now Ushman imagines that he is playing a character in one of these movies. And that as he sits here in the vinyl booth, staring into all the faces passing by the window, Stella is also sitting somewhere, watching the world go by; each of them looking for the other. And there is music playing in each of their ears. A romantic song whose tune would be familiar to the audience.

Ushman tries to remember the soundtrack from one of those movies they'd watched, but he cannot. It was only six months before the satellite was confiscated and Ushman was forced to pay a huge bribe to his local cleric in order to avoid a prison term.

The movie me, Ushman tells himself, would just drive up there. He takes the last swallow of coffee from his cup. The movie me would not hesitate to find her at her college and ask her to accompany me to the pond in the middle of the park that glistens from Mrs. Roberts's living room windows. And again, as the handsome couple skates in the crisp autumn air, the same sentimental song would play.

Of course, disappointed by his own fantasy, Ushman does not know how to ice-skate. But each time he has stood in front of Mrs. Roberts's windows and seen the figures going around and around, they look nearly mechanical. He wonders how difficult it really is. Perhaps it would come naturally to him. This is something he had hoped to try with Farak, when she finally came.

Ushman stares a moment longer at the passing crowds. There is still no tune playing in his head. He pays his check and begins the short walk uptown to his shop.

On the way, he passes one of his favorite New York department stores. This is the place, with its red awnings and well-dressed doorman, where Ushman liked to buy Farak gifts. Everything is so expensive and well designed. He is reminded of Mrs. Roberts and her desire that the Ardabil be out of reach. He remembers his own sense of triumph the first time he was able to afford something in this store, even though, or perhaps simply because, its price was inflated. A flicker of regret passes through his mind as he thinks of how he'd chastised Mrs. Roberts.

Ushman looks at his watch. It's a few minutes before noon. He allows the doorman to hold the door for him as he steps inside the store.

He walks past the jewelry cases, admiring a diamond and sapphire pendant in one. Next, there are hats and shawls and gloves. He'd once bought Farak a pair of brown leather gloves, lined with black fur. They were so soft and smelled so musky, Ushman let his hands linger in the box before he sealed it shut. He looks over the glove display and sees a nearly identical pair.

There had also been a teapot that he'd found upstairs. It was deep orange porcelain adorned with platinum wingspans as though a scattering of birds were flying across a full harvest moon. Ushman had it professionally packed and sent to Farak, who, later, when he asked about it, reported that it had arrived in pieces.

Several weeks later, however, his mother wrote to him about the expensive new teapot with which Farak had begun serving her tea. *It is foolish that she squanders your money on such poor taste. I always knew that this girl could not transcend her background. With this ugly pot and the awkward way in which she holds it—her knuckles white with exertion—she has proven it. Perhaps it is a gift that she has given you no children. Think of it.*

Never before had Ushman's mother mentioned their childlessness. Ushman read this letter over and over, trying to understand why Farak would tell him the teapot had broken, when, in fact, she was using it to serve his mother's tea. Eventually, like all of his mother's letters, Ushman crumpled it and placed it in the wastebasket.

A saleswoman approaches Ushman and asks if he needs assistance. Before he can stop himself, he has said, "I'm shopping for my wife."

The saleswoman directs him to a display of cashmere scarves folded carefully into a locked case. She opens the case and pulls out three or four wide scarves. Immediately Ushman has a favorite. But, he realizes as the saleswoman unfolds it for him, it is not for Farak. Even if she were still his wife. Even if this were not a charade. The scarf is for Stella.

It is a rich but pale shade of gray with fine black and red stripes at either end. It looks young and urban. The gray might nearly match the color of her eyes, he thinks. Ushman lays his hand on the cashmere. It is dense and lovely.

Just like the millions of other Americans who use the retail experience to fulfill some vague, yet particular, longing, Ushman asks to have the scarf wrapped up.

With the package under his arm, Ushman feels foolish and hopeful. He knows that the purchase of this scarf is unknown to Stella; and that it has no influence on determining if she calls. Yet Ushman feels that it is a marker. And that, somehow, it is holding her place in his life. Whether she knows it or not, he is ready.

Before leaving the store, he stops in the restroom. He is startled, however, when he hears a girl's voice.

"I don't want to," she says from inside one of the stalls, and Ushman wishes he had heard nothing.

"You have to, sweetie," says a man, who Ushman realizes is in the stall with her.

"Stop it," the girl says.

Ushman does not know what to do.

"Do it again," the man says.

The girl sighs, resigned. She is not crying.

"That's my girl," says the man.

Should he walk out and tell security? Is this a crime? There is no screaming. No call for help.

Ushman continues to stand still, his heart beating fast and loud. Without moving, he listens for more.

There is nothing, until he hears a zipper close and the toilet flush. In this moment of silence, which lasts forever in Ushman's mind, he has imagined the most horrible of abuses. He has seen the little girl's mouth and hands, reddened and fumbling. He's seen a bedroom with a quilt that she hides under and cries. He's seen the mother to whom all these things will remain hidden.

As the door of the stall swings open, Ushman is caught in his startled pose. He quickly walks to a urinal.

The girl is probably five, with thick black curls all over her head. The man, with the same black curls, is clearly her father.

"Wash up," he says to her, turning on the sink.

"Stop it," she says, just as she had in the stall. "I can do it myself."

The father catches Ushman's eye and shrugs.

"Sometimes I think it was easier when she couldn't wipe her own bottom," he says, laughing nervously, as the girl frowns at him and turns off the water.

Ushman forces a smile, then flushes and washes his own hands. He is confused. Was what he heard something truly innocent? Or is he being deceived? Is he guilty in his complicity? He studies the girl's intensity as she lathers soap between her hands. This task consumes her. She does not look up at Ush-man. He cannot see her face, what clues may be on it. Her father drums his fingers on the paper towel dispenser.

Ushman reaches for a towel and the man steps away from the dispenser, clears his throat, and paces behind his daughter.

Ushman dries his hands and picks up his package. He leaves them there like that. The girl still washing and the father pacing.

Outside on the sidewalk, Ushman realizes he's been holding his breath. He breathes deeply and feels the cool air travel deep into his lungs. This both refreshes him and fills him with regret. If only he were a wiser man. If only he felt stronger and less confused. Perhaps he could have done something. Something for the girl.

Or perhaps he would have made a fool of himself. Perhaps there was nothing to be done. Perhaps it was his own cor-rupt mind that presumed there was an assault when there was none. What does Ushman know about helping a child use the restroom?

He shakes his head and looks at his watch, realizing that he is late for opening his shop. The sidewalks are crowded now with shoppers and tourists. Ushman drops his head and walks quickly, inadvertently jostling those who are moving slower than he. This physicality fuels his anger, as though there were some conspiracy in the city to prevent him from walking freely.

When he reaches his shop, there is a small line of perspira-tion across his forehead. He unlocks the door and feels relief at the quiet, familiar air of the space. With a handkerchief, he wipes off his brow. Then he sets the package down beside his desk and looks out at the crowded sidewalk below.

"Filthy city," he says to himself as he sits in his chair, his legs quivering with adrenaline. This energy distracts him and he cannot sit still. Pacing across the room, Ushman tries to concentrate on his tasks. He looks at the stack of papers on his desk needing to be filed, the authentication materials awaiting his signature, the phone messages, the bills, the copy for his upcoming advertisement in the Metropolitan Opera's Playbill. All of this work stagnates in his mind and makes him more restless.

Impulsively, Ushman makes a decision. Leaving the package by his desk and the paperwork all undone, he turns the sign on the door to its closed position and he hurriedly walks the two blocks to his van. Again, he jostles the slowpokes and the gawkers, but he does not feel the impact of these contacts. Instead, he simply feels the motion of his feet beneath him, their utter decisiveness as he maneuvers the sidewalk, intent on his destination.

Ushman's van idles just outside the big black wrought-iron gates of the college. It is on the west side of Broadway, with Columbia University's much bigger campus shadowing it from the east. Ushman can see little more than the red-brick pathway beyond the gates. There is ivy and greenery covering the wrought iron on either side of the gates.

It is now nearly dusk. Ushman has had to travel around the campus on Claremont Avenue all the way up to 120th Street just once, when a traffic officer advised him to. Otherwise, he's been right here, regardless of the horns and cursing that his position has provoked. Though he's seen lots of young women wearing black leather jackets, he has not seen Stella. His back is growing weary and his eyes feel strained. He has studied each face on this block carefully, to be sure he does not miss her.

And then, in the twilight of the day, from two blocks away, he is surprised how easily he recognizes her. Before her features are clear to him, he recognizes the way she holds her head, the tailored black leather jacket, the pale hair piled onto her head like a haphazard halo. She is beautiful.

And yet so plain. Like the startling quality of a kilim that is unadorned. Her simplicity is strong and unapologetic. And Ushman feels proud that he has seen the beauty in this. As though his ability to recognize it makes him exceptional. She is not flashy or striking or exotic. She is not trying to stand out; she's trying to fit in. Ushman understood this about her instantly. And now he also understands that she will surely never come with him. He stands out. Like a sore thumb.

Ushman picks out the noise of his van idling above the noise of rush-hour traffic. He listens to its familiar rhythm. Stella abruptly enters the Chinese restaurant on the corner. Ushman watches her through the brightly lit windows as she orders food from the counter. He puts the van into gear just as Stella waves to a table of students in the back of the restaurant. She makes her way over to them and exchanges a hug with a boy.

A blond, handsome, American boy. He keeps his hand on Stella's back. Ushman places the van back into idle. Soon enough, Stella retrieves her thin plastic bag of food from the counter and is back on the sidewalk, walking straight toward Ushman's van.

She has her head down, and swings the bag at her side. Passing right by Ushman's big white van, she soon disappears inside the black gates.

Ushman rests his head on the steering wheel and breathes a sigh of relief. For once, he has done the right thing. He has not humiliated himself. He did not jump out of his van and approach her, claiming to have just been driving by, as he had planned while sitting here all afternoon. Ushman compliments himself once more for his restraint, though he cannot help feeling disappointed.

He is still alone.

Ushman has never felt that he understood when in life he should give up gracefully and when he should fight to the end. Tonight he decides that giving up is what he knows how best to do.

Ushman maneuvers the van into the southbound traffic of Broadway, looking only once in his rearview mirror at the campus behind him.

Six

It is late in the day. Ushman stands in his store, his hands clasped behind him, waiting. Like a character in a play, waiting for the plot point. The action that will motivate his next move. But there is nothing. No stage direction. No dialogue. No music. Ushman moves to the window. He looks at the sidewalk below. There are many people, hurriedly moving about. In contrast, Ushman feels so solitary and so still, as though he may be fading away. He wonders if this happens, sometimes. If ever a person is so totally alone and inconsequential that he simply ceases to exist. The cells that constitute his body could just sort of drain out through his feet, leaving only a puddle of murky water in their place. Like the unexplained liquid debris that sometimes litters the sidewalk, prompting Ushman to step around its cloudy circumference. But if this were true, Ushman reasons, then there would be no homeless people sleeping under cardboard or urinating in the subway tunnels. And gradually, as evolution worked its magic, loneliness and the people to whom it clings would become extinct. The world would be left with only useful, happy, interdependent people all desperately trying to prove their importance to the universe, for fear that they, too, could become the victims of natural selection.

But people's lives are consumed by minutiae. Not by the thought that a thousand years from now, some unknown genetic offspring may be in jeopardy because of our own reclusive tendencies.

What would happen if he vanished? Somebody would come for his rugs. Take them and sell them and make a fortune. As he had taken the gentleman's rug from Jackson Heights. Taken it away in the back of his van while a different van took the man's body away. He was just as alone as I, Ushman realizes. Nobody knew the contents of his life. The belongings in his house. The complexities of his mind. This similarity he could not recognize three months ago. Today, Ushman thinks, I am a different man. And if I disappear, let the cycle continue. Let someone else steal what is left of me from me.

Yes, good, Ushman thinks. Let somebody climb these stairs and take all these rugs. Let them have the bad luck that I have had. Let that theft follow their feet like a shadow. Perhaps then he, too, will die a better man. In this way, the world will be purified. Through sorrow and remorse comes redemption.

Ushman rubs his eyes and smiles at his own foolish philosophizing. He steps closer to the window and says, to nobody in particular, "You idiot."

It is then that he sees her. In the block just to the southwest. She is walking quickly, with a definite purpose. As she crosses the street, he can see her face clearly. At first he feels elated that he recognizes someone. Among all of those people, there is one that he knows. But then he realizes that she is coming here. He is her destination. As he has been so many times before. But for three months, since their last encounter in June, she has not come. There were a couple of phone messages that Ushman received, reminding him to be looking for a replacement for the rug in her den. He listened to each one with a lump in his throat, fearing the day that he would have to face her again, and then, when she made no mention of an appointment, he erased them. Ushman does not want her to remind him of his weakness that day, of the way he cried while her breath moved the hairs on his neck. He does not want to see in her face the smug smile of someone who knows your vulnerability, who has seen you depleted and reckless.

That morning that she stayed with him, as the sunlight traveled across the room, seems like years ago. Finally, she got up, touched his arm, and left him there, alone. To close his eyes on the room and sleep there, through the end of the day and the beginning of the next. To sleep through the recurring nightmare that has followed him from Tabriz to Queens to Madison Avenue.

In it, he is sleeping, with Farak at his side. They are in their home in Tabriz. He is awakened by the sound of a baby crying. As he listens more carefully, he realizes that the baby is somewhere in the house. And then, in a flood of panic, he realizes that they've had a baby. This whole time. Through all of the miscarriages and through all of their sorrow, they've forgotten that they already had a baby. A baby that needs them. A baby that is crying. Has been crying all along. In his dream, Ushman pushes off the sheet and begins to search. Beneath the bed, in drawers and boxes, in closets and in the folded towels. Everywhere he looks, the crying gets louder, more urgent. Ushman calls out to Farak. He needs her help. This baby needs its mother. Unbelievably, she keeps on sleeping. He would like to

shake her, but he hasn't time. He follows the sound of the crying outside. The garden is cool. He does not have a wrap. He
shivers. Then he hears the fountain. And, turning, with his arms
outstretched, ready to cradle the baby and deliver it to Farak,
Ushman sees the bird. The enormous white crane, with graying
feathers at its neck. It is pecking at the bench. At the same spot
where his father died. And with a sickness in his stomach that is
nearly unbearable, Ushman sees that the bird's beak is red. It
is mauling their baby. It has been methodically pecking at their
baby this whole time. All these years. While they worried and
argued and counted days. And now it is too late. The crying has
stopped. The bird flies away.

Over and over again, after Mrs. Roberts left, Ushman had
this dream. Finally, awakened by the daylight, Ushman went
home. His body sore and exhausted, he drove without care. He
did not obey traffic laws, and coasted through red lights after
he'd slowed to halfheartedly check for traffic. With one hand on
the steering wheel, Ushman thought of crossing the center line.
He did not think of his own death, but rather of a cessation to
this hollow aching in his gut. The worry and regret that is like
an iron sphere, rounding out its space in his abdomen, becoming heavier and more metallic every day.

Quite accidentally, Ushman made it home safely.

It is not difficult for him now to remember that taste in his
mouth and that weight in his stomach. In fact, seeing Mrs.
Roberts has made it palpable once again.

But now Ushman is trapped. He does not have time to leave
without being seen. He could pretend he is not here, hide in the
oversized closet and let her ring the bell, let the trill of it echo
through his shop until she gives up and goes away.

This is his plan. As he paces back and forth across his shop,

Ushman decides he cannot face her. Not today. He turns the
sign on the door to the closed position and opens the closet
door, ready to retreat into it. He checks the sidewalk once more
and sees that she has crossed to his side of the street. She is ten
paces away from the outside door when she stops. Standing directly beneath his window, she looks up. Ushman is concealed
behind the rug that is hanging. A splendid Bijar from Kurdi-
stan. Groups of red rose blossoms inside pale blue medallions
form a grid. It is like one in her entry, but the color scheme in
this one will not impress her. This gives him a small bit of relief.
But she is not studying the rug, rather her eyes are not focused
on anything in particular. They are simply gazing up. He stands,
quivering, behind the rug, waiting to make his escape. She takes
a few more steps toward the outside door and then stops. People
jostle her as they continue their hurried pace. She wrings her
hands, looking at the black leather gloves that cover her fingers.

Without warning, she turns away from the door, walks
south, against the flow of pedestrians, and then stops once more
beneath his window.

Again her eyes turn upward and she fidgets with her hands.
She has made her decision. With a slightly less purposeful
stride, she turns and retraces her steps, leaving Ushman standing in the window, shuddering with relief.

A few days later, just as he has forgotten his relief, Mrs. Roberts
does ring the bell. He has no escape. She stands on the other
side of the frosted glass door, taking off her gloves.

"You have neglected me," she says as he opens the door, startled by the reprimand in her voice.

She does not remind him of their last meeting, she shows no memory of his despair. And she certainly shows no sign of her own hesitation just three days ago.

Ushman extends his arm toward the center of his shop, welcoming her inside. It is just as it has always been. "I have just received my newest inventory. Please, please, come and see."

Ushman unfolds nearly every rug in the store, including ones that she has seen before, ones that she has taken home to live with, only to return them, unsatisfied, days later. It is a strenuous job. He is perspiring now.

She is looking at this last one carefully, her arms crossed in front of her chest. Once again, Ushman finds himself standing behind Mrs. Roberts, waiting for her opinion to be formed.

"You know, Ushman," she says, without removing her eyes from the rug. It is a Ghiordes prayer rug from the late nineteenth century that Ushman bought from a collector in Los Angeles. Its colors are subtle but stunning, with its arch formed from olive green and the border in navy and burgundy. "I do like this very much. But, from one end of the room, it would always look as if it were upside down."

He sighs. "It can be seen as simply an abstract element. It does not need to be oriented so that one is seeing the arch —"

She interrupts him by holding up a finger. He recognizes this gesture and is silent. "Tell me about the rug, Ushman."

She does this when she is nearly settled on her choice. But it is not so simple as choosing. Ushman must earn the sale. He must tell her about the rug so that she attaches to it, emotionally, as if it were a child in an orphanage.

"This arch is called a *mihrab*. It should be oriented towards Mecca when you pray. But for decorative purposes, it is irrele-

vant. This rug was woven in a mountain village in western
Turkey just before a massive earthquake destroyed the workshops in 1905. It is in excellent condition. A semi-antique, obviously. Its seven-row border symbolizes the seven steps of the
ascent to Paradise."

"And would you pray on it?"

"Of course. Absolutely. Five times a day," Ushman says,
smiling.

Mrs. Roberts does not smile. She is still staring at the rug.
"No," she says. "I mean, would you, now. Pray for me."

Ushman's smile fades. "I don't understand. . . ."

For a moment her face is serious, expectant. Then, quite
suddenly, she laughs. "Not literally, Ushman. I simply want to
see how it's done. You know. Show me how a Muslim would
approach this rug, at a time of prayer."

Ushman does not look at her face. But he knows, she has
that familiar look in her eyes. The desire, the longing.

He has a knot, suddenly, in his throat. Without understanding its purpose, Ushman feels that her request must be some
form of subjugation. Some reminder of his relation to her and
her country. A reminder that here, in his shop, she still wields
the power. A reminder of what she remembers of that morning
in June.

"I'm sorry," she says, when his silence fills the room. "I certainly didn't mean to offend you. . . ."

"Certainly not," Ushman says, knowing that he is beholden
to her. She is his customer.

For the sake of a sale, he will show her *salaat*. He has not
prayed since Ramadan last year. The ritual no longer feels like
it transports him to a place where he is whole. Instead, it only

reminds him of how much he has lost. So he is hesitant to begin. And Ushman is not a performer; there is no sense of drama in his chemistry. His motions are small and subtle.

He first steps out of his shoes and stands on the niche in the rug. With his legs slightly spread, he brings his hands to his ears, with his palms forward and his thumbs behind his ear-lobes. Under his breath, he recites the words. She does not hear them. He hardly hears them himself. But she watches his lips move as he truncates the prayer and bends quickly onto his knees, where he knows she wants him. Ushman does not truly pray. Instead, he looks up at her, to see that she is watching, to see that she understands his shorthand, to make it known that this demonstration is not sacred, and her observation of it is not intimate.

Her eyes, though, do not acknowledge this distinction. She is rigid with respect for this display. She clearly considers it to be an honor. This invitation into a world she does not know. Into a world she's seen as a tourist from expensive sailboats and chartered planes, but never really noticed. Never found par-ticularly charming or accessible or even very remarkable. Ush-man sees in her gaze a kind of distant epiphany. As though she is recalling things she might have seen while on elegant tours of Cairo or Istanbul. And as though the things she has seen are just now becoming relevant to her life. Because of Ushman on his knees in front of her. She is beginning to see the world more broadly. To understand that even as she strolled through the bazaar, looking for a trinket for her son, avoiding the eyes of lo-cal merchants who studied the expensive golden highlights in her hair and sparkling studs in her ears, Ushman or some-one like him was there. A man who may have spread a carpet beneath himself and said these very words, believing in Allah,

believing in his faith and his country with a vigor and convic-
tion that she now covets. Because this kind of devotion requires
desire. And this sensation of yearning seems to be, still, out of
her reach.

Ushman stands and wipes his face with his palms. "You
see?" he says, smiling casually. "It is a beautiful piece, with sacred intentions." Ushman is no longer desperate to sell this, or
any, rug. He doesn't believe his life will ever change.

Mrs. Roberts is still looking at the rug. "What does Islam
say about the afterlife, Ushman?"

"That for those who believe and live a good life, it is
Paradise."

"And for those who don't, there is hell?"

Ushman nods.

She smiles briefly. "Always there must be the faith. Belief.
Never is it good enough to just behave."

Ushman shrugs. He looks down at the rug again. "The
mihrab, the archway, is representing the doorway to Paradise.
Symbolically speaking there are—"

"I'm not speaking of symbols," she says, interrupting him,
her voice quiet and flat. "They don't interest me. I'm interested
in what is real. In what is urgent and absolute." Her eyes are
fixed on his face, as though she were deciding whether or not it,
not the rug, would be right in her den. As though something in
his face would either match her décor or not. As though she
might truly buy a forty-thousand-dollar rug based on his reply.

Ushman starts to shrug, but thinks better of it, so that his
shoulders pull up toward his ears and stay there, like a turtle
backing into its shell. "I think faith is required to protect religion from reason. After all, it is not a science. Allah, or God,
wants your heart, not just your mind. Your heart must believe.

Our actions can be . . . what is the word . . . hollow. Adequate, but hollow. Your actions cannot substitute for the contents of your heart."

Then, as he's finished speaking, Ushman allows his shoulders to drop, slowly. As he does so, Mrs. Roberts looks away, back to the floor and the rug just beyond her feet.

He lets her look a moment longer and then Ushman folds the rug over on itself. "Perhaps it is not the right rug for you," he says, noticing the tenor of the horns escalating outside, indicating that the afternoon is nearly gone. "Perhaps there will be one next month."

"I want it," she says, her voice still flat. "You'll bring it now?"

Ushman looks at his watch. He closes his eyes and then nods, extending his arms toward her. "Whatever you like."

"I won't be there. I'm on my way out. But my girl is there. She will let you in."

Ushman follows her to the door, still nodding his head. "Of course, of course."

She stops in the doorway and pulls on her black leather gloves that have a strong aroma of cedar to them. "And Ushman, make sure the arch faces the right way. Towards Mecca, you know."

"As you wish," Ushman says, closing the door behind her and looking at the Ghiordes prayer rug, folded over on itself, looking meek and sloppy, like a child trying to avoid being chosen for a difficult chore.

Seven

Without a crack of thunder or a spark of lightning, the rain begins. It is such a welcome distraction that Ushman actually breathes an audible sigh as he looks out of his apartment window. The street is instantly covered. Its slick blackness is beautiful the way a river is. Street and traffic lights are reflected and magnified in the water. Each drop of rain falls hard and leaves rings of delicate ripples in its place. It is mesmerizing.

He woke suddenly, without reason, and has not been able to sleep any longer. Instead, he sits in a dining room chair he's pulled close to the window and looks out at the night. He continues to watch the street, even when the rain ends, as suddenly as it began.

For a while, Ushman wished again that he might see his platinum-haired prostitute, who seems to have disappeared from the neighborhood. Raining or not, he would go quickly out into the night to meet her. But he's still sitting here, watching.

The *Times* delivery truck stops at the newsstand and its driver stacks four bundles of papers on a milk crate. The proprietor

covers them with a blue tarp in case the rain returns. Only because he is watching carefully, Ushman sees the brief moment
between light and dark. When the city is on the brink of day.
The sidewalk looks almost pink and then, suddenly, it is simply
gray again. The streetlights become redundant, the traffic becomes heavier, and the pedestrians are hurried, intent. The day
has begun.

It is not until Ushman is in the shower that he begins to feel
sleepy again. He lets his eyes close and appreciate this drowsi-
ness. It is this feeling, he reminds himself, that he will try to cultivate tonight.

He dresses without care in a pale blue oxford shirt and dark
blue jeans. Lifting a sweater from the hook in his closet, he
leaves his apartment without breakfast.

By the time he's driven into Manhattan, the sun has come
out. Its quality, though, is much different from the days before.
It is no longer warm on Ushman's hair and eyelids. In fact, it almost seems to make the air colder with its brightness. The block
between Fifth and Madison is long and in shadow. Ushman
walks quickly in the chill.

He has not been in his shop for ten minutes when the bell
rings. The door is frosted glass, but he can tell by the silhouette
that it is a woman.

Ushman rolls his eyes to the ceiling. Already, he thinks, Mrs.
Roberts has tired of the Ghiordes.

As he opens the door, he is shocked. He thinks, of course,
that he must be daydreaming.

But the girl is wet and cold and real.

"Stella," he says, holding out a hand. She places her fingers
hesitantly into his palm as he guides her into his shop.

She stands just inside the doorway, looking around. Ushman

excuses himself and fetches the folding chair near his desk. "Here," he says, "please sit."

But Stella doesn't move. There are circles under her eyes, her hair is wet, and she seems to be shaking.

"Are you all right?" Ushman asks, realizing that she may be hurt. He dispenses water from the cooler into a paper cup.

Stella puts her hand to her mouth, as if she's trying to hold something in. But his question, his voice, his hand extending the cup toward her—one of these things must have dislodged something. Moved a small piece of her aside. The piece that was strong, composed, in control.

The tears skim down her cheeks silently as she holds both hands over her mouth. Ushman puts his hand on her elbow and directs her body into the chair. Stella begins to heave and she bends her body at the waist, so that her face reddens with blood. Ushman kneels next to her. She shakes her head. He stands. He puts his hand just over her back, hovering.

Finally, she sits up a little and begins to rock gently backward and forward in the chair. She pulls her hands away from her mouth and wipes at her eyes. Ushman gives her the handkerchief from his back pocket.

"Are you all right?" Ushman asks again. She seems smaller than he remembers her. Her wrists are so delicate, he imagines the bones inside are like twigs.

Stella moans something akin to a laugh and nods her head yes. She is embarrassed now.

"Well, I am happy to see you again as well," he says, smiling.

Stella laughs again. "I'm sorry," she says, "it's just that . . ."

"Is there yet another pink jacket?" Ushman says, sitting near her on the stack of rugs. He cannot comprehend what is happening. That she has actually come to him.

Stella rolls her eyes. Keeping her eyes focused on the ceiling, she heaves a heavy sigh. As she lets the air out of her mouth, her head falls forward. "I've been up all night. I'm . . . I'm sort of a wreck." She looks at Ushman. His face is clean-shaven, his skin as brown as dirt. Stella's skin is pale with blotchy patches of red that punctuate her distress. "Did I tell you that my parents are in Italy?"

He shakes his head, raises his eyebrows.

"Traveling. That's why I was at Kennedy that night. It's a consolation trip. For their empty-nest syndrome."

Ushman furrows his brow, unfamiliar with the idiom.

"I've gone and now their house is quiet. Lonely. Like two old birds without any babies in the nest."

"So the two old birds fly across the ocean for some pizza pie?"

"Exactly." She smiles. Then her face goes limp again. "Only, yesterday, in Venice, my mother tried to kill herself. She jumped off a bridge into the canal."

Ushman stands up. It's an instinct. A refusal to sit with catastrophe. He puts a hand to his forehead, then lets it slide down the side of his face. "This is terrible. Was she . . . will she be all right?"

Stella shrugs, wiping her eyes again. "I suppose. My father was vague. He didn't say much about anything. About how she is. He only told me I could not come. I am not allowed." At this admission, her face begins to crumple again. The grief is heightened by the distance. Ushman is familiar with this sensation.

"He is protecting you. He is still your father."

"I don't need protecting," she says, bluntly, as though Ushman must accept this fact before the conversation can continue.

"Perhaps he needs to protect you. He needs to be able to do that, even if not for your benefit."

Stella's eyes narrow as she looks at her own hands. Then she nods, slightly, to herself. Her voice softens. "I couldn't stay in my room. I didn't want this to be the nightly drama on our hall. I just started walking. I got on a bus. I didn't even know . . ." She begins to cry again.

"They have good doctors in Italy, I think."

"Really?" She says, pushing tears from her cheeks back into her hair.

"Yes. I heard that once." It's true. Though Ushman realizes it must sound unreal. And insufficient. His mother's younger brother emigrated to Italy. Ushman's mother always told him it was because her brother had chronic pain in his stomach and there was superior health care in Italy. Of course, he died after just six months in Rome.

"My father told me that she was standing there next to him. They were looking . . ." Stella pauses, swallowing the hesitation in her voice. "He thought they were looking at some café, someplace to get a coffee from the Ponte della Paglia, when all of a sudden she's climbed, so quickly, so effortlessly, up onto the railing. And then she just dropped out of sight. Without a single sound. He screamed. He called out. There was a soldier, an American soldier, on the other end of the bridge. He ran to my father. He seemed to know. How could he know? My father didn't say a word to him. The soldier jumped in." Stella puts her hands on her thighs and sits up straighter.

"My father looked over the railing. She was gone. He only saw the soldier on the surface. And then the soldier dove. Just once. When he came up, he had my mother in one arm. As he swam to the base of the bridge, she dragged behind him. Her hair hiding her face. My father couldn't tell if her eyes were open or closed. There was a crowd waiting for the soldier to bring her up. A medic resuscitated her and my father rode in the back of the police boat with her. She looked at him, but never said a word."

There is a silence as Stella looks at Ushman. While she was talking, she was staring at one of the rugs. When she looks at him, she begins shaking her head. "This is so fucked up," she says, hanging her head again, covering her eyes with her hands.

"I will make you some tea," Ushman says, thinking both of keeping her with him and of comforting her. "Or would you rather go get a cup of coffee? I don't have any here."

Stella rubs her eyes. "I'll have tea, please. I can't go out there again. Not for a while. It feels like I've been walking all night."

Ushman sets about brewing some tea. She watches him pack the crumbled tea leaves into a small silver tea ball. Though he can feel her eyes on him, his hands remain assured and move gently through space. He pours hot water from an electric pitcher into a plain black ceramic mug and dunks in the tea ball. Steam rises. Stella folds her arms across her chest. Ushman notices her gesture.

"You're cold," he says. "Come." Ushman opens a small door across from his desk. It is just a closet. But he has managed to fit a cot in there, draped with a moss-green blanket. It was a necessity when his apartment was being painted and he couldn't bear the fumes. "Here," Ushman says, his arms outstretched toward the cot. "Rest and become warm."

She is still shivering, though she is standing close to him in the doorway. She steps forward, next to the cot. "Is it okay?" she asks. "Really?"

Ushman smiles. "In my country, no. But we are here in New York City. The things that are impossible here are very different from the things that are impossible in Iran."

"Thank God for that," she says, smiling tentatively.

Ushman nods.

Stella sits down on the cot. Ushman brings her tea and sets it on a small filing cabinet in the corner.

She takes off her shoes and sips the tea. Her socks are short white athletic socks, which reveal her ankles. Ushman notices the smooth white skin with guilty delight.

"Thank you," she says, picking up the pillow. A piece of paper floats to the floor. Stella reaches under the cot where it has fallen and picks it up. It is a photograph of Ushman and Farak.

She hands it to Ushman. His face is flushed. It is as if he's been caught in an indiscreet act. As if he were culpable for Stella's despair.

"I'm sorry," he says, glancing only for a moment at the photograph. They are sitting on a couch in Semah's apartment. Farak's hair is long and dark and falls in curls around her shoulders. Her eyes look straight at the camera, big and brown and spirited. She has the same smooth, unwrinkled skin as Ushman, but hers is a shade lighter. Her lips are full and red, but they are not smiling. They are open slightly, as if she's just said something to the person taking the picture. She is wearing a small gold chain around her neck. Ushman is sitting close to her and looks younger and happier. He has a wide smile that is almost mischievous.

Ushman quickly slides it into his breast pocket.

Stella shrugs. "She's beautiful," she says, lying down on the cot.

"I will not disturb you," he says as she pulls the blanket up over her chest.

He closes the door, his heart racing. His wife, his ex-wife, the only wife he ever expects to have, the woman with whom Ushman has slept, the woman who has fixed his meals and held his head in her hands, is not the woman in the other room. Farak is half a world away. Has never seen this shop or the street outside with its fancy pedestrians and pedigreed dogs. She may not even recognize Ushman now, with his graying temples and tired eyes.

But it is she to whom Ushman still feels tied. She whose picture makes him nervous and repentant about having this girl in his shop. He pulls the photograph from his pocket. It was taken at a birthday celebration. Farak was pregnant. For the first time. It was a carefree night.

The next day, she was on a bus, returning a skirt she'd borrowed from a friend. It was sudden, she told Ushman later, as though something had torn or cracked inside of her. The pain was indescribable. She could only say that it felt like she'd been impaled, as if on a skewer.

She got off the bus and hailed a taxi. The nurse at the hospital told her to sit on the toilet, which is what Farak did. They'd given her a pain pill, but she was still crying when Ushman got there. And still on the toilet. Ushman waited for her in the triage room.

Later, the nurse performed an ultrasound and confirmed that her uterus was empty.

Ushman had put the picture of Farak under his pillow as a place marker. A way to hold on to the past. Because it is the woman in the photo that he does not want to forget. The way her fingers looked laced through his, the feel of her skin, the sound of her breathing near him.

The subsequent miscarriages, the earthquake, her infidelity, the soon-to-be-expected-baby, her claim of desertion—the pain of those memories he tries to wash off of him every day.

The tea has filled the shop with its bitter smell. Ushman sits on the pile of rugs near the window, watching storm clouds darken the sky once more.

Eight

It is almost dark and Ushman paces across his shop. He stops in front of the window and looks down, watching the rush hour begin. The street is crowded with women in long dark coats. A few have scarves pulled tight around their ears. These figures remind him of home. Of women in their *hejab*, hurrying home for dinner and prayers. Though Ushman never came to sympathize with the Ayatollah's fanaticism, he has come to appreciate his country's policies. There is little ambiguity in Islam. Whereas in America, everything is negotiable. Everything is possible. These endless possibilities become exhausting.

Ushman hasn't eaten all day. He's been waiting for Stella to emerge from the closet. She's slept through one of his busier days: one designer, two tourists, and a young man shopping for his wife's wedding present. Each time the bell rang, Ushman cringed, afraid the noise would wake her. He was not being thoughtful so much as he was terrified of what would happen when she emerged. Ushman has exchanged more words with Stella, been more intimate with her, than he was with Farak during the time of their betrothal. Why, he cannot help but wonder, do people in America expose themselves so readily to complete strangers?

But he, too, has been revealing himself to her in his day-dream. Occasionally he would put his ear to the door, wondering if he could hear any sound of her. In this position, he would catch himself imagining that she was here by choice, not propelled by tragedy. He fancied that she was his new, American wife. That she did her studies in the closet of his shop just to be near him. That she would accompany him to the coffee shop on Saturday mornings and the waitress who seated them would no longer tell Ushman that he was a long way from home. That she would share the apartment in Queens and they might even buy a place in Westchester, where the trees are old and mighty.

These thoughts have made him smile. But they've also pumped him full of adrenaline and expectations. With an uneasy stomach, sweaty palms, and a clenched jaw, he feels as though these past few months he has been walking on a board stretched over a deep canyon. At any moment, the board could break, his feet could slip, and he would fall. Or, just as he is sure he can no longer balance—his legs weak, his head spinning— a hand may reach out. He imagines Stella is this hand.

Finally, Ushman hears noises of her awakening. He sits at his desk, pretending to be busy with paperwork. When Stella opens the door, he turns toward her.

"I can't believe I slept so long. Is it really five o'clock?" Stella pulls her messy hair up and away from her face, securing it somehow in back.

She is beautiful. Her eyes are wide and gray. Her face holds a glimpse of adolescence in its full cheeks and ready smile. Suddenly Ushman is afraid of her. Afraid of her beauty and self-confidence. She is not a match for him. She will never be the one to offer her hand to him. He is far too flawed, far too bitter.

She stands across the room from him, stifling a yawn. He is suddenly tired and frustrated with himself for indulging in his own juvenile fantasies.

"Come," he says, gathering his briefcase and keys. "I will help you find a taxi."

"Oh, my God. I'm so sorry. You probably had plans or something. You should have woken me." Stella rubs her eyes and smoothes her cheeks. She stands by the door, obedient and waiting.

Ushman opens the door for her. She waits behind him as he locks it and turns on the alarm. He can hear her breath, almost feel it on the back of his neck. She keeps talking.

"You're angry," she says. "I know. It was stupid to come here. I just . . . I actually didn't plan to. But I got on the bus and . . ."

"Stella." Ushman says it quietly. She doesn't hear him and continues to explain.

"I walked east, just without even thinking — "

"Stella," he says again, louder this time. He still has his hand on the doorknob.

"What?"

"Ever since I came to America, I have wished for my mother to die."

Stella doesn't say anything. She doesn't move. Her breath remains constant on his neck.

"I could explain. But is there really any explanation that could justify this desire?" He turns around to face her. His stomach is a wreck. "Is there?"

Stella looks down at her shoes, then back up. Her eyes look

clear and rested. "Sure, I think so. I don't believe in moral absolutes—"

"That is the problem with America. With Americans." He is angry. At himself for wanting to hear it and at her for telling him what he wanted to hear.

Stella raises her eyebrows and takes a step back. She places her palms against the wall behind her. "Are you accusing me of something?"

"Of being too forgiving. Of being ready to excuse me from hating her. Blaming her." Ushman cannot stop the words. He is full of rage, not for the girl, but for the way she's made him desire her. The way he sat in his shop while she slept and longed for her to change his life. To give him some part of herself. This desire now makes him feel weak and lost and hateful.

"I don't know what we're talking about, Ushman. Your mother or Farak?"

He doesn't answer. He cannot look at her.

"Are you angry because I slept on your cot? Because I came here when I didn't know where else to go? All I can do is apologize and go find another bus back to 116th Street." Her voice is incredulous. She cannot believe that he has turned on her.

Stella starts down the steps. Ushman watches the mess of blond hair on the back of her head jostle as she goes. She is about to push open the outside door, about to fade into the crowd.

"My mother is an invalid," he says, too loud even for the flight of stairs between them. There is nothing left to hide. She will know everything. If she's going to leave him here feeling this way, she may as well know just how worthless his life is. "Farak stayed in Iran to care for her. She stayed to care for my mother who should have died. She stayed and found a man who could give her what I could not."

Stella has her hand on the metal door frame. It is pale and motionless. She doesn't turn around. Her voice is quiet but insistent. Ushman strains to hear her.

"I don't know why you're yelling at me. I don't know how to make it right—whatever it is that I've done. And maybe it's not about me. I hardly know you. I hardly know anything at all." It is this last admission that makes her voice falter. But she has nothing more to say. Stella pushes open the door and leaves, without looking back at him.

It is dark out but still rush hour. There is a crowd of people waiting for the uptown bus. Stella stands in the middle, as if trying to extract warmth from the others' overcoats. Ushman sees the pale skin of her cheek illuminated in the light from a passing commuter bus. He imagines that he can see her jaw quivering, the way his is now.

Ushman walks closer to the bus stop. The cold air is exhilarating. He walks faster, trying to account for his heart's hurried pace. She is just a girl, he tells himself. Just a girl to whom you've exposed yourself and proven your own inferiority. Why, he asks himself, would you want to chase after her? Give her more cause to hate you?

Reaching past a couple of people, Ushman takes Stella's hand. It is cold. She turns her head. He pulls her out of the crowd. They stand in front of the glare of a jeweler's window. Ushman lets go of her hand.

"I am sorry," he says.

"Okay." Stella looks downtown, checking again for her bus. Her face is sullen, detached.

"Please," he says. She still does not look at him.

"I frighten myself with the things that I've told you. My life is . . . disheveled." Ushman begins to have a spinning sensation in his head, as though he's falling, spiraling end over end into darkness. He keeps talking. "And I feel ashamed about many things, but the most recent thing of which I am ashamed is what I said to you. I do not hate this country. It has been my refuge."

Stella sighs, impatient. "I don't care if you hate America, Ushman—"

He puts his finger to his own mouth. "Please, let me finish."

Stella acquiesces, but her mouth is held in a tight frown.

"There are many things I do not understand. But I do know why you came to my shop. And I was not mad. Not at all. You came because you wanted somebody to take care of you. And I failed—"

"You didn't. You let me sleep, you gave me tea—"

"My emotions are clouded by my own . . . how do you say? Luggage?"

She nods, trying to hide her amusement. "Baggage."

"Let me try again. Please." Ushman wants to reach for her hand again, but he does not. Instead, he says it again, "Please."

Ushman is not sure what it is he is asking for. He only knows that he doesn't want Stella to be anywhere else but here. With him. He does not want her to get on the bus that he can hear somewhere behind him, rumbling toward them up Madison Avenue.

"Your baggage is intense, that's for sure." Stella shoves her hands into her pockets. "And I don't like being yelled at. Ever."

"I am sorry," Ushman says, wishing he knew another way to express his regret.

She looks again for her bus. Then continues, "But those things you said to me—about your mother. About the way you feel about her. I don't know what you do in Iran, but we don't legislate emotions here. In my opinion there cannot be an immoral feeling. Morality is about intent and action." Ushman recognizes the same quality in her eyes from their first meeting in the airport, when she believed she had come upon a truth about the men working on the tarmac. It is a look that both seeks his approval and dares him to disagree.

Ushman nods, eager to agree with anything she says. Eager for her to simply continue talking. But she doesn't say anything else. Her cheeks are now pink from the cold and she is shivering.

"There's my bus," she finally says, motioning with her head.

Ushman is still dizzy, and though it is cold—his ears and hands are especially—he is perspiring slightly around his hairline and inside his shirt. He looks down at the concrete, puts a hand on the jeweler's window to steady himself.

"My car is around the corner," he says. "In a garage." It is a desperate statement. He is long finished with delicacy.

Stella looks at the bus, which has lowered itself to the curb for an elderly passenger to get off. "Thanks for the tea," she says, avoiding his eyes. Her body readies to fall back into the line of people waiting to board. It would be reckless of her to do anything else. Even if she knew him better. Even if he'd been decent and polite. She fumbles in her pocket for a MetroCard. It is not there.

She steps into the line anyway. Her hands continue to search her pockets.

Ushman steps forward. He presses six quarters into her gloved hand and backs away, still standing in the light from the jewelry store. She moves forward with the crowd. He wants to watch her go. Perhaps he will stand here all night, he thinks. Just watching the buses go by with their insides all lit up, as if in celebration.

She looks back at Ushman. He raises his eyebrows. Is it not enough money? Everything around her is a blur. The traffic lights and pedestrians, the taxicabs traveling north on Madison, the steam from the hot dog vendor on the corner. But he can see her face clearly. She wants something from him.

"I'll make you dinner," Ushman says, loud enough to be heard above the traffic. It is suddenly what he wants to do. He remembers what she said to him. Those words. Intent and action.

Late at night, on a talk show, Ushman once heard an actor talk about making his girlfriend dinner. At the time, Ushman had imagined that this was what he would do for Farak when she finally came to live with him in Queens. He would drive her home from the airport, carry her over the threshold of his apartment, and place her on the couch. *Rest there,* he would tell her, *I have prepared your first American meal.* It would have made a wonderful impression upon Farak. She would have taken off her shoes and told him about her airplane flight and the beauty of the George Washington Bridge as they descended through the dusk. This had been his intent.

Stella's face does not change. At first he thinks she may not have heard him. The woman behind her nudges her, anxious for a seat on the bus. Perhaps it is this nudge, this gentle reminder of the choice she must make.

"Okay," Stella says, finally smiling, and stepping out of line. "I'd like that."

Ushman is surprised. But he understands that she is trapped. She does not want to be alone. Even he can see that. He raises his eyebrows. "Really?" He will not question her motivation. She has agreed. She has offered him a way off of the board. He will not fall.

"You don't think I'd pass up a free dinner, do you?"

"Very good," Ushman says. "This way, this way." He touches her elbow only to guide her around the corner to the parking garage.

"It's not a car. It's a van," Stella says, as Ushman gestures toward his vehicle.

"You're right. And it has a nice sound system." Ushman smiles as he unlocks the van with his remote.

"Was that a joke?" Stella furrows her brow.

"No. It's true," he says, opening her door for her.

Stella laughs anyway.

"Listen," Ushman says as he starts the engine. He fiddles with the buttons on the stereo until he locates a station playing hip-hop. Suddenly the whole van is booming and thumping. There are speakers all around them, in front and in the back. The steering wheel shakes beneath Ushman's hands. Stella is clutching her seat. "See?" he says, turning it off. "Not a joke."

Stella cannot control herself. She throws her head back against the seat and laughs until tears stream down her cheeks. When she can finally speak, she says, "There has got to be a story here."

"You don't think I'm a hip-hop guy?"

Stella smiles. "You've got baggage, but not that kind."

Ushman shrugs. "I bought it from a lot in Queens. How do you say—as is?"

Stella nods. "Somebody had quite a party in this. You could be the coolest guy on your block."

"You don't think I am?"

"I guess I'll have to see your block," Stella says as she buckles her seat belt.

Ushman watches her hands on the buckle. She has long, bony fingers. When she's finished, he cannot take his eyes away. She catches him staring.

"What?" she asks, looking at both sides of her hands. "What is it?"

"You don't wear any rings," he says, thinking he must justify his staring with some observation. He then puts the van into gear.

Stella shakes her head. "Nope. I play piano and my teacher would always make me remove all my rings to play. It was a hassle, so I just stopped wearing them." She shrugs. He is now looking at her face. She matches his stare until a horn echoes across the garage, startling them both. Ushman takes his foot off the brake. Stella looks out the window. Silently, they coast down the ramp, through shadows cast by the massive concrete columns and bright fluorescent lights.

Ushman lives in a tall red-brick apartment building on a middle-class block in Flushing, Queens. He parks his van in a garage a block away from his building.

"That's mine," he says as he and Stella cross the street toward the green awning over the front doors.

"It's nice," she says.

Ushman is trying to recall the contents of his refrigerator. Is it true that he bought chicken at the market this weekend? Does he have a can of soup or enough rice for both of them? If only he had fresh olives or time to make a stew.

Everything he's ever cooked in America has been an act of remembrance. In effect, he has learned to cook by closing his eyes and picturing Farak's hands as they chopped and rolled and sprinkled and stirred. Here in his Pullman kitchen, he has seen her thread, marinate, and spice kebobs, chop vegetables, truss a chicken, sauté onion, soak lentils, stew potatoes, and form curry meatballs with her delicate fingertips. In the process, he felt close to Farak and invented a whole new cuisine. Persian, yes. But never exactly the flavor of his childhood or his marriage.

Stella moves to the back of the elevator to allow another gentleman to come in with them. He is a young guy, wearing sweatpants and headphones, with a radio strapped to his arm. His music is turned so loud that they can hear the drumbeat through his headphones. Ushman watches him look at Stella. He smiles. She smiles back. Then he looks blankly at Ushman. Almost imperceptibly, the guy shrugs.

Ushman feels for a moment as if he should step off the elevator and let Stella follow this man into his apartment. They are both young, beautiful Americans. They belong together.

The hollow beat of his music fills the elevator as the doors close and Ushman looks at Stella, ready to relinquish her to this athlete. She is standing quietly, leaning against the wood paneling. When she sees Ushman turn toward her, she rolls her eyes in the direction of Mr. Athlete. Ushman looks at his feet in order to hide his disproportionately joyful smile.

He is still smiling when the doors open on his floor. Stella follows him to his door. He opens the door for her and they stand together in the foyer, looking at his living room. The wood floor is covered by two rugs from Tabriz. There are large pillows scattered across the edge of one rug, but no furniture.

"Wow. A real apartment," Stella says, walking past his kitchen to the windows on the other side of the living room. There is no view, really, except the grid of lights extending farther east into Queens. "How cool. No shared bathroom, no hot plate on the stereo, no hair dryer under the bed."

"I will start dinner," Ushman says. "Please, make yourself relaxed."

Stella takes off her coat and hands it to Ushman. He hangs it in the front closet and then frantically rummages through his refrigerator.

He finds feta and two plums. They are set aside for dessert. There is some ground beef, which he quickly forms into small meatballs and sautés in a pan. He starts rice and chops leftover roasted eggplant into a gravy. In the cupboard there is leftover flatbread.

"May I do anything to help?" Stella asks, peeking her head into the kitchen.

Ushman just smiles. How strange to see this girl in his apartment, looking so casual, as if she might actually belong here.

"Yes?" she asks, not understanding his grin.

"Yes, you may." Ushman reaches for a tablecloth. "Would you mind setting our table?" He hands her a red linen cloth and points to an alcove beyond the living room. There is a small round dark-wood table flanked by two high-backed upholstered chairs.

Ushman finishes preparing their meal while Stella arranges the tablecloth, napkins, and silverware. He places the dishes on the table and they sit.

"It's really lovely, Ushman," Stella says, serving herself rice and meatballs. "I feel like a real person. Quite civilized," she says, mimicking a proper British accent.

Ushman nods his head. "I apologize for what I did to you in Manhattan. I didn't have any right to be angry at you. Especially after what you told me . . . after what you've been through today."

"You've redeemed yourself," she says, wiping her mouth. "It's delicious."

"I hope so. I've never made dinner for anyone. Other than myself."

"No?"

"No."

"How could that be? You were, I mean, you are married."

"I never fixed dinner for Farak."

"Why not?"

"I don't know. It's not customary. Even when she was not well. Her sisters or her friends would bring food to the house. They would feed her in our bed. I would eat at the table. Alone. Or with my mother."

There is silence.

"Iran is a different place. Totally different from America. It is very, how do you say, sheltered." Ushman is trying to explain his marriage.

"Where I come from, where I grew up, it is also very sheltered."

"You are not American?"

"Yes, of course. But I grew up in the South. The American South. In a small community of very traditional people. Divorce wasn't really tolerated. Homosexuality. Premarital sex." Stella blushes. Ushman clears his throat. "Not a lot of men cooked dinner there, either, is what I'm trying to say."

"I forget. New York City is so big. It seems like a whole country to me. But there are many other regions of America."

"Many," Stella says, laughing. She takes another bite of food. "My father has never made me dinner."

Ushman leans back in his chair. "Is this true?"

"Yes. Men in my family don't cook. Certainly not like this. Who taught you?"

"I taught myself, really. From watching. From watching the memories in my head. It's funny, at the time, in Iran, I wasn't aware that I was watching. I didn't pay attention. It was just there. In the background of my life. Like a song you've heard over and over without noticing. And then, all of a sudden, you realize that you know the words."

Stella is staring at Ushman's hands as he pushes the lingering rice around on his plate. She reaches for her water glass and raises it toward him.

"Here's to men cooking dinner," she says, waiting for Ushman to raise his own. He does, and they clink their glasses.

"When my parents said they were going to Italy, I had a hard time picturing it," Stella says, putting her glass down.

"Why?" Ushman asks.

"Because they are so American."

Ushman looks blankly at her.

"You, know, so plaid sport coat and comfortable shoes. So T-bone and baked potato. So buffet-loving. So Protestant. So prude." Stella makes gestures with her hands as if they were walking through each set of adjectives. "It's a whole state of mind," she adds, twirling her finger next to her head.

Ushman laughs, covering his mouth. He doesn't quite understand all of her references, but she is so animated, so lovely.

Stella is encouraged by Ushman's amusement. She, too, is laughing now. But she continues, sitting up straighter in her chair and banging her hands against the tabletop for emphasis. "When did they become interested in pasta and wine and naked sculptures? And why hadn't they been interested in those things when *I* was living at home?"

Ushman understands that she is not looking for an answer, but he shrugs anyhow. She mirrors his shrug, her energy now contained. Then, after she's given it some thought, she reaches one hand across the table toward Ushman. "Hey, hey," she says, thumping her fingertips near his plate. "Maybe I'm on to something here. Maybe it was just too much nudity? Is that why she did it?"

Ushman smiles, though he hasn't followed her logic. Stella, however, is amused. She laughs from the back of her throat, short coughs of hilarity. She holds her napkin to her face in order to cover her mouth, and her laugh turns silent and internal. Then, eventually, she uses the napkin to wipe at her eyes. When she's finished, her face is red and lonely.

Ushman doesn't say anything. He simply sits there with her in silence. Secretly, he is grateful to her mother for jumping off that bridge, whatever the reason. Because with that single, unexpected motion, her mother pushed Stella out into the streets of Manhattan, onto the East Side, and, eventually, to Queens with him.

Stella fidgets with the napkin in her lap. A wisp of hair falls in front of her face.

"I can make tea," he says, uncomfortable with the silence.

Stella doesn't look up. "Um," she says, her mouth twisting into a pucker. Ushman does not want her to go, but he braces himself for her excuse.

"I sort of wrecked your napkin," she says, grimacing. "Sorry." Stella pulls the napkin up from her lap and hangs it in front of her face so that she is hidden. It has little smudges of black all across it, like soot.

Ushman does not respond right away. He is still waiting for her to tell him she must go. So, again, there is silence.

Stella slowly lowers the napkin until Ushman can see only her forehead and her eyes. "Okay?" she asks. "Or do you have to kill me now?" Her voice is perfectly modulated.

For a moment Ushman thinks it is a serious question. He is ashamed. He cannot imagine she would think this of him.

But as she lowers the napkin even farther, he can see her mouth. A perfectly mischievous grin that reminds him of her youth and its resiliency. He imagines the lengths her emotions have traveled today. And yet here she is, creating her own small happiness.

Ushman reaches his hand out to her. She places the napkin in it. He bows his head, trying not to smile. Trying to follow her lead. He pretends to inspect the napkin. "I will wash it and your life will be spared."

"I am sorry," she says, wiping beneath her eyes with her fingers. "Am I clean enough for tea?"

"Yes, absolutely," Ushman says, tossing her napkin onto his shoulder. Together they clear the table, and Ushman prepares a plate of dessert and two cups of tea. They sit together in the living room, side by side, on his own rugs from Tabriz. Ushman shows Stella how he sips the tea through a sugar cube held between his front teeth.

"This is the way in Iran," he says, placing a cube between Stella's own teeth for her. His finger brushes against her bottom lip. She puts the cup to her lips and drinks. Then she holds the cube between her thumb and forefinger.

"It's good," she says, "but what about conversation?"

Ushman smiles, displaying his own sugar cube.

"Yeth, ith ith juth thumthing you learn to do. A wight of passagth."

Stella laughs. Ushman removes the sugar cube and chuckles at his own joke. He feels so relaxed. So confident. So American.

They each finish their tea in silence, watching the lights of Queens, which seem to grow brighter out the window. Stella puts down her cup and casually leans her head on Ushman's shoulder. He stiffens. The smell of her hair and her clothes and her skin fills him. Then, as casually as she placed it there, she removes it.

"I should get home. My father may have called again."

It was just a friendly gesture, Ushman tells himself. Everything is different here. She can touch me like that, lay her head on the place just above my heart, and then take it away. It does not mean anything.

"I will take you," he says, standing up with their teacups in his hands.

"You don't have to. I could take the subway. But I have absolutely no idea where I am."

Ushman smiles. "Me neither," he says.

The drive into the city is filled with the noises of Ushman's daily commute. The volume of it is less at night, but there is still a cacophony of horns, diesel engines, brakes, radios, and speed. Ushman, though, travels slowly. He would like to think of something to say to Stella. Something to make himself indispensable to her. Something that would make her want to stay in this van with him forever. Instead, he watches the endless pairs of tail-lights ahead of him and begins to hum.

"What's that?" Stella asks.

Ushman shrugs. "Just a tune. I don't know the name."

They are in Manhattan now and Ushman enters the park, headed west. The road is winding and dark compared to the Queensboro Bridge. Stella looks over at Ushman.

"I have midterms next week."

"Exams?"

"Yes." Ushman can feel her steering the conversation into banalities as they approach the Upper West Side. He doesn't want this evening to end in small talk. He doesn't want it to end without some sort of understanding.

"I'm divorced," he says.

Stella looks out the window, then back at him.

"Really? I thought—what about Farak?"

"She divorced me. On the grounds of desertion."

"Why did you tell me that you were married?" Stella's voice is curious, not accusatory.

"I don't know. In my mind, I am. I was. It all happened so far away, it's hard to know what's real sometimes."

"When?"

"When she became pregnant. When she arranged for my mother to stay in a ward and she moved out of our house. When she went to live in Istanbul with the baby's father."

"Oh." Stella's forehead is wrinkled with worry.

"Until tonight, I didn't like to think that I was divorced."

"And now?" Stella points to her building. Ushman does a U-turn in order to pull up right in front of Barnard's gates. He puts the van into park and leaves his hands on the wheel. She is waiting for him to answer. Ushman takes a deep breath and turns to look at her. She has her hands folded in her lap. Her head is cocked, her eyes studying his face.

"Now," he says, "it seems like the right thing."

She smiles. Like some sort of miracle, she does not laugh or fidget or look away. She just looks right at him and smiles.

Ushman reaches his hand across the empty space between them. He touches her cheek with his thumb. It is the place he intends to kiss, but as he begins to place his mouth there, near his own thumb, Stella turns her head so that it is the corner of her mouth that he kisses. Half of her lips. A lingering-half-lip kiss. And then she is shy. Her face is flushed and she opens the door.

"Thank you for dinner," she says, standing on the sidewalk. "And the ride."

"You're welcome. I will keep your mother in my thoughts. May I call you?"

She nods. "Please."

Ushman watches her walk away from his van and into the big black gates. He could sit here all night, thinking that she might turn around and come back to lean in his window, say one more thing. Give him one more kiss. But he also cannot wait to walk back into his apartment and smell her there. Wash

the dishes she used, study the smudges of her eye makeup, and
remember the weight of her head on his shoulder.

He has done the dishes and walked carefully around his apartment twice, remembering her in every place she'd been. Now it
is just another sleepless night and Ushman sits and stares at the
empty street below.

Without a reason, without really any deliberate thought,
Ushman finds himself out, walking toward the bodega.

A part of him begins to forget the singularity of this evening's circumstances, of this girl's character. By doing so, he begins to anticipate a predictable outcome of their meeting. He
imagines that Stella is a loose college girl, one of those who
spend their spring break topless on MTV. He imagines another
date like the ones he's seen so many times on American TV. A
date in which, sometime during the evening, Stella would excuse
herself and then emerge from his bathroom wearing a black lace
negligee. This fantasy leaves him excited and terrified.

The bodega is a neighborhood place and as soon as he's in
the door, Ushman wonders why he's here. He doesn't want another orange soda. Regardless, now he's here and he's nervous
and he averts his eyes from those of the clerk as he enters. He
wanders to the back of the store and finds himself standing
right in front of the display of condoms. Of course, he thinks,
this is why I'm here. For the first time tonight, Ushman feels in
control. Like a man.

But as he looks at the boxes, each with gold lettering, yet
each slightly different, he becomes overwhelmed. Is "ultra sen-

sitive" intended for a man like him, with overwrought emotions? He does not understand the vocabulary of condoms. "Ribbed" is something he cannot quite imagine, nor how that would be "for her pleasure."

Looking at the display, Ushman finds himself plagued with doubt and regret. He has managed to invite another problem into his life. Tonight's date will never turn into anything resembling the fantasy in his mind. It will only serve to remind him, when the spell has been broken and Stella's moved on to whatever it is girls like her move on to, just how lonely the rest of his life will be. Just how cruel this American life will become. With its endless possibilities and constant disappointments.

Suddenly there is a woman standing next to him. She does not study each box, but reaches knowingly for an economy-sized black one. Her hands are small and her fingers thin. Ushman keeps his head forward, but as he moves his eyes to see her face, he realizes that he knows this woman. She is the prostitute who had been in his kitchen just a few months ago. The one he has often longed to see again. She looks different under the fluorescent lights of the store. Her hair has grown out to expose its natural black color. She is wearing a sweatshirt and a short leather skirt.

Apparently, she recognizes him as well.

"Are you getting pussy for free yet?" she says as she adjusts a package of toilet paper under her arm. "It's never as good as when you pay for it."

Ushman pretends he has not heard her.

"You need relief? You come to me. I have my own," she says, shaking her box of condoms as she walks away from him.

Ushman turns and walks to the middle of the shampoo isle.

He stands there, sweating, until he sees her leave the store. Then, without hesitation, he selects the same package she had and completes his transaction without further incident.

Despite this humiliation, Ushman eagerly takes the box of condoms home and places them in the drawer of his nightstand. As he lies in the darkness, trying once again to sleep, he thinks of it there. The shiny black cardboard, as seductive as a photograph. A black and white photograph of a pinup girl. Like the ones his uncle kept in a saucepan under the kitchen sink. When he found them, as a boy, he marveled at the stretches of skin between the ladies' bikinis. This was his first confirmation that women, indeed, had a form as magnificent as he had imagined.

Nine

There is another dinner planned at Ushman's apartment. Stella has called him at his shop to tell him that her mother has been moved to a clinic somewhere outside Padua. She will survive. Her father is continuing with the tour group. As she tells him this, she sighs audibly into the phone.

"Does this concern you?" Ushman asks.

"No. I mean, yes, of course. I suppose he doesn't know what else to do. But it seems wrong. As if sightseeing could possibly be the proper reaction to this event. She jumped off a bridge." Stella says this with some anger in her voice.

"Yes," Ushman says, excited and distracted by her call.

"He's very pragmatic, my father." Stella sounds now as though she is choosing her words carefully; trying to be kind, trying to find an explanation. "He probably figures that if she's going to be hysterical, she's going to be hysterical. He might as well go to Rome and see the Colosseum. Life goes on."

Ushman murmurs some agreement, though he's not sure if that's what she wants. He is nervous.

"I mean, as long as she's not dead, life goes on," Stella says, laughing a short, shallow laugh.

Ushman just listens, trying to find his way.

"This totally sucks," she says finally. Is she crying? He cannot tell. Her voice is thin and resigned.

"You are very brave."

"I don't know why I'm telling you all of this. It's just . . ." her voice falters. Then, stronger, she says, "I don't want anyone here to know about it. I don't want to be 'the girl with the crazy mother who jumped off a bridge in Italy.' "

"I will keep your secret."

"Thank you," she says warmly.

"Will you come for dinner again?" Ushman blushes, ashamed by his clumsy invitation.

It is as though she can sense his self-doubt.

"I have another secret," she whispers.

Without thinking, Ushman whispers, too. "What is it?"

Still whispering, she says, "I'm a virgin."

Ushman's stomach drops. He thinks of taking his hand off the receiver, as if even that much contact with her could be criminal. Instead, he clutches it more tightly, afraid to move.

"I know it's kind of a bomb to drop," she continues, speaking normally now. "And personal. But I want to come for dinner and I just, I thought I should be up front. You know, so that, whatever . . ."

Ushman tries to regulate his breathing. He cannot speak.

"I hope I haven't totally freaked you out," she says. "I didn't want to misrepresent myself. And then there would be some awkward moment that . . ."

"Um . . ." Ushman hesitates.

"It's not like I'm a total prude or anything. I mean, it's not like I'm not interested in . . . Oh, man. I always do this. I tend to think I can prevent awkward moments by just being honest, and then, boom, I bring the awkward moment right to me."

Ushman feels as though he has been found out. He thinks of the far-fetched fantasy he'd concocted last night, the one that drove him to the bodega and to the absurd purchase that lies, even now, in his nightstand.

How ridiculous his fantasy seems now. Hearing her voice again, he wonders how he ever thought that such a smart, likable girl could be promiscuous. It gave him a way to understand what she may have been thinking, having dinner with a man like him. It gave him an expectation, a map upon which to locate himself. In the dark of night, he'd convinced himself that they were at the beginning of a sort of extended one-night stand.

But now. She must want something Ushman cannot fathom. She must want to be close to him; to construct a relationship.

For what purpose? he asks himself. Certainly he is not the most eligible man she knows. He saw her, that night, hugging the student in the Chinese restaurant. That boy—blond, American, college-educated—is without question a better match for her. Anyone would be.

Ushman is not dependable. He is foreign, divorced, quickly going gray, with big feet and no friends. There is no logic in their companionship.

"Okay, you have to say something, or the awkward moment just balloons into an insurmountable barrier."

"I expect nothing," he lies, forcing himself to finally speak.

Of course, there is an even farther-fetched fantasy that Ushman has about this girl. One that he has not given language to in his own mind. It is only a nebulous feeling. A buoyancy beneath his feet, a fluttering in his chest. She may be his second chance.

"Don't lie," she says, unafraid to tease him. "It's not that I'm uninterested in sex. I actually tried to lose my virginity. It's a really ugly story. I'll tell you tonight."

"I look forward to that," Ushman says, laughing despite himself.

"So, I checked the subway map. It's not so bad getting to you. I can take the number 7 and then—"

"I will come for you after work."

"It's no trouble. You could meet me at the corner of—"

He does not allow her to finish. "Stella, I will pick you up. Please, let me do that."

There is a pause. She gives in and her voice is cheerful with self-mockery. "Okay. I'll be the girl whose mother jumped off a bridge and whose virginity is up for grabs."

"I think I'll know you."

After delivering three rugs to a customer in Greenwich Village, Ushman climbs the steps of the Metropolitan Museum of Art. He is part of a panel discussion this afternoon. The wind has picked up and he pulls the collar of his wool coat up around his neck. The curator's assistant is waiting for him inside the door. She is young, probably a peer of Stella's. He cannot fathom ever asking her to dinner. He is bewildered when he realizes how extraordinarily he's behaved with Stella. As if that night in the airport he had not only purchased a ticket to Paris, but also another man's courage.

This girl's face is wide and her eyes are drawn, as if they

have been stretched to fit. She is not nearly as attractive as Stella, yet Ushman feels as though she is completely out of his reach. She accompanies Ushman to the gallery where the discussion will take place. There is an awkward silence between them as her heels echo across the floor.

Ushman dutifully takes his place behind a long table at the front of the room. There are folding chairs, half of which are already occupied, mostly by elderly couples. They watch Ushman as he removes his coat and drinks from the cup of water in front of him.

There are three other members of the panel, all of whom are looking through the catalog of this current exhibit. Standing again, Ushman extends his hand to each and reintroduces himself. Their faces are familiar, but he hasn't bothered to retain their names. Then, he, too, looks at his own copy of the catalog.

The exhibit features Middle Eastern textiles from the seventeenth and early eighteenth centuries. Ushman is the only non-scholar on the panel. The curator had employed Ushman to help furnish her apartment with kilim, and ever since, she has called upon him to serve on relevant panels. Probably for the look of authenticity that he adds. For the firsthand knowledge of looms and dyes and patterns and terrain that are so familiar to him. It is good business for Ushman. He has found many clients through the museum.

Including Mrs. Roberts. When she comes in, with a thick black scarf still wrapped around her neck, Ushman nods and smiles. She sits in the front, across the aisle from him. Without fail, she attends every exhibit and discussion that the museum hosts. Her presence this afternoon is no surprise.

He must go to her and say hello. It is not what he wants to do. Instead, he'd like to pretend she didn't come in, he'd like to forget about the disaster of his real life and linger on the prospect of his date tonight. The carpets of Iran, the culture of Islam, and the craft of textiles are the landscape of his unhappiness. This afternoon, he'd rather be somebody without any knowledge of the intricacies of the way in which the Turkish knot influenced the Iranian knot. He closes the catalog and sighs.

"How are you, Mrs. Roberts?" Ushman awkwardly extends his hand, but she is busy unwrapping her scarf and doesn't notice. He drops his hand to his side.

She places her scarf on the back of her chair and then looks up at him. "Very well, Ushman. And yourself?"

He nods. "Quite well. Thank you."

"We are enjoying the prayer rug," she says, smiling at him. "You did get my check?"

"Yes, thank you. Are you settled, then, on your decision?"

"Nearly." She has a coy look in her eyes.

"I'd just like to get the paperwork finalized," Ushman says.

"I'll call you next week. You know I don't like to rush these decisions. I'm so looking forward to the discussion."

"It is a beautiful exhibit. And it's very nice to see you again." Ushman bows his head and turns away from her. He goes back to the table and occupies himself once again with the catalog.

His favorite is a Polonaise carpet given to the museum in 1950 by John D. Rockefeller. So-called Polonaise because when it was first exhibited in Paris in 1878, the coats of arms woven into the rug were presumed to be Polish. Though it was later proven to be one of many like it that were produced in Isfahan for the Shah Abbas I and his court, nobody bothered to rename the style. Ushman always likes to imagine the weavers of the early seventeenth century, producing these elegant carpets that were exported to all of the finest European cities as gifts from the Shah.

When his mother was a girl and the Russians still occupied Tabriz after the Nazis had surrendered, she had told Ushman, she stood on a stone wall near the side of her house and watched three young blond Russian soldiers awkwardly roll her father's Polonaise carpet. A merchant who owned many of his own workshops, her father had numerous expensive and precious carpets in the house. But his favorite had been the Polonaise. He had bribed other soldiers so that they would not take it. But these three were intent. Strangely, they were moved by the patterns in the carpet, more so than they were by her father's money. Or perhaps they were just cruel. Perhaps they had heard, from other soldiers, how much he valued this rug, how meaningful it was to him.

At the request of the Shah, the Americans were on their way to force the Russians out of Iran. It would be their first engagement of the Cold War. But they would not be there in time to prevent this theft. They would not be there in time to alter the events of that afternoon. When the Russians had gone and the floor in her father's study was bare, Ushman's mother sat down on the stone wall and watched through the window as her father, Ushman's grandfather, carefully took a hunting knife from the cabinet in the corner of the room and pushed it through his rib cage and into his heart.

He fell to his knees and then onto his chest, forcing the knife farther into the muscle.

Ushman likes to imagine that the Polonaise in this very exhibit might have been his grandfather's. That perhaps Mr. Rockefeller bought it in Paris from a Russian collector just a few years before donating it to the museum. If he were a better man, Ushman would send the catalog to his mother. He would listen to her complaints about the American soldiers, who prohibited her father's burial ceremony in the interest of securing the neighborhood. He would never tire of her complaints. He would sympathize. Instead, Ushman resents his mother for not running faster to save his grandfather. For not pressing harder against his wound, or calling louder for help. For Ushman has witnessed his mother's self-pity all of his life. And he's sure that, even at twelve years old, his mother sat there on the wall, already transforming her father's tragedy into her own pathetic narrative.

No, Ushman does not share this Polonaise with his mother. A private musing, it is soothing to think of the myriad paths this very Polonaise traveled before it ended up here, in the finest museum in America. And how is it, Ushman wonders, that he is sitting here with it—the only Iranian in the room? And, perhaps, it's rightful owner. Its richness speaks to him of the romance in his heritage; of Iran's royalty and civility and his grandfather's honor. In deep hues of orange, yellow, red, and brown silk, with silver and gold brocading, it is a true masterpiece.

Happily for him, though, the audience this afternoon seems more interested in the other carpets. Those from Syria, Turkey, and Iraq. Ushman could speak about all these carpets. On other panels, he has spoken more frequently and enthusiastically, gratified by the audience's appreciation of his expertise. But this afternoon Ushman can think of no suitable way to convey his proximity to the greatness of these historical treasures. He does not have the energy to boast. He would like someone else to do it for him.

Ushman is certain he has told the curator this story of the Polonaise in his past, but she is staring blankly at her notes, twisting her hair around her forefinger. He looks at the audience. Mrs. Roberts has her head cocked, listening, or daydreaming, intently. Two of the men have their heads hung forward, sleeping. The more alert members of the audience are straining to hear a particularly soft-spoken panelist.

Looking at these old American faces, their eyes set deep into their faces, and thinking of the historical path of the Polonaise, Ushman feels restless with the smallness of the world. His own mother's face, looking much like theirs, lying somewhere in Tabriz, looking out her window at the clouds forming into the same shapes they do all over the world. Some of the very same shapes hanging over Manhattan right now. And this carpet, or one very much like it, a memory behind his mother's eyes, a texture of her dreams, a piece of her chemistry. And this same carpet hangs here, in front of Mrs. Roberts, who will, no doubt, hold its picture in front of her husband as his body betrays him the way Ushman's mother's body betrays her. Death will come to each of them, to all of us, in different ways, but it will leave behind the exact same quiet. It will take with it the memory of this carpet and the shapes of the clouds that have moved across each land.

Ushman shuffles his feet under his chair. He is determined to cultivate something of his own, some small, precise moment that he can hold on to tightly, thinking of it until his very last heartbeat, pressing it so strongly against his eyelids that it may even leave an impression, a small pattern against his tissue, changing his anatomy forever. With relief and anxiety, Ushman reminds himself of this evening, of his date with a beautiful American girl.

Ten

He cannot believe that it's true, but she is actually standing there at six o'clock, on the corner of Broadway and 116th Street, wearing an orange woolen poncho and baggy jeans. She has headphones covering her ears and she's bouncing to the beat. For a moment Ushman hesitates. There is no possible connection he could have to this girl. They did not learn the same songs as children, she does not know how the banks of the Talkheh become awash with color from the rising or setting sun. In her heart is the memory of a different landscape. She is from a different world; her trajectory, even momentarily, could never mirror his own.

Against his better judgment, he stops and lifts his hand from the steering wheel in recognition. When she climbs in and smiles as she pulls off her headphones, he reminds his cynical self how nice she smells. Her eyes are welcoming, familiar. She is not a stranger. No more so than any other person in this world would be. Even Farak, with whom he thought he shared so much—culture, values, heritage, homeland—even she was never truly known to him. If she was, he would not be here, alone, in America.

For the first time since he's met her, Stella is wearing lipstick. She looks strange but lovely. Ushman concentrates on this.

"This is a nice color on you," he says, gesturing to her poncho.

"You like it?" she asks. "I just got it at a thrift store downtown. One of the ones that sell new and used clothes, where everything's sort of the same price regardless." She laughs. "I went with some girls from my dorm. What about you?"

"Me?"

"Yeah. What did you do today?" Stella's eyes are eager and accepting. Her curiosity is unjaded.

"Just work," he says, remembering the events of his day, beginning with his early morning at the bodega.

"Oh," she says, pushing her face close to the windshield, "I almost forgot. There's a lunar eclipse tonight. Do you think we can see it from your place?"

"Absolutely. And if we can't, we'll go up on the roof." Ushman has never actually been on the roof of his building, but he's overheard other residents speak of it.

"It should be amazing. I had astronomy this morning. It's a required course—meaning I'd never take it unless I had to—but it's actually mind-blowing once you realize that time and space are just huge." She stops and looks over at Ushman. "Am I talking too much? I'm just excited. And nervous. I can't believe what I said to you this morning." She buries her head in her hands.

Ushman just drives.

Then, suddenly, she sits up and looks right at him.

"But then, I'm sitting there in astronomy and the professor is lecturing about the timeline of the universe. Are you aware that humanity is just a blip? Not even a blip. Just a fraction of a fraction of what the universe has been and will become? Talk about perspective. I figure I can't feel so entirely stupid about saying what I said because, first of all, it's true. And second of all, there will be no remnant of me or my stupidity. No fossil or geographical shift that can document, really, even the most important historical human beings, let alone my paltry admissions."

She looks at Ushman and he smiles, finally. The intensity of her voice and the rapid pace of her speech thrill him.

"Okay, now I really am talking too much." She sits back against the seat.

"It's just that you talk so quickly. I must concentrate to follow your logic."

"I know. Especially when I'm excited. I'll try to speak . . . more . . . slowly." She winks at him.

Ushman smiles. It is true that she speaks quickly, but he has understood everything she's said to him. He wants to prove this.

"There must be something that lasts. Something that is indelible," Ushman says.

"Not that I know of. But I will let you know if there's anything in the next lecture to give us hope."

"Please do. Now," Ushman says with authority, "let's get some take-out food and watch the eclipse in Queens."

"Take-out. Fantastic. Can we get Chinese?"

Ushman nods. She's like an exuberant child. If she wasn't so charming, so wide-eyed and genuine, he'd be suspicious of such enthusiasm.

"In the little white cartons? I love that. My parents aren't fans of Chinese food, so we never got take-out when I lived at home. This—you, here, Chinese—is the beauty of leaving home," she says with genuine affection.

"Indeed," Ushman says, imagining the freedom she must feel. Ushman never left his parents' home. Not until he came to America. He never lived in Iran without the dread of his mother around every corner. Even when he was a newlywed, when his mother was confined to her bed, she was still there. Her smell, her voice coming at them through the dark, her hair that had to be brushed. "I never . . ." He starts to tell Stella this and then changes his mind. "I never ate Chinese food until I came to New York."

Stella looks at him. He senses that she knows it is not what he was going to say. She looks away from him, out her window, as if she isn't interested in anything inauthentic.

"It's true. Okay, one time in Istanbul there was an old man selling egg rolls from a cart. I was with my father and he bought us each one." He recalls eating the exotic treat out of waxed paper as together they watched oil barges lumber down the Bosporus.

"And?"

"A little greasy, but good."

"There's a Chinese place on the corner across from my dorm."

"I know," Ushman says, remembering her face through the big glass window and the boy she had hugged. "I mean, I saw it when I picked you up."

"The crazy thing is that they also have fried chicken, hamburgers, and club sandwiches on the menu. Who goes to a Chinese restaurant for a burger and fries?"

Ushman shrugs.

"I find it very suspicious. There should be a police investigation. Maybe sociopaths are identifiable as those people who order burgers at a Chinese restaurant."

Ushman laughs. "But the proprietor puts it on the menu. They shouldn't make the offer."

Stella raises her eyebrows. "Now you're on to something. We can blame it on insecure restaurateurs. They are the sociopaths."

Ushman laughs. "Maybe. It is worthy of study, right?"

"Absolutely. Does your Chinese place serve American food?"

"No," Ushman says. "Not even soda. Only tea."

"I like the tea you made. With sugar cubes between our teeth."

"I am happy to make you tea."

Later, on the roof, Ushman and Stella sit on milk crates and watch the earth obscure the moon. It has been a gradual process, as if they were watching a sculptor carve away his stone. For Ushman it reminds him of what Stella told him in the van. How large are time and space. He could not have imagined caring about an eclipse just a week ago. But now, tonight, he watches it carefully, simply because Stella does.

Their Chinese food has been eaten and Ushman has made tea. They are both looking up at the sky. The moon is no longer illuminated, not even a sliver. Its true nature is revealed; it is simply a cold, dim rock. Without the sun's light upon it, there is no magic, no romance. As they sit in this momentary darkness, waiting, Stella reaches out her hand and places it on Ushman's knee. Her eyes remain skyward, but Ushman looks down, at the sight of her hand. Its own paleness so absolute against his own dark pant leg.

He feels strangely liberated, here on the roof, under an eclipse. Her skin is so fair and smooth and warm. Ushman lifts his index finger, hesitating only for a moment before resting it on her pinky. Delicately, as though he hopes he will not be noticed, Ushman traces the stretch of her bones. Each finger's knuckles, each knuckle's circumference. Astonished at how easy it is to touch her, Ushman continues, using just his finger, to trace the landscape of her bony wrist, and then, guiding his finger into the loose arms of her poncho, the slope of her forearm, its invisible hairs tickling his finger. By the time he has reached the crook of her elbow, her skin is riddled with goose bumps. He cannot see them, for only her hand is revealed on his leg, but he feels them as he traces his way back down her arm.

"We should go inside," she says, still looking up at the new sliver of moon that has revealed itself.

"You're cold," he says, standing up, letting her hand fall from his leg.

"No," she says, finally looking at him.

He recognizes the longing in her eyes, but he cannot believe it is for him.

"What about the eclipse?" he says as she takes his hand in hers.

"It's purely academic now, don't you think?"

"I didn't mean to . . . I hope I didn't . . ."

"Sure you did . . . and, yes, you did. Now follow through." Her voice is sure and steady.

Ushman leads her through the small door back into the hallway and they travel down the elevator, quietly. In his apartment, they sit on the floor by the windows and Stella takes off her poncho.

"Do that some more, please," she whispers, placing her head down on the carpet.

Ushman smiles, totally unconvinced that a girl who asks for things in such a manner could really be inexperienced. But he does not say anything. Instead, he is grateful to oblige her. Ushman sits on his knees, bending over her, as if he were inspecting a carpet. It is with the same critical eye that he looks at her: her pale eyelids, long fingers, flushed cheeks. Then, using the motions he uses to feel the density and fiber of a carpet, Ushman continues his journey across her skin, this time using the tips of all of his fingers. Beneath his touch, her body responds and informs him of its utter willingness. Almost without thinking, Ushman allows his hands to travel across even the most sacred places. Though she is fully clothed, her body could not be more revealed to him. Ushman is surprised at his natural affinity for this American girl's body. It is as though he recognizes it, as though he has been returned to an all-but-forgotten home.

He almost forgets that her body is actually inhabited, until she opens her eyes and puts her own hand to his cheek. Gently urging him toward her, she places her mouth against his. It is not so much a kiss as an exchange of breath.

Then, suddenly, she lets go of him and covers her face with both hands.

"What is it? What's wrong?" Ushman asks, remembering the delicacy of the situation.

"I'm embarrassed," she says, still hiding. But her voice is not shy. "I'm so inept."

"You? There is no shame in purity. I am the one who should be ashamed." Ushman sits back on his heels, his hands at his sides.

"No, don't say that. I've never, I mean, felt like, anything like that. I didn't know you could do that, without doing the other." She takes her hands away from her face and her eyes show him something new about her. Something extremely tender and needy.

"I didn't really, either. It's not been my experience."

Stella reaches out her arms and embraces him. Her breath is still rapid and hot on his neck. He closes his eyes.

"Okay," she says, letting her arms drop from around his neck. She props herself up on her elbows. "Ready for the story? My near miss?"

Ushman sits back on his heels. "Continue," he says, startled by the way she retains her self, even now. She is not distant or terse the way Farak sometimes was.

"It was prom night. He drove a VW bug. I was wearing a black dress. We'd had some wine coolers." Stella is smiling, setting the scene in her memory.

"What are these things? Prom? Wine colors?"

"Coolers. But colors is good. They are like colors. Fruit-flavored wine that turns kids on to alcohol. And prom? It's like a school dance. Fancy clothes, loud music, big expectations. Yes?"

"Okay. Continue, please." Ushman likes to imagine her in a fancy black dress.

"That's all. We had some kind of unspoken agreement that we'd do it. I don't even know how we established that fact. We'd been dating a little while and it was as if the event demanded it. So we both knew what was meant to happen and all night we had a terrible time because all either of us could think of was getting back in his car and the condoms in the glove box and it just became a very stressful obligation."

"So what happened?" Ushman blushes at the mention of condoms hidden away.

"I decided to just go through with it." Stella rolls her eyes. "I wanted to be done with it. I wanted to be able to move on and not have my 'virginity' be the only thing on my mind every time I kissed a boy."

"How many boys have you kissed?"

She shrugs. "Not many. Maybe ten."

Ushman laughs. "This is a lot. Ten boys. I guess it's typical in America." He studies her lips. Though he's been married and with two prostitutes, still Stella has kissed more lips than he. He does not like to think of this.

"The land of heathens, right?" Stella nudges his arm with her elbow.

"I thought that was all Islamic propaganda," Ushman jokes, trying to cultivate a lightheartedness about her past.

"Hey, I *am* still a virgin, right?"

"How can this be? With—what do you call them—wine coolers and a black dress?"

Stella buries her head in her hands. She mumbles something Ushman cannot understand.

Gently, he pulls her hands away from her face. She giggles and turns, hiding her face in the carpet. Ushman lies down beside her. "You must tell me," he says.

She turns her face toward his. In a playfully serious voice, she confesses, "He fell asleep. On his best friend's couch while the rest of us played pool."

Ushman shakes his head. "One too many wine coolers?"

"Exactly. He was belching in his sleep. It was disgusting. I got a ride home from his friend's father. I was humiliated. An unwanted virgin on her prom night. The next day I had a piano competition and I flopped. My confidence was totally compromised." Stella pushes her bottom lip out into a pout.

"That is a sad story," Ushman teases her. "You should have told me that one in the airport when we met."

She smiles. "Yeah, then you *really* would have given me your card. . . ."

"But you must have been relieved that you didn't let such a careless boy—"

"Now I am," she says, looking at Ushman and raising herself back up on her elbows.

Ushman is always surprised at her directness.

"Now it won't be clumsy and adolescent and insignificant." Her face is close to his. She does not hide her face now.

"You're sure it won't be?" Ushman says, but it is the word insignificant that is stuck in his mind. Is he something more than another boy she has kissed? And if so, what could he possibly mean to her?

She nods. "Oh, yeah. I'm sure," she says, with complete satisfaction in her voice. Her hair falls forward over her shoulders. Ushman reaches out and lets a strand slide through his fingers.

"I will treat you honorably," he whispers with sincerity, though he no longer has a clear idea of what that means.

She leans into him and he puts his arms around her warm torso. The moon is full again and its brightness shines in on them, illuminating their unlikely embrace.

Eleven

When Mrs. Roberts calls on a Tuesday morning, it has been nearly two weeks since he delivered the prayer rug to her apartment. Nearly two weeks since he carefully placed its arch toward the east, the sound of his own rubber soles chirping on the wood floor. The maid watched him silently from the corner. Ushman pitied her, working all day every day in this apartment. Its rooms quiet and smelling faintly, always, of disinfectant. He imagines her own apartment to smell like that of laborers in Tabriz: of cooking oil and warm meat and burning mustard seed. In a veil and manteau, she could look Iranian. But there is something about her eyes, their wide, gently sloping lids, her thin, pearlike figure, her thick, strong fingers, that is Western. She smiled at him, faintly, as he stood and waited to follow behind her as she showed him to the door.

"I've made a decision, Ushman," Mrs. Roberts says as Ushman listens to her voice come through the telephone. "I know that you were anxious. . . ."

"Simply anxious for you to be satisfied," he says, searching on his desk for her invoice.

"Well, as beautiful as it is, I'm sending the prayer rug back."

Though disappointed, Ushman is not surprised. He finds her check, attached to the invoice, and tears it up.

"Can you come this afternoon, Ushman? I'd like for you to also take the rug in my entry for cleaning."

For a moment, Ushman cannot picture the rug. Then he remembers. It was one of the first ones she bought. A Bijar that came to Ushman by way of Paris. It is a grid design of small medallions containing groups of red rose blossoms on a camel-colored field. It is reminiscent of the nineteenth-century Aubussons, but the colors make it also quite modern. It is a very rare rug, and when Mrs. Roberts purchased it, he understood that she had great potential as a customer.

He would like to send a runner to pick up the rugs, but Ushman knows better. Mrs. Roberts would only rebuke him for it later. And when someone has spent as much money as she has on his rugs, he can certainly justify the most personal of service.

"I can come at three o'clock," Ushman says, making a note to himself on her invoice.

"Very good," she says, and hangs up.

It is the first time that Ushman has been to her apartment since kissing Stella. For some reason, this makes him timid. He does not look directly at the maid, though she smiles at him warmly. And, when Mrs. Roberts meets him in the den, he looks past her, to the windows and the sky beyond.

"Ushman," she says, her voice sudden and stern. "You did not bring another for me to try?"

Ushman stands, turning his hands over in front of him, empty. "I did not. I have received nothing new since you were last in."

"Well, you must call Farak. She must find me something exquisite."

Ushman looks at his hands. He places them at his sides. He is ungrateful to Mrs. Roberts for speaking Farak's name. He finds that his throat is blocked. He cannot make a sound. Instead, he nods.

"I want something that will lift this room up. Don't you know? Something delicate and rare. Will you describe the room to her?"

Again Ushman nods.

"Well," she says impatiently, walking to the windows and turning away from him. "Will you?"

"Yes. I will make it a priority," Ushman says, his voice thin.

"Just remember how hollow this room is, how empty it feels without anything covering the floor."

"I will remember," Ushman says, speaking more firmly now. His voice is his own again. "We will find something truly perfect."

"I do hope so," she says, turning to face him again. She smiles, briefly, then walks out of the room, stopping only to watch Ushman as he lifts the rug onto his shoulder.

Ushman loads the prayer rug and then makes another trip up to collect the Bijar rug for cleaning. On the second trip, he does not see Mrs. Roberts. The young maid is standing in the hallway waiting for him. She holds open the door for him while he works.

He carefully folds the rug and realizes that as she's standing in the hallway, the maid has begun to sing. It is not a tune he knows. Her words are in another language, incomprehensible to him, but its effect, as the tune floats down the hallway toward the elevator, is melancholy.

Ushman lifts the rug onto his shoulder and walks through the open door past the girl. He pushes the call button for the elevator and waits. She continues to hum until he is standing in the elevator. As he pushes the button, he hears her tune abruptly end and the door to the apartment close again in silence.

Twelve

Ushman has looked over Stella's shoulder now four times. She is studying what appears to be an astronomy textbook. Each time, he hopes that she will look up and also not look up. He wants to spy on her. It's true. He wants to watch, uninhibited, unafraid to roam over every inch of her with his eyes. To study the way her hands move and the pale curving places behind her ears. But he also wants her to see him. To sense his readiness. To shut her book and put on her coat and walk with him to his van.

He is supposed to be in the periodicals section, has told her he likes to browse the weekly news magazines for photographs of Iran. This is half true. He used to force himself to study the magazines looking for Farak's face. Looking, more specifically, for proof of her pregnancy. For a widening of her manteau where it would normally hang straight. During the hot summer months in the city, Ushman wanted to see his wife. He didn't like sitting there, in the vinyl armchair, among elderly women with overstuffed shopping bags, but it was cathartic. As if each time he looked for Farak's face and her pregnant body and didn't find it, there was still hope. This lack of evidence was a recantation of their phone conversation. Innocent until proven guilty.

She never mentioned her pregnancy to him again. Not after that first time on the phone. Even as she arranged for his mother to be moved into a medical facility, even as they spoke of his belongings still in the house, even as she read him her forwarding address. And so he could accept that she was having his mother moved, that she was packing up his remaining things, that she was moving away from their home, and still tell himself that there was no baby. Not until he saw its form. There had been no intimacy. No mixing of blood. No bodily betrayal. Until he saw its result.

But today Farak is only on his mind as a testament to the way life can change. A testament to the wonders of time passing and democracy. He has glanced at the covers of the magazines with a kind of lovely detachment. For the first time, he feels that his own life has also immigrated to America. He is no longer a body moving through foreign spaces, layering clothes on the useless form, the lonely, isolated form of himself. There are things around him that are beginning to feel real and pertinent to his life.

This public library, for instance. It is the place where Stella is studying for her midterm exams. This rather small East Side branch near his shop, furnished with fabrics in shades of yellow and green, will now evoke a memory of today whenever he passes it. He will remember the brown sweater she is wearing today. The exact sensation of her hand on his as they climbed the stairs to find her a carrel. He is nostalgic for Iran, part of him sad that he is finally feeling more at home in New York. And he still misses Farak. He misses how comfortable he was with her. They were true family. The past did not need to be explained. Their feeling about Islam, their halfhearted practice, their allegiance to Iran regardless of regime. All these things were an unspoken foundation of their lives.

But, to his surprise, the excitement when he is with Stella is more powerful, even, than the longing for his past. That excitement keeps him from staying in the periodicals section. Instead he paces in front of the shelves of books that surround Stella's carrel. Occasionally a title catches his eye and he pulls out the book, looks at the table of contents, closes it, and replaces it on the shelf. The whole time, Stella is in his peripheral vision. He knows each time she turns a page, or makes a note, or rubs her temples. Ushman thinks that she must sense his presence. But her concentration is uninterrupted. And he finds this quality very seductive.

Stella is less hurried than other Americans Ushman has known. She does one thing at a time. When he speaks, she listens. She does not fidget with her hands or chew her lips or drum her fingers on the table. She is still and she looks at his eyes and she listens. When she studies, she does not wear headphones or suck on candy or shake her knees. Her focus is incredible. And so he circles her carrel slowly, like a moon around its planet.

It is already dark when they are back on the street together, headed toward Ushman's van. Effortlessly and publicly, their hands are entwined. Ushman feels their skin touching at every nerve ending in his body. He wonders, for a moment, why it is that he never had these sensations in Iran. In a country where this touch has no threat of police intervention, Ushman did not expect such an extreme thrill. The kind of raw adrenaline rush that is usually a by-product of danger or rebellion. Nobody on 61st Street has looked twice at them, and certainly nobody has noticed their hands. But perhaps it is exactly this anonymity, this disregard that thrills him. Walking with a girl — a girl younger, paler, and prettier than he is handsome — on a crowded sidewalk in the middle of Manhattan is utterly unremarkable. Whatever occurs between them is their own.

Until what occurs between them is determined by the skinny African man on the corner of Fifth Avenue. He has a brief-case open on the sidewalk, but he is leaning against the wall, smoking a cigarette. Stella's eyes drift to the gold watches lining his case, and Ushman slows his pace to allow her a longer look.

When the African sees her hesitate, he drops his cigarette and comes toward them, chanting, "Fendi. Gucci. Rolex. Good price. Fendi. Gucci. Rolex. Good price."

Ushman is not unfamiliar with street vendors like this one. When he first got his shop on Madison, Ushman passed a guy every afternoon selling umbrellas, purses, and watches. He was an American guy with a big gut, gold teeth, and a ready smile. Ushman still sees him sometimes farther north on Madison. One day after work, Ushman bought a Rolex from the man. He sent the watch to Farak. It had a gold face with diamonds surrounding it. Ushman wrote a nice note, asking her to think of him each hour of the day.

Farak had given the watch to his mother. Presented it, he supposed, as the gift of a dutiful son. Ushman heard about it in every letter his mother wrote for six months. She was ecstatic. She had raised a good and loyal man. America had not changed him.

Just like the rest, Ushman threw this letter away. Her slanted, quivering script made him sick to his stomach.

"A watch for your lady. Fourteen-karat. A watch for your lady."

Ushman looks at Stella. This is all new to her. He holds out his hand, gesturing to the watches. "Do you want to try one?"

Stella glances at the vendor, then at Ushman. Quietly, she says, "No, thank you. Just looking."

She places her hand on Ushman's elbow. Ushman recognizes her hesitation, her reluctance to engage the city. It reminds him of himself.

"Go ahead, if you like," Ushman says.

"No, it's okay," Stella says, her eyes lingering just for a moment before she looks away, down the street.

The traffic is loud, but Ushman hears the vendor quite clearly. His accent seems to have dropped away as he says, "White bitch."

Stella's hand tightens around Ushman's elbow. She is almost pushing him, urging him to move on. But Ushman knows she has heard the vendor's insult and his pride prevents him from walking away.

But what Ushman doesn't understand is that this man is hunting, mainly, for a captive audience. He, too, is alone in this city, half a world away from his family, his children, the house he built with his own hands. He only wants somebody to hear him, to look him in the eyes, to explain the inequality of pain. To acknowledge that the warm, the well-fed, the carefree shoppers dropping thousands of dollars in brightly lit boutiques along Madison Avenue, for the most part are white. And the people he sees wandering the subways, shaking milk cartons for change, huddling over grates, crouched against buildings, for the most part are black.

So when Ushman hesitates, searching the man's face for an apology, he does not get it. Instead, the vendor raises his voice.

"Yes. I'm talking about your white cunt bitch."

Ushman speaks, if only to drown out these words. "Stop. You know *nothing* of her. Please, have some restraint."

Their voices elevate so that passersby begin to turn their heads, noticing the disturbance.

Stella has her hands deep in her pockets. Her head is down, but the crosstown wind is suddenly stinging her eyes, making them water.

"Do you put your cock in her, brother? All they ever want is the big dark cock."

"Shut up!" Ushman shouts, but the vendor continues.

"Make her work for it, man. Make her wear this African nigger's gold watch." He is holding a watch out to Ushman, swinging it in front of his face.

Ushman looks to Stella. He sees tears on her cheeks. The vendor continues to shake the watch near Ushman's face. Ushman swats at the watch and knocks it out of the African's hand. It flies toward Stella and falls on the sidewalk near her feet.

Ushman and the vendor both look at it.

Stella picks it up and offers it to the vendor.

"Keep it, whore," he says, his white teeth shining under the streetlight.

Ushman takes the watch from Stella's hand and places it back in the man's briefcase.

"Let's go," Stella says, motioning to Ushman with her head.

But he doesn't move away. Instead, he leans in closer to the vendor, so he does not have to shout.

"What is your problem? You don't speak to people in this way. Not anyone. Especially not a woman on the street. It is filthy, indecent, sickening."

"You think she's taking you somewhere? She's not going to let you in to where she's going. Even if she wanted to, she couldn't." His laugh is thick with disgust.

Ushman holds the man's gaze for a moment, seduced, some-how, by the violence of his eyes. Finally he turns away and puts his arm back on Stella.

"He's crazy," Ushman mutters, loud enough for the vendor to hear.

"The watch is cracked," he yells. "You owe me fifty dollars." The vendor lights another cigarette and leans against the wall.

"Fuck you," Ushman says, leading Stella away. It is the first time he's said those words in English. They are caustic in his mouth, like acid.

The vendor calls out, "Enjoy the ride, asshole. You'll be back here, like me, selling crap on the street. This is as good as it gets for us. You know it. You know it's true." His laugh is swallowed by the sound of horns announcing a bottleneck at the end of the block.

Ushman's hand is shaking against Stella's back. They walk in silence. Ushman feels as if he will never be able to say an-other word to her. He is grateful for the people around them. They distract him from the hollow feeling in his chest borne from his sense of responsibility for what's just happened.

"You can't engage those people, Ushman," Stella says, as they turn the corner. It sounds like a reprimand. Like one of her big truths. Ushman drops his hand from her back.

"I only meant to correct his thinking."

"About what?"

"About you."

They are walking through the parking garage toward Ushman's van. His voice echoes across the concrete.

"He was speaking poorly of you. Of us."

"No. He was just angry." Stella's voice is tired, deflated.

Ushman opens Stella's door for her. As they turn out of the garage and head toward the Queensboro Bridge, Ushman sighs and looks out the window.

"I was angry, too, Stella."

"Yeah, I know." Stella crosses her arms over her chest.

"Okay. So let me . . . let me express myself. I cannot allow him to say those things simply because he's crazy."

"Whatever." Her face is turned away from him. She does not want to talk.

"I don't like that word. Say something else."

There is a long silence. Ushman is afraid she may never speak to him again when she shifts in her seat. She looks right at him.

"Okay. I'll say something else: You're wrong." Her eyes study him, wait for his reaction. The tone of her voice suggests she is daring him to disagree.

Ushman rises to the challenge. She is smart and he wants to know what it is that she thinks he doesn't understand about what happened on the street.

"I like these words less," he says. "But if I'm wrong, tell me why."

Now she seems eager. "He's not your adversary. You've already won."

"I didn't want to fight."

"But he did." Her voice is pleading. She wants Ushman to agree with her. To have some revelation. "He wants to take you down so that he feels one person closer to the top of the heap," she continues earnestly, "because he's way down there. He's an immigrant, poor, uneducated, alone. His pain is not something you can argue with, Ushman."

Ushman shrugs his shoulders. "You pity him."

She nods.

"I do not." Ushman clenches his jaw. He says it again. "I do not."

"I grew up in the South, Ushman. The American South. White guilt is in my blood. I've been surrounded by inequality and bigotry my whole life. I would not want to be on the receiving end of it."

"But your pity only adds to his degradation."

"I don't know what else to feel." Here her voice betrays her dismay.

"Outrage. Don't let him treat you poorly just because he's suffered. We all suffer. Skin color, money, nationality. There is no measurement of pain."

She interrupts, "You are wrong—"

"You already said that," Ushman says sternly.

"But you *can* quantify pain. Even in the courts."

"Who is this?"

"The legal system. There is a formula to figure suffering and its fair compensation. Different degrees of suffering are compensated differently."

"This is absurd. Individual suffering is absolute. There is no relativity."

"Since when? The day we met, in the airport, your sad story trumped mine tenfold."

He cannot keep from smiling. "True. But I do not know what you felt. Your poor young heart may have been breaking."

Ushman looks over at her as he brakes for a red light.

Finally she looks at him, full of goodwill again. "It was" — Stella laughs — "it really, really was." He can see she holds no grudge.

They have entered Queens and the night gets darker as Manhattan's skyline drifts away behind them. Ushman takes a deep breath. They are both quiet, watching the lights from storefronts go by.

"Should we get Chinese?" Ushman asks as they get closer to his home.

"And eat out of cartons. Yeah, yeah." She nods enthusiastically.

"See?" he says as he pulls the van into the parking lot of his neighborhood Chinese restaurant. "Joy, too, is absolute. The little cartons do for you what jewels do for others."

Stella nods, and then, with her hand on his shoulder, she whispers, "I like jewels, too."

"I will make a note of that. Lo mein?"

She smiles. "And Kung pao."

Ushman unbuckles his seat belt and takes Stella's hand from his shoulder. He holds it in his own, studying it, though he knows Stella's eyes are on his face. He thinks of her life before him, of her childhood home, the smell of Alabama dirt, the piano notes in her head, the things he cannot ever know. Finally he looks up and smiles, suddenly shy.

"Later, you have to ask me to tell you some things about supernovas and comets and such. I need a little quiz."

Ushman raises his eyebrows, feigning arousal.

"Just for a while, please."

"Yes, of course. Teach me all that you know of the heavens."

Stella leans in to kiss him. Her lips are smooth and warm. In his peripheral vision, he can see the glow of the Queensboro Bridge. He closes his eyes and lets it fade away.

After a few weeks of two or three dates a week, they've now seen each other seven days in a row. Ushman realizes he has never dated anybody before. Not like this. In university, he had only one girlfriend. A neighbor. They had a verbal agreement that they were, in fact, involved. But nothing physical ever occurred between them. Except for one day, as they walked together, a motor scooter tried to pass an idling taxi. It came uncomfortably close to the curb. The noise of its puny motor just beside them made the girl jump. Ushman reached for her hand. It was nearly covered by her chador. He held on to her cool fingers for a moment after the scooter had passed. Ushman knew he was touching her inappropriately, but he did not immediately let go. Even when she gently tugged. Instead, Ushman rubbed his index finger across her palm proprietarily. It was instinct. He was trying to mark her. To use this rare opportunity to indicate how he would like to possess her. She tugged harder and Ushman let her hand go. She then verbally terminated their involvement.

His father was obliged to whip him for this disgrace.

Later, when Ushman went with some school friends to a religious ceremony in Qom, an elderly cleric offered to arrange a temporary marriage for each boy in the group. There were women, lots of them, called *sighas*, offering this arrangement, just for the night. Of course, there would be no marriage without a gift from a groom to his bride. Ushman and his friends could not determine a better use for the spending money with which they'd been sent. The women, still covered by their veils, eagerly accepted the *mahr*.

As is Islamic law, the cleric had each couple sign a contract that limited the duration of the arrangement to just one hour. Then, still in a group, the cleric recited the marriage formula in Arabic and dismissed the boys with their wives.

With his palms sweating, Ushman followed his *sigha* to a small house not far from the main thoroughfare. Inside, she removed her *hejab* and directed Ushman to wait for her in the bedroom.

It was a sparse room, with only a mattress on the floor and a dim light hanging from the middle of the ceiling. In the corner was a small tea set and some books stacked in a pile. Ushman could not discern their titles.

He stood, nervously shifting from one foot to another. When his *sigha* returned, she was wearing pink lipstick and bright blue eye shadow. Her cheeks were darkened by rouge. Ushman also noticed that her hair, which was auburn, was hanging around her face in exaggerated curls. She had taken off her robe and was wearing only a black bra and panties.

"Lie down," she told Ushman. "I cannot stay more than thirty minutes."

Ushman did as he was told. She expertly removed his pants and underwear and guided him through his first marital intimacies. The whole time that he was with her, Ushman did not remove the shirt that his mother had pressed for him that morning.

When their consummation was complete, Ushman felt obligated to make conversation with his *sigha*. She ignored his petty questions and took hold of Ushman's wrist.

"The marriage is complete," she said, picking up his clothes from the floor. "If you are not satisfied, there will have to be another *mahr*."

Ushman nodded that he understood. Then he dressed himself and left her there, still in the bra that he'd wished he'd had the nerve to ask her to remove.

When Ushman decided to marry Farak, he did not dare compromise their engagement with any physical contact, nor even too much conversation. He did not have much confidence in his own desirability. And there was nothing more he felt he needed to know about Farak. She would be his wife. A permanent wife. He had offered her a *mahr* of five hundred gold coins. In a permanent marriage this gift is a symbolic gesture, a form of flattery; not an actual payment. Unless, of course, he divorced her.

Ushman patiently waited until after their wedding day to reveal any of his many defects to Farak. Then, he assumed, he could not be rejected.

With Stella, Ushman is experiencing the strange phenomenon of revealing oneself without a marriage contract. Of displaying one's flaws without any guarantee of companionship.

Ushman has never been more afraid.

Stella, however, is more accustomed to the phenomenon of dating. Ushman admires the fearless way in which she does not adjust herself to please him. She does not change her language, the youthful slang that is a part of her vocabulary, nor hide her family's personal strife. She is irreverent and innocent and clumsy. And as they spend more time together, reveal more of themselves, Stella has become more of the girl he imagined her to be the first time he saw her in the airport. Friendship appears effortless for her. She knows exactly what questions to ask, how to make him comfortable, when to just be quiet. He, on the other hand, feels as though he is at once becoming the man he always imagined America would make of him and the fool that he always feared America would expose him to be.

Some nights, after dropping Stella off in front of the big black gates of Barnard College, he must literally pull the van over on 59th Street, step down, and jump in place, just to feel his feet beneath him. As he does this, the cold night air on his face and the adrenaline in his blood combine to make him feel as though his life is just beginning. For that moment, his body and mind both are twenty years younger. His cynicism, defeat, and reluctance are gone. There is nothing but hope and energy and joy. And as he jumps, like an eager child, up and down, he feels like there may truly be redemption for him.

Watching the cars whiz past him, wondering what a crazy man they imagine him to be, Ushman smiles. He tells Stella this story tonight after she has finished schooling him on the rings of Saturn, Mars's dust storms, and a comet's lifespan. She laughs with him, flattered that she has made a middle-aged man so foolish with desire. Ushman pulls her into him.

His attraction to her has become overwhelming. Though each night they continue to undress each other and Ushman caresses her body until they are both quivering with anticipation, he has not pressed her to go further. A small part of himself is behaving this way because he wants to believe that there will be another wedding night for him. That he will have another bride and that she will be this girl, American and chaste.

And so, a few nights later, when their usual repertoire of touching is interrupted by Stella's voice in the dark, he hesitates. "I'm ready, Ushman," she says, and he opens his eyes in order to see hers. She is there, beneath him, her hair spread out on the pillow. When she sees his eyes, she nods and speaks again. "I am."

Ushman swallows. His physical need overwhelms any other uncertainty. "I bought something, just in case. I hope it's all right. I only wanted to be prepared."

She smiles. "It's fine. Thank you."

He leans over to the nightstand. Stella watches.

Ushman readies himself. He is gentle with her, despite his impatient desire. She keeps her hands pressed into his back the whole time, so that when they are finished and she finally lifts them he feels a chill where her sweaty imprints are left.

Immediately he is worried about her. He is disappointed that he did not stop himself. Never before has he so dishonored a girl and her family.

"Are you all right?" he asks as she lies next to him, quietly breathing.

"Mmm-hmm."

But she is not. He can see that she is pressing her lips together, trying to keep herself composed. And her eyes, though clear and open, have a look of panic.

Ushman places a hand on each of her pale cheeks. "Please," he says, "tell me what has happened. Are you hurt?"

She shakes her head, but two perfect tears emerge and roll down her temples onto Ushman's index fingers. "I don't know. I'm fine. Just emotional. It's been such a long time coming for me. And now it's over, and . . ."

"You're disappointed?"

"No," she shakes her head. "No, no. I'm spent. And surprised, I guess, that it all changes like this."

Ushman still has his hands on her cheeks. "Nothing changes," he says automatically.

"We are lovers now," she says, and the sound of this word from her mouth makes Ushman feel cheap. As though he is a character from a romance novel.

"We were before," he says gently, careful not to deflate the milestone for her. He has caught a few more of her tears. Her face in the darkness surprises him with its hunger. She has absorbed everything he's said, as though she will rely on these words for sustenance. "You are lovely," he says.

"And tired," she says, turning in to his body. "May I sleep a little here, with you?"

Ushman places his arm around her. "It's early still. I will wake you in time to drive you home." Her desire to stay, to sleep, assuages his guilt. He reminds himself that this is not Iran. It is America. She had not expected to remain a virgin. Here, her honor is more complex than an intact hymen.

"Midnight?" she says sleepily.

Ushman runs his fingers down the length of her back and listens to her breath become regular.

The telephone wakes her before Ushman has a chance. It is his cousin, Ahmad.

"*Een pesar khaleh-ye to ast.*"

"*Salam,* Ahmad."

"I have not seen you at prayers."

"It's been very busy."

"Are you alone?"

"Yes," Ushman lies.

"I have news."

"Tell me."

"It's Farak. I have a letter from my sister."

Ushman looks at Stella, half uncovered on his bed, her eyes open.

"And? What is the news?"

"The baby. She has had the baby. A little girl."

"Alive?"

"Yes. And healthy, I presume. That is all it says. A baby girl born three weeks ago."

There is silence on the line.

"I thought you'd want to know."

Ushman still does not speak.

"It is the will of Allah, Ushman."

"And Farak's, too, Ahmad. Do not forget her will."

Ahmad ignores Ushman. "I am coming into Manhattan tomorrow. Should we have lunch?"

Ushman hardly hears his cousin. The room is dark, still, and the only light seems to be coming from the bed, from Stella's naked body. She is so pale, her skin looks nearly transparent, like wool stretched thin across a loom. Her brow is furrowed. Though he is speaking Farsi, Stella has understood Farak's name. She is not looking at him. Her arms are above her head and she is looking at the ceiling. It is an attempt to give him the sensation of privacy.

"Ushman. Lunch tomorrow?"

"Tomorrow is not good, Ahmad. Call me next week."

"Don't be a recluse, Ushman. You will become depressed."

"Good advice, cousin. Thank you for the call."

Ushman hangs up the phone. Stella is sitting up now, with her back to him. She pulls her sweater on over her head. He sees a spark of static electricity as her hair rubs against the wool. There was a time, during the long, cold winters in Tabriz, when Ushman would comb oil through the thick ends of Farak's hair before bed so that she would not sparkle with electricity as she shifted under the weight of their many wool blankets.

Stella gathers her hair with a rubber band. She turns to face Ushman.

"Are you okay?" she asks.

He nods. He doesn't want to tell her, to say it aloud. But he does not have the energy to invent an explanation of the phone call.

"Farak has had her baby. A girl. It was my cousin who called. His sister is in Tabriz. She takes figs to my mother sometimes. She seems to hear everything about everyone. Even about Farak in Istanbul."

"Oh. And the baby is . . . healthy?"

Ushman shrugs. "Evidently."

"That's good news. I mean, it must be weird, but still, it's good, right?"

Suddenly Ushman wants to be alone. He does not want Stella's big, well-meaning eyes trying to decipher his face. Strangely, for a moment, she reminds him of the prostitute. Of his own dishonor. He looks at his watch.

"I'll take you home," he says as he pulls his undershirt and pants from the bed. He moves to the living room, to stare out at the lights of Queens while he dresses himself.

Thirteen

Ushman merges into traffic on the Queensboro Bridge. They have been driving in the same silence that descended upon them in the apartment. It is a stale silence, but Ushman is surprised and grateful that Stella has granted him this. All he wants right now is to be alone. To get her home and return to his more predictable, more comfortable routine of solitary misery. He glances over at her once and sees only that her whole body is turned away from him. Out her window, the lights of northern Manhattan are reflected in the East River. They sway in the gentle current of the water. This view, which he's noticed every night for the past week, is suddenly painful. As if the city's reflection of itself is a symbol of life's inherent loneliness. At the end of the day, the city, too, is left with only herself. There is no sign of life visible in the darkness. Just the skyline.

Finally, as he sensed was inevitable, Stella begins to question him. Though it is not about Farak.

"So," she says as they are heading north up a deserted Central Park West, "did that totally suck for you? I mean, just technically speaking." She is still staring out the window, her breath making the window opaque.

He blinks hard. "Are you asking about my phone call?" He is defensive, his tone cold.

"No. About the other."

"Oh," he says, dismayed. His tone remains unchanged. "About the, uh, the intercourse." He does not want her to think he is afraid of saying it.

"Yeah, the intercourse." Her voice, its American inflection, annoys him.

"What a stupid question. This is not something you ask."

For the first time, she looks away from the window and at him. Her voice is loud. "Don't call my question stupid. I'm not begging for compliments. I'm simply fact-finding. I have a life ahead of me, you know. I'm interested in your perspective. For future reference."

This is the first time she has mentioned any future. And Ushman is not in it. His feet buzz, his chest aches with anger and regret. He would like to call her some awful name. To shame her. To make her feel as disposable as he knows he is.

It is on the tip of his tongue, but he does not say it. Instead, he remembers the curve of her backbone, barely visible but for the moonlight. She is a girl. She has revealed herself to him, given herself to him, though he does not deserve it.

"Okay, fine," he finally says. "For me, it was . . ." He hesitates. He does not know how to fix what has happened to this night. "It was just right."

Something about the phrase, spoken with his accent and two hands on the wheel, makes him wince. *Just right.* He sounds like the salesman he is, talking about the way a rug fits in a room. Not like a man speaking to a woman about their own intimacy.

"Uh-huh," she says, and looks out the window again. Are there tears on her face? He cannot tell.

"Stella, it's true," he says, softening the tone of his voice. "It could not have been better."

"Unless, maybe, you unplugged the phone."

Ushman is silent for a moment. He turns west onto 110th Street. As they pass Amsterdam, he looks up the avenue to the Cathedral of St. John the Divine. The apostles on its façade are lit from below and their shadows creep up the stone in long elegant stretches.

"It is not your concern—what I was told on the phone—it is not anything for you to worry about."

"Are you living in a freaking vacuum, Ushman? Look at me. I'm sitting here next to you. We just, we just . . . fucked, didn't we? Of course it's something for me to worry about."

Ushman's face is washed in a red glow from the stoplight. A single disobedient tear falls from his eye and draws a slender, vertical path down his cheek.

"This is not your sadness, Stella. I do not want you to be a part of it."

"Tough," she says, pushing the hair away from her face. "You can't pick and choose."

"Oh, no?" Ushman shifts the van into park. He looks at Stella, his cheek still wet. He is angry. "It's a democracy, isn't it? This is the beauty of America." Ushman's voice is bitter and sarcastic. He can sense Stella recoil. He continues. "I am free to tell you goodnight and take my sadness back across the bridge where, in solitude, I can imagine the baby girl that my wife holds in her arms, that was born through her hips; the same hips that I slept against for eleven years." He closes his eyes and more tears escape. His voice, however, does not lose its pitch. "I

do not want your pity. I do not want your arms around me because of the pain in my life."

"You are a hypocrite," Stella says, tears gathering behind her
own eyes. "You made me dinner, that first night, because I was
in pain. You took care of me, maybe you even pitied me —"

"I did not —"

"I don't know that. Pain brought me to you that night. Don't
tell me that pain is not a reason to give love. Are you so
masochistic that you will deny yourself comfort? Why this pain,
about Farak's baby, is suddenly off limits, I don't know. Maybe
because you love her." She does not look away, but wipes the
tears from her face without embarrassment.

Ushman averts his eyes from hers. "It is not love, Stella. It is
shame. This baby, this little girl, has proven that I was the one
to blame. I was the one who could not give Farak what she
wanted. It was not her deficiency. It was not the earthquake. It
was me. Only me."

"You can't be blamed for her miscarriages, Ushman," she
says quietly.

But he interrupts. "You don't understand. You don't know,"
he says, exasperated.

Perhaps Stella wants to reach out for him. To put her hands
over his, as they continue to grip the steering wheel. But she
does not. Instead, she closes her own eyes and rests her head
against the back of the seat, allowing him some privacy to hang
his head over his chest and sob.

Behind his eyes is the bulging grayness of his pain. His loneliness. His stale anger and self-pity. The tears cause this pain to
swell. The pressure in his head becomes so great that he is afraid
of the sound that may come out of his mouth if he opens it.

Finally, he can contain it no longer, and he wails the way his mother did when his father was found, shot dead. He does not beat his chest as she did, but he mourns out loud until he has nothing left but whimpers.

They sit there this way, the van idling, for what seems like forever. When his crying has subsided into deep breaths of exhaustion, Stella opens her eyes and reaches across the divide to put her hand on the back of his neck. It is cool against his hot skin. She smoothes the rough black stubble around his hairline. He does not flinch. In fact, he raises his head and turns toward her, leans into her arms. He feels as though he has never before had someone care for him. To rest the entire weight of his head on her, to succumb to the warmth of her breath on his ears, to shudder and have her hold him tighter—these things humble him as he wonders how he's survived this long without them.

"I apologize," he says, without raising his head, "for my behavior. Often, I forget that my life is here. That I actually have an effect on the people around me. For so long, I've left my self, my identity, in Tabriz. In New York, I've been simply a merchant. It is difficult to believe that anyone, especially you, might care to . . ."

"I get you, Ushman. I get that you have this whole other life and that those experiences are not separate from who you are." Her voice is earnest and Ushman smiles, reminded of her innocence.

"You are sweet. I hope that never is there so much sadness in your life."

"There you go again, discounting my misery. . . ." But her voice is playful, and Ushman sighs.

"May I have a second chance to end this evening properly?"

There is quiet in the van. A restful kind of quiet as if Ushman's outburst has had some restorative effect on them both.

Stella answers him with a tentative kiss. The warmth of her mouth, its saltiness, its softness, replaces something in Ushman. Whatever loss he's suffered, whatever shame he's felt, is erased by the urgent hunger of his body for hers. Though their kiss remains gentle, even diminutive, they each, with their hands, hold the other's face, keeping it there, just so, lest their embrace ever end.

With the same reckless abandon of their first meeting, Ushman finally pulls himself away, only to coast down the hill and around the corner to the first space on Riverside Drive. Without a word, he turns to the back and pulls a carpet to the center of the van's cargo area. It is folded carefully, just back from cleaning. Ushman does not think to whom it belongs. He simply unfolds it halfway, so that its colors are a blur of darkness that will protect them from the cold metal of the van.

Ushman reaches his hand for Stella. Her fingertips are already cold and they send shivers up his spine. Taking them close to his mouth, Ushman lays his breath on them. The heat of his body, his desire for her like none he has ever known, warms them.

Without any interruptions, Ushman and Stella lie together on the antique carpet—the sparse fall foliage rustling across the roof, the halos glowing pink around the streetlights outside the van's windows, the metallic din of Persian music on the radio— and undress each other, slowly, lingering on each new part of their nakedness.

fourteen

 "It's snowing," she says to him when he answers the phone.

"You're awake?"

"You're not?"

"I am." He is not. He has been having the nightmare. But this time, he found the baby before the bird killed it. He rushed it to Farak's arms, where it was bloody against the white sheets, but she held it in her arms. Ushman tied tourniquets in every place he could. He kept ripping the sheet to fashion another and yet another.

"I wanted to hear your voice as I look out the window at this new and perfect world." Ushman doesn't know what she is talking about.

Stella eagerly tells him that the entire campus is covered in snow. And it is still falling. The tiniest little flakes falling in such a dense mass that it is difficult to see anything but the white blur.

"I've never seen anything so beautiful. Everything looks calm and serene. The city's noises seem far away."

Ushman opens his eyes and looks out the window. He watches the snow fall thickly in Queens as she continues talking.

"Do you know what I woke up thinking about?"

"Tell me."

"It's funny, as diligently as I avoided backseats in high school down South, in Manhattan I ended up screwing in a parked car."

Ushman can still hear the sheets ripping to form another tourniquet. He looks outside. It is a snow shovel, scraping against the sidewalk.

"It was thoughtless of me. I only—"

"I'm kidding, Ushman. It's great. The irony is perfect."

Ushman closes his eyes again. She is a beautiful girl. So early in the morning, though, he finds it difficult to speak so freely. She doesn't seem to notice.

"I miss you. I still feel where you were." Her voice is quiet but unashamed.

"Me, too. The bed is cold."

"That's not what I mean."

"My English is not very good this early in the morning."

"Shut up. I'm trying to flirt, the stress on *trying*."

"I'm flirted."

"You're funny."

"Did you sleep?"

"The snow woke me up. And my father."

"Is there news?"

"Not much."

"Has she improved?"

"I guess. It's hard to tell. My father's English is not very good."

"You're funny." Ushman smiles, realizing nothing is so very different about the relationship between children and their parents in America or in Iran. Everywhere in the world there is be-wilderment about those who have borne us and those whom we have borne. "I'm not opening the shop today. But I have a deliv-ery in Manhattan later. Can I pick you up?" Ushman opens his eyes and looks at his side table. It is still early.

"Around five?"

He pulls the page off his calendar so that it is current. "In my—English word of the day—toboggan."

"You're funny."

"I do not lie. It's right here on the calendar. *A long narrow flat sled without runners, made of thin boards curved back at the front end: now used for the sport of coasting down a prepared slope or chute.* I will show you later."

"I'm flirted. I'll eagerly await the arrival of your tobog-gan, sir."

"And I look forward to your prepared slope, madam."

"Ooh la la. It's a whole new calendar. English vocabulary and naughty wordplay."

"Don't get too excited, Stella. I'm certain that I cannot sus-tain it."

"What is tomorrow's word?"

"For you, I'll look. Diastema. Oh, no. *A gap or space between two teeth.*" Ushman cannot contain his laughter.

Stella giggles. "You're kidding me."

"Not at all."

"You've got your work cut out for you."

"Indeed."

"I've got to pee."

"See you at five."

"Indeed."

fifteen

By the time Ushman drives into the city, everything on the road is slush. There are still deep drifts of snow along the gutters, but they are black and imprecise from the city's struggles. There is no trace of the peaceful, calm world that Stella described to him this morning. Now the snow looks ugly, even threatening, its rapid disintegration like an exhibit of the city's corrosive effects. But as he drives through the slush, his van becoming covered in a kind of gray ice-mud, Ushman is not discouraged. Instead, he is only looking forward to his trip uptown and his commiseration with Stella about the mess. And their eventual exodus to Queens, where the slush is not quite as black as the stuff along Madison Avenue.

This morning Ushman put on his fur-lined boots that Farak's uncle had given him as a wedding gift. Her parents were both killed during the first year of the Iran-Iraq war. Her father's brother was responsible for finding her a place in Ushman's father's workshop and, eventually, accepting Ushman's marriage proposal. The boots were all Farak's uncle could afford as a dowry. Ushman's parents were disappointed with his choice anyway. But when his mother saw the boots, she clucked her tongue.

"All my sacrifices, and he chooses a girl with nothing to give. Nothing but these ridiculous boots." At the time, Ushman did not defend the gift from Farak's uncle. He knew that his breath would be wasted on his mother. Instead, he wore them often during the winter months, and thought of them in his own mind as a symbolic gift. *To keep us grounded, on solid footing*, he would say to Farak in their dim bedroom, as she would pull them off of him and warm his icy toes between her hands.

He has never worn them in America, but this morning he dragged them out from the back of his closet and pulled them on to walk through the snow to the market. He bought chicken, the Farsi-language Tehran newspaper, and the cheese streusel he has admired so many times before. A surprise for Stella's breakfast. He's hoping she'll finally accept his many invitations to stay the night. At home he prepared chicken kebabs for their dinner and read the paper. From a cabinet in his closet, he retrieved a white taper candle and stabilized it on a saucer, sinking it into its own warm wax. He put this on the dresser in his bedroom with a matchbook beside it. The snow was still falling and he imagined it would make the room feel warmer tonight as he and Stella removed their layers of clothes.

Unexpectedly, there is actually a parking space in front of Mrs. Roberts's building. Ushman cannot remember the last time he was able to pull in next to the curb. He has a roll of plastic in the back of his van that he wraps around the rug. Heaving it onto his shoulder, he slams the back doors and is careful of his step, as the boots make him a little clumsy.

Ushman has an informal partnership with a rug cleaner in

Queens. He brings in his high-end clients' rugs, and receives twenty percent from the rug cleaner. Ushman is happy to give the old Armenian man the work. He does an excellent service. And it pleases Ushman's clients that he handles everything about their rugs. He appraises, brokers, cleans, and restores. Ushman enjoys their esteem.

And now, with the rug on his shoulder and his van parked neatly next to the curb, Ushman feels amenable. The doorman calls him "sir" and rings the elevator for him. He is looking forward to picking up Stella later and lighting the candle in his bedroom. He notices how quiet and smooth the motor is on this elevator. As it slows, Ushman imagines the cables gliding in the darkness above and below him.

The same young maid answers the door. She does not look at Ushman's face or eyes. Instead, she opens the door, watches him walk through, and motions for him to unburden himself. "I will get Mrs. Roberts," she says as she clicks the door shut. Ushman stands in the entry, wishing he had not worn his snow boots. His feet are hot and he feels like a clown in the refined, uncluttered apartment.

He can hear Mrs. Roberts's shoes clicking from somewhere deep inside. She is getting nearer. Ushman kneels and removes the plastic from the rug. Using his pocketknife, he cuts the twine with which he secured the rug this morning.

"You're here," she says, holding her hands together as if in prayer. "Even with the snow." She raises her eyebrows and motions in the direction of the den where there is a bank of windows. "The park is stunning. You must see it before you go."

Ushman nods and smiles. "I knew you were anxious to have this back."

"Yes. How did it clean?"

"Perfectly," Ushman says and he unfolds the rug on top of the pad that's already in place. "I'm told there were no problems. As you can see. . . ." Ushman stands and stretches out his arms, gesturing at the rug. And it is then that he sees it. Or he thinks he sees it. A small dot of burgundy that is not a part of the pattern. A piece of Stella's virtue left on the rug.

Mrs. Roberts, however, is looking at his boots. Ushman, too, looks down at his feet. "Snow boots," he says with a nervous laugh. He looks again at the rug. Thinking of the whiteness of Stella's skin, her thin eyelids fluttering against his cheek, Ushman begins to perspire.

"They look awfully warm. I always wanted Mr. Roberts to have a really good pair of snow boots. Especially being a skier. But he prefers slippers by the fire après-ski. Or he did. I don't know the last time we skied. Probably ten years. Maybe more."

"They have a good sole. Lots of traction."

She finally moves her eyes from his boots to the rug. "It's beautiful, Ushman. Just beautiful." Mrs. Roberts kneels and puts a hand on it. Ushman is sure she will notice the mark. He readies himself to express dismay. But she stands and turns away from it. "Now," she says, "you must come see the park."

Ushman circles the rug, looking at the stain from all angles. Will she notice? Will anyone? How soon can he reasonably recommend that it be cleaned again, and will the stain come out? It is fairly inconspicuous, he decides as he listens to Mrs. Roberts's heels click-clack across the floor. Reluctantly, he follows her in his clumsy boots.

She is standing in front of the windows, waiting. Her hair falls in stiff curls around her shoulders. The black tunic she is wearing is punctuated by a thick silver belt. Ushman crosses the living room and stands beside her.

"This is not why I live in New York, Ushman. But it's why I refuse to winter in Florida or Scottsdale or St. John. Winter is a beautiful season. It cannot be missed."

Ushman is indeed impressed by the perfectly blanketed park. Each tree branch, each hill, each bench is covered by clean, pure white. He can see faint black paths worn by sledders and dog walkers. But the vastness of the park is accentuated by the endless bright snow. Every corner is softened, every trash can is altered. It is a much different landscape than the Queensboro Bridge. Ushman takes a deep breath. He wishes he could show this to Stella.

"Would you care for a glass of water?" Mrs. Roberts says as she turns to him.

Before he can answer, she has opened a sliding panel halfway across the room to reveal a wet bar.

"I would offer you something a little stronger, but I'm told that your faith doesn't allow it."

"True," Ushman says, nodding.

"So often religion takes all the fun out of life." Mrs. Roberts winks and hands Ushman a tall glass of water. He thinks of his van parked on Riverside Drive in the middle of the night. He thinks of the stain on Mrs. Roberts's rug. Ushman looks back out at the park and drinks his water.

She continues. "It is meant to protect us, I suppose. And to comfort. But it has become transparent for me. Perhaps in the Dark Ages, when there was so little explanation for things. But with science. And what we now know of life. It seems ridiculous to believe the tenets of a fictional text of any religion written thousands of years ago." Something about the cadence of her voice indicates to Ushman that she is asking a question of him.

"I'm not a scholar. And I'm not a cleric. I'm not even a very good Muslim. But I believe. The way children do. Without a second thought. Life is complicated enough without questioning your soul and its destiny."

She is looking at him, her eyes watching his mouth move as he speaks. When he is finished she says nothing, but forces her mouth into a smile and sighs, "Hmm." It seems that it will be all she says. But then she takes a deep breath and adds, "But isn't that exactly what makes life complicated? The destiny of one's soul? What else is there, really?"

Ushman cannot help but laugh. He also cannot help wishing he were having this conversation with Stella. He has no desire to explain himself to Mrs. Roberts. He's not even sure if what he's said is the truth about himself. In some ways, he is still selling. Still saying whatever it is that will continue to convey an image in which she can invest. But he can see in her eyes that he has initiated an argument.

"Am I so shallow? You think I don't understand the complexities of struggle?"

"I know that you do," Ushman replies, hoping to defuse her attack.

"Well, you're wrong. I have no idea what it's like to choose between selling drugs or working a six-dollar-an-hour job. I don't know what it's like to sacrifice new shoes for a child's medicine. But I do know that in those sacrifices is the question of the divine. The destiny of one's soul is decided by one's reaction to the struggle. How does one behave under duress? Any kind of duress. This is morality, Ushman. This is God's territory."

Ushman looks down at the boots he is wearing. He thinks of Farak, and the sacrifices she's made. For his family, for him, for the tailor, for her baby. Certainly not all of them condoned by Allah. But Ushman has no doubt of her soul's destiny. Farak may have committed adultery, she may have abandoned him when he wanted her most, but Ushman still knows the balance of her heart. This is what he means to say when he tells Mrs. Roberts that he believes.

"Often," he begins quietly, still looking at the boots, "people behave poorly under duress. I know I have. But I believe in Allah and the wisdom of the Koran."

Mrs. Roberts smiles, satisfied. "I admire your faith," she says, looking toward the northern tip of Manhattan. In the time they've been talking, the day has turned to night without any sunset to warn of the transition. "And I admire your honesty."

Ushman, once again, is chagrined by her esteem. Her rug is there in the entry with Stella's blood on it. What kind of a believer is he, really? He should just tell her, just point it out, feign surprise, and remove it to be cleaned again. But the stillness of the air in the apartment and Mrs. Roberts's grateful eyes render him mute. He looks at his watch. It is the only way he knows to excuse himself from her presence.

"I apologize, but I am meeting a friend for dinner."

A table lamp turns on automatically in the corner. She raises her eyebrows. The room glows orange. "How nice. It must be gratifying for your wife to know that you've made friends here. That you do not insulate yourself from society."

"Indeed," Ushman says, averting his eyes from hers. He has told none of his customers about the divorce. "Give my regards to Mr. Roberts."

"I will," she says, the click-clack of her heels following Ushman to the door. She stands at the edge of the rug as he crosses it. Ushman yearns to mop the perspiration from his forehead.

Again, he remembers Stella's naked body. So perfect, so pale, beneath his. He stands a moment longer on the rug.

The young maid appears to open the door for him.

"Make me a drink," Mrs. Roberts says to the girl. And then she steps onto the rug in order to rest her hand on Ushman's shoulder. She says to him, "This is what brings me closer to the divine." She lifts her hand and is gone.

Ushman steps off of the rug and passes through the open door. As it closes behind him and he stands in the wide hallway, he can hear the faint rhythm of Mrs. Roberts's stride fading away somewhere deep inside.

Sixteen

Stella paces in a small circle, checking her watch. Ushman has spotted her from two blocks away. She is wearing a black watch cap and a long black jacket, and her blond hair shines in two long streaks over her shoulders. Ushman is suddenly perturbed by the length of the red light. At the base of his stomach is a dread that at any moment, Stella may decide to wait no longer and disappear forever into the noodle shop full of handsome students in sweatshirts and baseball caps. Finally, though, Ushman idles the van at the corner and Stella crosses through the packed trough of snow that has been made by pedestrians. Her face is flushed from the cold. In a gesture of utter confidence and beauty, she presses her lips against Ushman's cheek before settling into her seat. She sighs, rubbing her hands together.

Her confidence gives him confidence. "Cold?" he asks, taking one of her hands in his.

"Mm-mm," she nods. There are gloves covering her fingers, but he can still feel the chill coming from her skin. "I'm glad your toboggan is heated," she says, smiling.

He nods. "Yes, it's a first-class model."

Stella smiles. She leans her head against the back of the seat, closes her eyes, and laughs. Ushman is still holding on to her gloved hand. She laughs so hard there are tears coming out of the corners of her eyes. He chuckles out of camaraderie, but retains enough composure to wipe the tears from her jawline.

When his fingers touch her face, she opens her eyes and lifts her head off of the seat. Her laughter fades to a smile and she lets Ushman wipe the rest of the tears with his thumb.

"You should not laugh at the misfortune of others. The bulk of my toboggan cannot be helped."

Stella breathes carefully, one hand resting on her stomach. She is fighting back laughter. "Please, stop. I don't know why it's so funny to me."

"Perhaps you've been studying too long. How did you fare? On the astronomy?"

"Okay, I think. The world was all so beautiful this morning. I sat in the classroom, my scarf around my neck, and out of the corner of my eye I could only see white. Out the window, it was just perfectly calm. And white."

"Leave it to Manhattan," Ushman says as he merges the van into Broadway traffic.

"Did you run your errand?"

Ushman nods.

"Are we having dinner?"

"I prepared kebabs."

"You spoil me."

"I see you have a bag. . . ."

Stella briefly touches the backpack between her feet.

"Yeah, I brought a few things."

"Kebabs are a small price to pay for your face on my pillow all night long."

"On the pillow, okay, but I have my own set of requirements," she says, winking at him.

Ushman blushes. He is still unaccustomed to her candor and her playfulness. Especially from a virtuous girl. Only after several years of marriage did Farak speak openly with him about their intimacies. And then only in a whisper, usually in the dark. He wonders if all Americans speak so openly. Would Mrs. Roberts speak so candidly to Mr. Roberts?

He remembers his earlier conversation with Mrs. Roberts, the view from her apartment, and the stain on the rug.

"Stella," he says, "are you religious?"

She doesn't scoff or even seem surprised by his unexpected change of subject.

"No, not really. I think common decency goes a long way. But not because it's in the scriptures."

"Why, then?"

"Just because it makes sense. To treat people the way you'd want to be treated. It's like a formula that, if everybody followed, would lead to great harmony. Are you religious?"

He nods. "A bit. I've become more so in America, I think. Simply because it's comforting. In Iran, religion is used in order to control people. To maintain power. The corruption made it easy to disregard." Stella blinks. Then she takes a deep breath and looks at her hands.

"There's something very beautiful that I learned in astronomy. About the universe. I promised you that I would tell you if I learned about anything indelible. Remember?"

"Yes, of course. Please. . . ."

"Well, there is this finite theory of energy. It says that the universe contains only a certain amount of energy and that that measure of energy simply converts from one form into another. Existing forever, changing constantly. So that a star might contain energy that was once a part of the ocean or a part of a person's heart. So, energy lasts, Ushman. It remains, after all."

Ushman looks at the steel cable on the bridge that they are driving on. There is energy there. And in the engine of his van, the hum of his heater, the electricity of his headlights. "That is beautiful," he says. "It's what I hoped for. Something that lasts. To think that the same energy contained in my grandfather's body might be here now. Somewhere."

Stella adds, "Maybe in the moisture that produced this snow."

"Yes." He smiles. "Yes."

"But it's not reincarnation. It's not recognizable, traceable energy. It's just atoms. Reassigned."

"And those atoms have no memory?"

She shrugs. "No. This is just my theory that I sort of invented out of my astronomy textbook. Don't go changing your religion." She laughs.

"It's a nice theory," Ushman says as they leave Manhattan behind. There is even more snow on the ground in Queens. Covered with a layer of grime and exhaust, it is hard to imagine that it just fell this morning.

"I have a question for you now. What is it that first made you notice me?"

Ushman smiles. "It is not a trick question?"

"No, I'm just curious. I won't be mad."

Ushman reaches a hand to the back of his own neck. "Here," he says. "The length and curve of your neck."

"Really? That's so weird. I would never have guessed." She closes her eyes and smiles, satisfied.

"It is exquisite. Hidden, mostly. But when you lift your hair and it is revealed . . ."

He doesn't finish his sentence. Stella smiles. She places a hand on the back of her neck, as if it has suddenly become dear to her as well.

"This part of you reveals your nature. Tender, delicate, but able to bear great weight."

"I like that," she finally says. Then, quieter, she adds, "I like you, Ushman."

Ushman takes his eyes from the road in front of him. He stares at her, without a smile, without a trace of frivolity. His eyes look far into her, documenting the very truth of her emotion. Finally, he looks away.

"You flatter me," is all he says, his voice shallow and uncertain.

Stella giggles. "Why does language always make things so risky? Of course I like you. You already know that. But I feel totally self-conscious saying it."

"Because words make it real. You cannot take it back. You cannot claim you came with me because you were just bored or hungry."

"I suppose that's why people get married, too. Get the license, pay the band, make it real."

Ushman shrugs. "Maybe," he says. "Maybe that is why."

There is silence between the two of them as Ushman longs to speak with Stella more openly. He would like to tell her that she will make a wonderful wife. That she is a gift he never hoped he could deserve. But Ushman does not want to jinx his good fortune, this perfect moment.

The streetlights and traffic lights are surrounded by thick halos. Their fuzzy perimeters obscure the darkness, making beautiful pastel globes. It may snow again tonight.

"This morning seems like long ago," Stella finally says, looking toward Ushman. "It all gets so ugly so fast."

"You mean the snow?"

"I want to wake up and have it be like it was this morning. So quiet and still and bright."

"I do have a surprise for the morning."

"Is it clean, fresh snow?"

He smiles and shakes his head. "No."

"Is it the chance to sleep in without the interruption of hair dryers or radios or yoga poses?"

"I can't do my yoga poses?"

Stella laughs. "If you're doing yoga poses, I'll for sure wake up to watch."

"Why do you think that might be funny? You think I am not limber or strong?"

"I know that you are both limber and strong. But I'll still be waking up to watch."

"I don't do yoga."

"I know."

"Do you?"

"No. What's my surprise?"

"Shall we look up the word in my English dictionary? I believe it means that you cannot know ahead of time."

"Come on. . . ."

"No, no." Ushman shakes his finger at her, thinking of the streusel he will serve to her. "I choose my words carefully. It is a *surprise*."

"Okay, okay. I'll wait."

"What have you heard from Italy?"

"I had a call from my mother. Acting like she's at some kind of spa. As if she's finally decided that massage therapy is not some weird New Age activity."

"Did you speak to her about what happened?"

"What did happen, Ushman? Because unless I had told you about it, come directly from my dorm room to your office, I would be starting to believe that it was all a dream." Stella's voice is bewildered, frustrated.

"Be grateful your mother does not display her weakness to you. My mother reminds me all the time of each of her many frailties."

"Oh." Stella's voice softens. "Maybe that's why you don't like to talk about your life. Are you afraid of droning on like your mother?"

"I do not like to complain."

"I wish you would. And I wish my mother would." Stella reaches over and grabs his shoulder. Ushman looks at her. "I don't want to pretend," she says with her eyebrows raised. "What is the point of having a relationship if it's all pretense and niceties? Why bother?"

"Pretense and niceties can be nice."

"Only for a short time." She lets go of his shoulder and rests her head against the seat. "Not for a lifetime."

"But a lifetime of complaints . . . ?" Ushman cannot remember a time, even as a small child, that his mother did not tire him with her list of grievances.

"Shall I go?" Stella asks.

"To Italy?"

She nods.

"Why not? Perhaps in person she will tell you what it is you want to know."

"I don't want to go. I can hear that she has reconstructed what happened. She has recast it as an accident. An anecdote. I don't want to go along with that delusion. I don't think I can." Ushman admires her enthusiasm for the truth, but he also wonders if one day she, too, will outgrow this fixation.

Ushman pulls into the parking garage, nodding to the attendant.

Stella continues. "Part of me says that whatever has happened is about her as an individual—an adult. And I should not interfere. We're not, necessarily, friends." Stella looks down at her gloved hands. "And then I feel ashamed that I'm able to distance myself in that way. She is my mother. I am her only child. I should be there."

Ushman perfects the position of the van in his usual parking space. He cuts off the engine, but continues to grip the steering wheel. "It is hard to know, when someone is so far away, what your role is in their life. But, without a doubt, if you can, you must go." Ushman takes the key from the ignition and holds it in his lap. He looks over at Stella, then back at his hands. "It is better to go and be disappointed than it is to stay here and be disappointed. If you are forever excluded from the truth of what has happened, you will blame yourself. Because you didn't ask. You didn't go and see for yourself."

Stella fingers the bag between her legs.

"I know what I am talking about, Stella."

She nods, still avoiding his eyes.

"But you didn't ask for my opinion. I'm sorry for the lecture. You will make up your own mind."

Stella picks up her bag and steps down from the van. As she comes around the back to meet Ushman, she sees his boots. He looks so out of place in the bulky fur boots in the middle of a concrete parking garage. They are not urban footwear. He looks as if he should be herding sheep. Or riding a camel.

"Are those your toboggan boots?" she asks, unable to hide the smile that is threatening to turn into laughter.

Ushman reaches for her bag and puts it over his shoulder. He then takes her gloved hand in his. "Well, I couldn't very well coast down the prepared slope without them, could I?"

Stella's laughter echoes through the parking garage. Ushman does not laugh, but he is smiling as he wraps his arm around her, guiding her out onto the icy sidewalk.

After dinner, Ushman lights the candle on his dresser. Stella follows him into his room and watches as he flicks his wrist back and forth to extinguish the match. She stretches herself out across his bed and sighs.

Later, as they watch the beam of a streetlight outside his window, waiting for a snowflake, Ushman remembers his mother's latest complaint: the food at the elder home. "At least," she said to him as clearly as if she were next door, "Farak knew how to cook. Peasant girls always do. But she betrayed us, Ushman. There is no seasoning here. No flavor in the food. And my neck. Cramping all day long."

"She is not a peasant," Ushman said, defending Farak, a habit he has not broken.

"Do not argue with me, Ushman. I know about life. However she was born, she turned out a peasant."

Ushman would like to stop calling his mother. Would like to pretend that she had the courage to jump off a bridge. No American soldier could save her. She would sink like a brick.

Feeling guilty, Ushman strokes the back of Stella's neck. He concentrates on the rhythm of Stella's breath, places his hand on her back, and feels her rib cage moving in and out, in and out.

"Ushman?" she says, her voice suddenly timid.

"Yes?"

"Is everything good, for you, I mean, this . . . what we just did?"

"You must ask?" he says, rubbing his hand across the back of her neck.

She covers her face, though he cannot see it anyway, and nods.

"If you must ask, then I've done something wrong."

"I mean, I got the feeling that, yes, you were enjoying yourself, but you are so concerned about me, I wondered if you are concerned enough about yourself. Do I need to be doing something more?" She is still hiding her face, speaking into her hands.

Ushman sighs. "Men are simple, Stella. Most of my pleasure comes from seeing you enjoy yourself. It is a beautiful thing."

She turns her face to his. Her eyes are wide and serious. "Did Farak enjoy herself?"

Ushman closes his eyes. Of course she is curious, he tells himself, as I would be if she had had a husband in a distant country. He tries to think. It is startling that in this moment, he can remember very little about their lovemaking.

"There was a time . . . But you will see, someday, with someone else, that each experience is very much unique." As he says it, a lump forms in his throat. Is it true that there will be a someday? Another man for her? He does not want to think it possible.

"I'm sorry, I didn't mean to . . . I just, not to compare, or anything. I didn't want that. Really, I'm just curious. Because you're the only person I know, like this, who's been married. Who's been in a relationship for so long. Who knows how it is that things . . . evolve."

Ushman stops stroking her. "There was a time," he says again, "that I thought our intimacy would never change. And then she became pregnant. And very quickly, it seems, we were in a cycle of loss. She lost five babies before they were anything more than a stain of blood. And to become pregnant again was our way to respond. Or my way, I suppose. Finally, she didn't want to try anymore. And by then her body had become her enemy. And my body its conspirator. That is why she sent me here. To America. She couldn't live with two enemies any longer."

Stella has been listening so carefully to Ushman's voice that she hasn't allowed herself a breath. She lets the air out of her lungs and lowers her head, once again looking out of the window. Ushman notices the taper that has sunk into a pile of wax on his dresser, the flame struggling to survive.

"Last night . . ." she says, turning away from the window and placing a hand on his face, "last night, when you said her name on the phone, it sounded completely different than when you say it in English conversation. It sounded like it belongs in your mouth. I could hear its familiarity on your tongue."

"She had a baby girl," Ushman tells her again, as though she doesn't already know. As though this is some kind of explanation. Then he closes his eyes.

Stella rests her head on his chest.

Ushman knows that she can hear his own heart, beating beneath her ear. He feels it gently rocking her head. He imagines his heart forming from nothing, growing its cells inside his mother's uterus, then continuing to beat, even here in Queens, so far away from Iran. And he imagines the baby's heart, Farak's baby's heart, beating in a cradle in Istanbul.

Where, he wonders, is the energy from those fetuses? Those five unfinished hearts?

He opens his eyes and looks across the room. Outside of the window, millions of perfectly formed snowflakes have begun in an unhurried descent.

"It's snowing," he says quietly.

Stella nods. "Joy," she whispers, and closes her eyes.

"Absolute," he says, stroking the hair away from her forehead so that he can kiss it. He pulls the heavy wool blanket over both of them. The flame on the candle is finally swallowed by its own heap of wax. Darkness is everywhere except for the white of the snow as it falls past the window. Ushman's heart continues to drum beneath Stella's ear, becoming a lullaby.

Seventeen

Ushman studies a photograph of the Ponte della Paglia in a guidebook of Venice. He then closes his eyes and imagines being somebody on that bridge. A tourist, just standing there, disoriented and maybe a little nauseous from the smell of the canals. Looking toward the Bridge of Sighs and the old prisons of the Doge. There are birds squawking overhead and a gypsy singing off-key. All of a sudden a woman, an American, is up on the rail. For a moment she just stands there, calm and reflective, as if this were nothing out of the ordinary. And then, without a shriek or a hesitation, she steps off, into the dark water below. How shocked Ushman would have been, and how torn between horror and anticipation as the uniformed soldier dove in after her; yet another body swallowed by the thick black water. Ushman realizes that this scene is one that Stella must frequently imagine. He winces, as if for a moment it is his own pain. He is filled with an urgent tenderness toward her.

Putting the guidebook away, he pulls a phrase book from the shelf.

Ushman calls her three times while she is in her room, packing. The first time he says, *"Arrivederci."*

"I thought you had a meeting."

"I do. Right now, however, I am in a bookstore on Fifth Avenue. *Posso lasciare un messaggio?"*

"I already packed my phrase book, Ushman."

"Unpack it. You must carry it with you."

"What did you say?"

"I said you must carry it with you."

"I mean in Italian. What did you just say?"

"I asked if I could leave a message."

"Say it again."

"Posso lasciare un messaggio?"

"Nice. Will anybody in Italy sound like that?"

"Persian Italian? I doubt it."

"Damn."

"Mi dispiace."

"What's that?"

"I'm sorry."

"Me, too."

Ushman has never before been in a bookstore in Manhattan. Its size and volume are spectacular.

"It's like a palace, this bookstore," he says as he sits in a velvet armchair, flipping through the phrase book. "And they invite you to sit and stay, as if it were your own palace. All of your own books."

"You'd think this is a very literary country."

"Well, I'm not alone here. I mean, there are many other people pretending this is their own personal library."

"Key word: pretending," she says, laughing.

The second time he calls, he says, *"Ho fatto una prenotazione."*

"Are you still in the bookstore?" she asks.

"Yes. I have a reservation."

"At the bookstore?"

"No. That's what I said. In Italian."

"Where?"

"When you come back. A restaurant downtown. Very fancy Italian food."

"Are you in the food section now?"

"Yes. I'm late for my meeting. But I want to take you to dinner. Out. A nice date. When you get back. *Ho fatto una prenotazione.*"

"I'll be dreaming of kebabs."

"You can show me what to order at the Italian place. You will order for me. In Italian."

"I'm going for three nights, Ushman. You already know more Italian than I do."

The third time he calls, Stella is zipping up her bag.

"You should be in the taxi," he says.

"I've had some distractions."

"Really?"

"Some Italian guy keeps calling."

"Beware of those Italian men."

"They are persistent."

"Forgive me. I just wanted to tell you to travel safely. *Ti penso sempre.*"

"Translation, please."

"Look it up in your phrase book. But first, go get a taxi. *Ciao.*"

Ti penso sempre. I always think of you. Ushman had seen the phrase in the book. It was not something he would have said had the book not suggested it, but it was also not untrue. He is

dreading this long weekend, this American Thanksgiving, because there are three days ahead of him in which he has no
chance of seeing Stella. Somehow, he cannot remember how it
is that he filled his time before she came along. He does not recall being bored or restless. He certainly never before wan-
dered into a bookstore. What he does not remember is that grief
and anger were his constant companions. They occupied all of
his free time.

In a rush, Ushman decides to buy the guidebook. He tucks
the sack under his arm and hurries to his meeting downtown.

Later, Ushman drives to a Middle Eastern restaurant in Flatbush. He does not care to go home yet. He feels sullen and useless. The sound of an airplane overhead makes his jaw clench.
He orders a dinner plate of souvlaki, salad, and hummus. Taking out the guidebook, he regards the palazzos, cathedrals, and
the countryside of Italy. It is a beautiful country, he decides,
thinking for the first time of traveling somewhere other than
Iran. Looking at a map, he traces the route from Venice to
Padua, where Stella's mother is now. As the familiar tang of feta
and tomato lingers in his mouth, he finds himself once again
trying to conjure images of a woman on another continent. Is
Stella just now boarding a water taxi? Does it sway in the cur-
rents, calming her? Or does the crush of different voices, all
speaking Italian, disorient her? Or maybe she is passing the
row of water taxis, and, instead, hailing a land taxi that will
travel west, away from the ancient city of Venice and into the
busy afternoon traffic of the Veneto.

These thoughts occupy his mind until he has finished his

dinner. Just as he is settling his bill, his cousin Ahmad walks in. Ushman closes his eyes, cursing coincidence.

"To inja hasti," Ahmad says, smiling broadly. He is a short, square man with a long graying beard and a wide face.

They embrace. He smells of saffron and tea.

"Can you sit with me? Have some dinner together?" Ahmad asks, gesturing at a booth. Ushman knows that Ahmad's bride is pregnant and he would like to boast about his happiness.

"I just finished," Ushman says, holding the guidebook behind his back. "I have an appointment. In Manhattan."

"In the dark? You are too busy, Ushman. Work does not disguise your pain."

"You don't know what you're talking about." Ushman has never liked his cousin's presumptuousness. As if his piety gives him access to everyone's private life.

"You have been shamed. I know. It's not Tabriz, but you cannot walk around—even in this country—and pretend you have not been wronged. But Allah has begun to serve her a just revenge."

Ushman understands that Ahmad is speaking of Farak.

"You've heard news?" This is Ahmad's redemption. Without fail, he has news from Iran.

Ahmad looks across the restaurant, nodding and waving at acquaintances. He is active in the local mosque. Ushman is sure that these social exchanges are meant to heighten the suspense and value of his information. Ahmad looks out the window and strokes his beard, nodding. Then he brings his eyes back to Ushman.

"Well?" Ushman says, annoyed at these childish tactics.

Ahman smiles. "The baby is marked. *Allah Akbar.*"

"How? What do you mean?"

"A blotch of purple across her temple. A terrible mark."

Ushman rests his hands on the counter.

"Ugly," Ahmad adds as punctuation. Then again, *"Allah Akbar."*

"Is it dangerous?" Ushman asks, looking at his hands, waiting to hear the words.

"A warning to all. Farak betrays you, betrays Allah, moves to an unholy place where she leaves her face uncovered. Hah," Ahmad says, spitting into his own shoulder.

Ushman presses his hands harder against the counter and looks at his cousin. "Is it dangerous, Ahmad?"

Ahmad shrugs, his performance over. "A birthmark. But it will prevent her from committing the sin of her mother. No man will have her. She will die unwanted."

Ushman's chest heaves. He feels as though he cannot breathe.

"I need some air. Goodbye, Ahmad."

"Come to prayers, Ushman," Ahmad calls to him.

Ushman leans against his van. He feels for a moment as if he might vomit. There are still patches of black snow on the ground. He spits, then kicks the snow with his shoe. Ushman gets in the van and rests his head on the steering wheel. He curses Ahmad. His vigor, his pleasure at delivering this news. News of anybody's misfortune. A baby's, even. When his own child is being formed. Ahmad is Allah's worst disciple.

His head aches with an image he cannot remove. Farak watching her child sleep, rubbing her hand across this mark, pitying the girl only while the baby's eyes are closed. Ushman cries into the crook of his arm slung over the steering wheel. His tears feel hot against his cheeks.

He curses himself. He himself has wished for something terrible like this. Something unnamed and vague, but still, something vengeful. And now he cries. It is only since he has met Stella, since his own sorrow has faded, that he is so undone by Farak's. Only now that he has something to cherish does he want the universe to be forgiving.

Did he cause this? By wishing Farak to experience remorse. Yearning for her to lose the baby. Anything that might return her to Tabriz. Even there. Even if she never came to New York. Even if he had to live with pretending forever that she would. Better that than somebody else having her, making her happy. Just wash his mother for the rest of her years. Ushman had wanted the world to prove Farak wrong. To prove that there was not a better life. That this desire of hers was a foolish one.

But look, now, at his own desire. At the book under his arm. Has his hypocrisy reached across the oceans and caused Farak's baby to be disfigured?

He tosses the guidebook to the passenger's seat and wipes his face dry. He starts the engine and drives toward Flushing, his mind awash with disbelief, sorrow, and contempt.

Tomorrow is Thanksgiving. There is more traffic than usual for a Wednesday night. Drivers with their minds on parades, American football, and pumpkin pies. Ushman relies heavily upon his horn.

When he reaches the parking garage, he is irate. He grinds his teeth and jams the gearshift into park. Before he's cut the engine, he is startled out of his fury by an abrupt knock on the passenger's-side window. He looks over, expecting a vagrant. It is a familiar face, but one that he does not immediately recognize.

This time, her hair is red, primary red like the stripes in the

American flag. Her skin is still pale and her eyebrows are painted on in high black arches. Ushman reaches over and rolls the window down a crack.

"Gobble, gobble, right?"

"Pardon me?" Ushman says, confused.

"Turkey day tomorrow. Cowboys and Indians, you know?"

Ushman nods. "Yes, sure."

She smiles. The space between her front teeth is so wide it is nearly vulgar. Diastema.

"What is it, then, that you want?" Ushman asks, then wishes he hasn't.

"I'm lonely tonight," she says, blinking too fast and sticking her lip out, as if to pout.

"I'm not," Ushman says and rolls up the window. He shuts off the engine, takes the guidebook from the passenger's seat, and steps down from the van.

It does not surprise him that she is standing at the rear of the van, her hands twisted behind her back, her white legs bare and shivering.

"Please, John," she says, following him as he walks quickly out of the garage.

"That is not my name," Ushman says, shoving the keys deep into his pocket.

"Twenty dollar and I call you whatever you like."

Ushman shakes his head. He almost pities her, having such an ugly face. He looks closer at its ugliness, as if she is Farak's ugly child. As if this were the fate that awaits her, too.

But then, he thinks to himself, her ugly face did not prevent me from inviting her into my kitchen. It did not prevent me from being grateful for her presence. Ushman realizes that her

livelihood relies not upon how attractive she may be, but upon
how defeated a man is at the moment she finds him.

Though Ushman has had this moment of clarity, it does not
make him feel any more in control of what is happening.

"No, thank you," Ushman says simply, walking toward the
exit.

Her heels echo across the garage as she walks with him.

"You from Mexico?" she asks, grabbing his elbow, jogging a
bit to keep up with his pace.

"No," Ushman says, allowing her to hold his arm.

"You look like a spic."

Ushman ignores her.

"But spics aren't usually so quiet."

"I'm from Iran," he says, crossing the street as she follows
him, her heels chattering against the asphalt.

"I'm Vietnamese. You got family here?"

Ushman does not answer her question. He is struggling with
how easy it would be for him to allow her to follow him all the
way home, make him a scrambled egg or a bowl of noodles, and
stay with him for the night. Suddenly he notices that she is
quiet. In this silence, he has begun to enjoy the weight of her
hand on his elbow, the empty space beside him now filled.

Then she speaks again.

"My parents brought me, when I was eight. The kids at
school threw rocks at me. My father chopped his fingers off at a
slaughterhouse. He smokes rock now. My mother does nails
at the seaport. She watches the boats all day. The ferries and
whatever. My brother is still in Vietnam. He was our ticket out.
They traded him for my place on the boat."

"Shut up," Ushman says suddenly, pulling his arm away

from her. "Your sad story does not concern me. You do not concern me. I simply do not care."

They have stopped walking and Ushman is turned toward her, looking down on the black roots of her hair. He expects that she will cry. That inevitably he has hurt her feelings and she will expect him to give her some consolation. He imagines that he might be able to do this, if she will just be quiet. To hold her, to do some good, would ease the tremor behind his eyes. He turns to look up the street at the awning of his building.

For this reason, he does not see it coming. He first hears her throat making a scraping sound, digging deep for its innermost contents, and then he feels the warm sting of her saliva on his cheek. It begins to slide down, toward his mouth. He cringes and curses something unintelligible. Ushman does not want to wipe it with his coat sleeve. He reaches for his handkerchief in his pants pocket.

She just stands there, one hand on her hip.

Ushman turns and walks away.

"I'm just making conversation, John. Why you gotta be so rude?"

Ushman does not stop walking. He does not reply.

"A man always thinks he's got the last word. Well, listen to me." She is yelling now and stomping her feet in agitation. "Listen to me, mister. Your cock tastes like shit. Like a rotten dog shit." Her voice is loud and it seems to echo down the block. Ushman's neck burns with anger. It is nearly too much for him. He would like to turn and run at her, knock her down, make her knees bloody on the sidewalk. Instead, he scrapes furiously at his own cheek until the skin beneath his handkerchief is raw and throbbing with pain.

He reaches his building and abruptly enters the lobby,

pulling the door closed behind him. He holds the handkerchief to his face, its burning causing his eyes to water. A few of his neighbors are gathered around the elevator waiting. Hurriedly, he joins them. Though he can still hear her shouting, and his face flushes at its pitch, Ushman realizes that her voice means nothing to these people. They do not know that it is he who has provoked her fit. They do not care that her complaints may be justified. In fact, they may not even hear her voice at all. For them, it may be drowned by the other background noise. The bass from the car around the corner, the beating of a hammer on a pipe, a child crying from an open window, the banter of a bet being made in front of the newsstand, a woman screaming about her baby brother, lost forever in a faraway place. The common, meaningless sounds of other people's lives.

Eighteen

Ushman stands in front of the windows in Mrs. Roberts's apartment, staring at the sky. He is looking for the airplane from Venice upon which Stella is due to arrive at any moment. He had planned to be there, at the entry to the international terminal, just where he'd been standing when he first saw her. It would have been a surprise. He looked forward to leaning against the wall and watching her before she noticed him. And then to have her notice him, among all the people around them, for each of them to see only the other. It is exactly this feeling that he'd dreamt about when he hoped Farak would one day join him. And exactly the feeling that had driven him to the airport so many nights, including the night he met Stella. This afternoon, however, he would not be fantasizing, or pretending or despairing. It would have been a true reunion. He would have been legitimate.

But he received an urgent plea for his presence from Mrs. Roberts. So he waits in her living room, searching the sky. He sees nothing, though, before Mrs. Roberts enters, clearing her throat.

"Ushman," she says, closing the door behind her. "Sit down."

Ushman feels a surge of adrenaline, but he smiles and sits on the edge of an oversized leather chair.

"We had Thanksgiving dinner here at the apartment. My son and daughter-in-law, my sister, a few close friends." She pauses and looks at the backs of her hands. "Do you, did you, celebrate Thanksgiving, Ushman?"

He shrugs. "I had turkey meatballs and watched a little football."

She throws her head back and laughs. "You're fully Americanized now."

Ushman laughs with her, but in truth he spent the last two days in his apartment, afraid to go out, afraid of the girl whose anger shamed him, afraid of his own remorse.

"Well, anyway, as I was saying, the children were here. My son is an artist. He has a studio downtown. You'd like him, really, I think. He was admiring the Bijar when he was here. I'm not sure when he saw it last. But for some reason, its beauty captured him this time." She pauses again. "Remind me, Ushman. Is this one that your wife chose?"

"Yes," Ushman lies. Though Mrs. Roberts knows the actual history of the rug, he knows that she prefers this version. "Farak chooses everything from Iran," Ushman lies again.

Before she left for Turkey, Farak assigned her duties of choosing, buying, and shipping rugs for Ushman to her friend Semah. Ushman does not trust Semah. Not the way he trusted Farak. Semah sent him sloppy rugs. Rugs made with Americans in mind, replicas of Chinese rugs, Afghani rugs. Rugs in pale greens, blues, and pinks, with low knot counts and inferior wool. And the prices she quoted him were inflated, Ushman knows.

It was only one time that he asked Semah to send him rugs. Mainly because he wanted to retain the connection to Farak. But when he opened the shipment, it only exacerbated his grief. The rugs Semah sent were like a measuring stick of all that he had lost. He sold the rugs at cost to a dealer in Westchester. Since then, he has started using a friend of his cousin who lives in Tehran and travels to the weavers four times a year. Because of the added middleman, Ushman's prices have gone up. But nobody in New York seems to notice.

"She has wonderful taste," Mrs. Roberts says. "I hope someday we will have the chance to meet her."

Ushman folds his hands in his lap. "And I, also," he says.

There is a long silence. Ushman feels as if Mrs. Roberts is waiting for him to say something else. Finally, she resumes her train of thought.

"As I was saying, about my son. He was admiring the Bijar in the entry hall when he noticed something. Let me show you." She stands and turns, walking toward the closed doors.

Ushman sits a moment longer, trying to think clearly, to decide upon his strategy. She waits for him in the doorway. He quickly walks across the room. As he reaches her, she continues to talk. "I had my dry cleaner come by this morning. Do you know what he told me, Ushman?"

Ushman shakes his head. They are standing just a few feet from the rug. From here, he can see the dark stain, can't believe he ever thought she wouldn't notice.

"It's blood," she says to him and the tops of his ears burn with shame.

He walks forward and kneels next to the spot. She stands behind him and cannot see that he closes his eyes and curses to himself. Then he stands and looks at her face. "I agree. This is terrible."

"It didn't happen here, Ushman. Every drop of blood here is very well accounted for, believe me. And I can't believe that your cleaner would have let something like that happen. This is what troubles me, Ushman."

Ushman puts his hands in his pockets so she cannot see them tremble.

"I cannot imagine . . ." he says, but does not finish the sentence.

Mrs. Roberts looks into Ushman's eyes. He feels obliged to return her stare. There is a brief moment, as he remembers the way he felt lying next to her on the stack of rugs in his shop, that he considers telling her just what happened. Her eyes seem to be asking for a confession, a clandestine revelation.

But Ushman does not speak and he does not turn away, either. They stand there, staring into each other's eyes. It is, finally, Mrs. Roberts who looks away and breaks the silence.

"You must check with your cleaner, Ushman. You must be assured that he does not let the rugs out of his sight after they are cleaned. This could be a great liability for you."

Ushman nods enthusiastically. "I will do that. And I apologize, Mrs. Roberts. I will take it immediately and have it cleaned. I will watch it myself."

"That's not necessary, Ushman. My dry cleaner is sending someone over later. He will spot-clean it and then we'll see where we are. I just wanted you to see it. I wanted you to be aware. You do understand?"

"Absolutely. Thank you so much for bringing it to my attention."

"You're welcome," she says, smiling a brief, indiscernible smile. "And now—" But before she can finish her sentence, the young maid is running through the hall, yelling. The sound of her feet hitting the floor drowns out whatever it is that she's saying. Ushman does not understand the words, which she continues to repeat, until she is running the other direction with both Ushman and Mrs. Roberts behind her.

"Come quick, come quick," she says over and over again, until they are all three standing in the bedroom off of the hall looking at Mr. Roberts lying peacefully in bed. Looking closer, though, Ushman notices that Mr. Roberts's eyes are open, but not seeing. They are empty and do not move toward the door.

"He's gone," the young maid says quietly, almost to herself.

"I can see that," Mrs. Roberts says, pushing past the girl to the side of the bed. The girl backs out of the room and stands respectfully, waiting in the hall until she is beckoned again.

Ushman follows her and they stand there together, quiet and tense. The girl closes her eyes and begins moving her lips. Ushman watches her until, finally, she makes the sign of a cross over her chest and opens her eyes. Ushman looks away, embarrassed by her faith. Perhaps because she has seen that he was watching her, participating in her prayer by observance, she reaches out for him. Her warm hand takes his own and squeezes it gently, both offering, and taking, comfort. Then, looking away from him, she lets his hand go.

Ushman is startled by her touch. He can't help but feel flattered.

And then ashamed.

The man is gone. Dead.

There is the ambiguous, yet particular sound of grief coming from inside the room. Mrs. Roberts seems to be walking around the bed, viewing him from each side. Tending to his arms, his feet, his head. Touching his still-warm body for the last time. When her voice calls out it is flat, as if coming through a poor connection on the telephone.

"Ushman," she calls. He looks at the maid. Then he pokes his head in the door. Mrs. Roberts is sitting on the bed. She has her husband's hand stretched out on the inside of her arm. His fingers are spread. His eyes have been closed. She does not turn to see Ushman's face in the door. He walks into the room so she will know he has heard her.

Slowly, Mrs. Roberts pulls her arm out from beneath her husband's hand, but she does not stand. "It must be so hard to die," she says, crossing her arms across her body. "To let go, with so many people wanting you to stay." She stays like this for a while, bent over his body.

Then, without notice, she stands and turns to Ushman, her face blotchy with spent tears. She extends her arms and he moves toward her to catch her embrace. With his arms around her waist, she lets go and he is holding the weight of her up. Her arms are hanging at her sides and she shudders with an inaudible sob.

Ushman doesn't know what to say. Any words of comfort seem entirely unfit. As he holds her frail body erect, he puts his mouth close to her hair and says, "Shh. Shh. Shh."

He looks at the bed. At Mr. Roberts's body. Ushman closes his eyes and can remember, so clearly, holding Farak just like this. The weight of her body dependent on his arms. Her hair in his mouth as he could say nothing but "Shh." In Tabriz, though, it was not a body on the bed, but a pile of bloody towels. And she bled still, even as he held her. His shoes became damp with the blood. A scripture from the Koran echoed in his ears. A verse he did not even remember learning. *Recite in the name of thy Lord who created all things, who created man from clots of blood.* He did not say it out loud. He did not dare speak, knowing that Farak desperately wanted somebody to blame. He simply held her, as he holds this woman now.

Of course, in Tabriz, Ushman, too, was weeping. His tears falling into Farak's hair. The taste of salt in his mouth and his vision blurred.

But here in Manhattan, his eyes are clear. He simply stares at the man whose wife is in his arms. There is no remorse. Only envy.

For these two, having lived a long life together. The man with his wife at his side, still stroking him even after he's gone. This is not a true time of sadness. There is nothing tragic here. But he accepts that, for she who is left behind, who knows not what she will have to face without him, who has no faith in an afterlife and lives in desperate search of desire, his lifeless body is terrifying.

And so he holds her until the shuddering stops and she gently puts her arms around him, turning her cheek against his chest, and sighs. Then, pulling away from him and straightening her skirt, she says, "I can't believe this happened while you were here, Ushman. I am so sorry. I certainly didn't mean to—"

Ushman holds his hand up to stop her. "Please," he says, "there is no need for any apology. May I call somebody for you? The doctor? Your son?"

"Charles is in Berlin. An art show. Our doctor lives downstairs. I'll ring him. I'll do that now," she says, and calls for the maid to bring her the phone.

Ushman is left alone in the room. Feeling obliged to make some gesture of goodbye, he touches the sheet gently where it slopes over the arch of Mr. Roberts's foot.

Sitting in a small wood-paneled study with Mrs. Roberts, Ushman glances at his watch and sees that Stella has probably already called his apartment. Mrs. Roberts notices that he's checked the time, but she says nothing of it. She does not excuse him. Instead, she sits next to him in a matching armchair and stares at the tapestry on the opposite wall.

"You know, we were once in New Delhi. It's where we found that tapestry, there. But when we were coming home, our plane was canceled. The airport was crowded and hot. I saw three nuns approach our waiting area. With them, sort of in the middle of a triangle they were making with their bodies, was Mother Teresa. I am not, as you know, a religious person, but Mr. Roberts is. I pointed her out to him. I told him that he should go to her, seek a blessing. He refused. Men have that — what is it? Ego?"

Ushman shrugs. She continues. "Something that stops you from reaching out. A fear of rejection, perhaps. But from Mother Teresa? I couldn't take it. He sat there, fanning himself, while a saint walked by. So I stood up, I walked over to her. She took my hand, signed my boarding pass and blessed me."

Ushman now, too, is looking at the tapestry.

"I went back to where he was sitting. I told him that she'd

blessed me. I knew he resented it. Wished that I were fearful and obedient. But then, do you know what? Years later, not too long ago, actually, we were at a cocktail party. The hostess was a beautiful young woman and she was wearing a large garnet crucifix around her neck. Halfway through the evening, I noticed the two of them across the room. She was engrossed by something Mr. Roberts was saying. I moved closer so that I, too, could hear his voice. He was telling her about the time in New Delhi. Except he was telling her that *he* had been blessed. That Mother Teresa had taken *his* hand, signed *his* ticket, and given *him* a holy blessing."

Ushman is quiet, wondering why it is that she feels comfortable sharing this with him.

She continues. "I didn't blow his cover, Ushman. I listened quietly until he was finished. I watched this woman put her hand to her cross and smile at him so sweetly. Then I laid my hand on his back so that he knew I was there. So that he knew that I heard him lie about Mother Teresa for the softening effect it had on this beautiful woman. So that he knew that I was standing there, and did nothing to correct him. So that he knew that I knew the worst of him. For some reason that was important to me. Like an insurance policy. He could never again suggest—overtly or otherwise—that his faith made him superior. We never spoke about it."

She closes her eyes for a moment and a brief, sad smile forms. Opening her eyes, she says, "I never told him that I actually thought it was sweet. A kind of homage to me. An appropriation of my own life to win another woman's esteem."

Ushman turns his signet ring around and around. "There is always something left unsaid, it seems."

"Is there? What will you wish that you'd have told your wife? Assuming, of course, she precedes you."

Ushman is stunned. He has not anticipated that his comment would elicit any question. Certainly not of this sort. He does not welcome her curiosity. He is anxious to find Stella, to be with her.

"There are many things. It is different. Being so far apart, you know. There are things I'd like to tell her, just about New York. Things that we do not take the time to speak about on the phone."

Mrs. Roberts turns her chair more completely toward Ushman. "When was the last time you spoke with her?"

"Farak?" Ushman does not need to clarify of whom she is asking, but he feels his resolve weakening. He feels as though Mrs. Roberts is looking for some consolation in the drama of Ushman's own life. He is tired of continuing to speak of Farak this way. He is tired of being constantly pulled into his past. He knows he should resist the impulse to speak honestly. This can only lead to trouble.

"Of course, Farak. How often do you speak?"

Ushman sighs. He bows his head so that his eyes see only his own hands. His resolve stiffens. "Once a week. About many things, but mostly business. Or my mother." Ushman pauses, only to keep his voice from faltering. He has not given in. He has not told her anything he shouldn't. "It is very difficult, to live this way. To be so very far apart. And alone." Ushman can feel the perspiration forming around his hairline. He does not look at her. Though it is a lie, it is the first time he has spoken the truth of it to anyone.

Mrs. Roberts has suddenly stretched her hand out to cover

his own. She looks into his face. "My God, Ushman. I've wondered. Of course, I knew. You have such a tragic disposition. But to hear you say it, I feel . . . just devastated."

"You are a very good customer. I do not want you to be concerned about my personal life."

"But you must be in so much pain."

Mrs. Roberts is still clutching his hand. Ushman does not like the coolness of it. Awkwardly, she lets him go.

Ushman shakes his head and shrugs. "No more than you," he says, and cringes, knowing that he has given her some part of him that she has desperately wanted. For so long, she has longed to know the detail of his pain. To be inside his exotic life of longing.

"Yes," Mrs. Roberts says under her breath, her eyes flattered by the comparison, "yes." She wipes a lingering tear from the corner of her eye.

The maid opens the door and announces that the dry cleaner has come to spot-clean the rug. Mrs. Roberts looks to Ushman.

"Ushman, would you mind? Send him away. I do not want to be occupied with that now. You can take the rug, can't you? Will you have it cleaned again for me?"

Ushman stands, relieved to be excused from the small room. "Of course. I will take it with me now."

"You have to go?" The way she says it, Ushman understands that the only acceptable answer is no.

He searches in his pocket for his keys. "Let me deal with the dry cleaner. I will then load the rug in my van and make a call. Perhaps I can stay a little longer."

Mrs. Roberts seems not to have heard him. Instead, she

addresses the girl. "Poach a chicken breast for Mr. Khan, Maria. I'm sure I cannot eat tonight, but I will sit in the dining room with him and make some necessary phone calls."

Ushman excuses himself and walks through the apartment to the foyer. There he finds the dry cleaner: an overweight middle-aged man wearing a skullcap and loafers.

"Sir," Ushman begins, his voice echoing, "Mrs. Roberts asked me to inform you that there is no longer a need to spot-clean the rug this evening. There has been a death in the family and she will send the rug out for cleaning at a more opportune time."

The dry cleaner looks at the spot, then back at Ushman. He shrugs. "You the doctor?"

Ushman shakes his head. "No. Actually, I am a rug merchant."

"You mean she bought the rug from you?" He has a strong New York accent.

"Yes."

"And there's been a death in your family or hers?"

"In hers."

"So . . . why the hell are you here?"

Ushman makes a hand motion that indicates the dry cleaner should lower his voice. He is angry that this man can express himself the way Ushman cannot. "I was here, actually, just by coincidence. To examine the spot."

"You mean the old man just died? Like while you were looking at the spot of blood?"

"I'm afraid so."

"That's creepy," he says, and picks up his small leather satchel. "I'm outta here. You want help with that?"

Ushman is kneeling at the edge of the rug, beginning to roll it up. Before he can answer, the dry cleaner is kneeling next to him, forcing the rug over on itself.

"Thank you," Ushman says, pushing in unison with the man.

"Yeah," he says, standing up. "Tell her that I'm sorry about the old man."

"I will. Thank you." Ushman extends his hand and the two men shake.

It is bitterly cold. Ushman sits in his van, his legs trembling.

"I'm stuck," he says into his cell phone. "It's a long story. Too long. I've missed you."

"You said that already," Stella says, sulking.

"Her husband just died, Stella."

"You said that, too."

"I want to see you, but I don't think it's possible tonight. This is a terrible situation."

"Doesn't she have family, Ushman?"

"Her son is an artist. He's in Berlin."

"The guy really just died? While you were there?"

"It's incredible. My timing is awful."

"You can say that again."

"This woman, she is so rich. And worldly. And I used to like the fact that she appreciates my rugs. She understands their beauty, their craft, their intricacy. But now I have come to pity her. And it does not feel good. I don't like staying because of her misfortune. I feel dishonest."

"Then come be with me. I need to see you." Stella's voice is confident.

Ushman does not say anything. How can he refuse?

"She gives me no choice, Stella. I'm sorry."

"No choice? What does that mean?" Stella scoffs. "Like she'll stick you with a steak knife if you leave?"

Ushman thinks of the young girl upstairs, fixing his dinner.

"I cannot explain. Maybe tomorrow. Can we meet tomorrow? At the Italian place in the Village? I want you to tell me everything. About your mother, her health."

There is a silence.

Stella sighs. "I guess. If this friend of yours is more important than I am."

"I'm not her friend. I'm a place holder."

"You are whatever you choose to be, Ushman."

"Did you come back from Venice a philosopher?"

Finally, she laughs. "Leave me alone. I'm tired."

"I'm not making fun. Did I say already that I missed you?"

"I think so."

"Just in case I didn't: I missed you."

"Got it."

"Okay, I'm very cold, so I'll go back upstairs now. Get some sleep. We'll talk in the morning."

Ushman locks the van and walks back into the lobby, cherishing its warmth. He tries not to let himself wonder what Stella will do now. How she will fill this evening that is so suddenly empty.

Upstairs, Mrs. Roberts is waiting in the dining room. There is a place laid for Ushman. A poached chicken breast, steamed carrots, wild rice, and a roll. He hasn't realized how hungry he is until he sits down.

Mrs. Roberts has on reading glasses. She smiles faintly at him. "Did you make your call?"

He nods. "And I'll take the rug to get it cleaned again. It's already in my van. Thank you for the dinner."

"You're welcome. I have to make these calls, Ushman. I wish now that I'd acquiesced to Mr. Roberts's suggestion that I hire a secretary. How silly is that? To hire someone to make phone calls? This is my life, Ushman."

"Yes," he says, fingering his knife. "Is there anything I could do to help . . . ?" As soon as he's said it, he regrets it.

"Oh, would you? At least call the newspaper for me. The obituary is here. But it's not typed. I don't think I can fax it like this. And I don't know that I can bear to read it right now."

Ushman swallows a bite of chicken. "Of course, of course." He tries to understand what it is that she's just asked.

"Finish your dinner. I'll call my son. Then you can read this over, see if my writing is legible, and we'll call the *Times*."

Ushman continues to move food around on his plate, composing bites and sipping water, while Mrs. Roberts reaches her son, in a distant hotel room in Berlin, and tells him that his father is dead. She does not mention that the rug merchant is sitting across from her at the dining room table. He does hear her say, though, that the maid will stay the night with her. She will not be alone, she tells her son.

When she hangs up, she tells Ushman, "He'll catch a plane tomorrow. How is the chicken?"

"Very good," Ushman says, surprised that he has cleaned his plate, given the circumstances.

"I'm glad. When you're ready, let's go to the study."

Ushman wipes his mouth with his napkin and pushes his chair back.

"Are you sure that there isn't somebody else who would be better suited to help you with this?"

"Absolutely not. Don't doubt yourself for a moment." She stands and gathers her papers. Ushman follows her into the study.

She directs him to take a seat on the sofa, beneath a brightly lit floor lamp. She sits next to him and hands him a sheet of paper. Across the top is written, in capital letters, Mr. Roberts's full name, and beneath that it says, *Obituary*.

"Go ahead," she says, "skim it and make sure that you can decipher my writing."

Ushman does just that, but her handwriting is textbook perfect and he has no trouble reading any of the words.

When he's finished, Mrs. Roberts finds a business card among the papers in her lap and dials the number on it. She reaches an editor at the *Times* who seems to understand exactly what it is that she would like. Ushman doesn't know if this is customary or if this is a favor for the Robertses. Either way, he takes a deep breath as he hears Mrs. Roberts say that she has asked a dear friend to read the obituary for her. Mrs. Roberts then passes the phone to Ushman and folds her hands in her lap.

Ushman reads the biographical details of her husband's life into the phone as clearly as he can, so there are no mistakes. While he does so, Mrs. Roberts sits next to him, her head bowed, silently weeping.

Nineteen

 The restaurant is on a narrow block just south of Christopher Street. Ushman has parked the van in a space just a few blocks away. Stella is meeting him at the restaurant. Ushman offered to pick her up. She declined, explaining that she would be downtown this afternoon, shopping for a warmer jacket.

Ushman sits at a table adjacent to the window. The tablecloth is red-and-white-checked. There is a small votive flickering and a carafe of water on the table. He watches the dark street for Stella.

He is nervous in a way he hasn't been since that night on the roof of his building. All of a sudden he feels as though his broadcloth shirt buttoned up high and the navy cashmere sweater sloping over his shoulders cannot hide the mad beating of his heart. Surely the maître d' who lit the votive with his short, immigrant fingers knows that Ushman is terrified. Knows the look of a man who does not feel as though he belongs. And why should he feel at ease here? The other patrons are all young, wearing tall boots and glitter around their eyes. They are drinking martinis and eating rolls of salami and olives. Ushman can remember sitting in a café with his school friends in Tabriz and how they would ogle the occasional German or Russian tourists, scoffing at their huge shoulders and big pink noses. But these foreigners were not trying to belong to Iran. They were not dating a local girl, or setting up shop in Tabriz. How, then, would he and his friends have behaved?

Ushman takes a deep breath, reminding himself that this is America; the country of foreigners.

Just then, he sees her. With her head down, to avoid the crosstown wind. He breathes a sigh of relief. Just as she looks up, probably to check the building number, she sees him. Jaywalking, she crosses the street, her smile never fading. Ushman is terrified by her beauty. She looks different to him. More confident, more relaxed. He cannot believe she is coming in the door, her eyes still looking only at him.

And when the maître d' shows her to Ushman's table he feels a thrill radiating deep within him. And as he stands to embrace her, his fingers seem to be tingling.

"*Ti penso sempre,*" she whispers in his ear as they embrace. She says it as he had taught her. In phonetic Italian. Ushman holds on to her tightly, smelling the cold air in her hair, the sweet gloss on her lips, the down feathers in her jacket. He fights back tears in his eyes.

This is wrong, he thinks. Wrong to feel such happiness when I've done nothing to deserve it. His good fortune does not make any sense.

"Do you like my jacket?" she asks, a smile in her voice.

Ushman pulls away and looks at the black puffy jacket that is covering her from her neck to her knees.

"You are lovely."

"Even in this?"

He nods. "Especially in that. It looks warm. Yes?"

"Incredibly. And on sale, too."

"Perfect."

The maître d' returns and takes the jacket from Stella. She sits down and smiles. "I can't believe we're here. There were so many times this weekend that New York and you, especially you, seemed so far away. I didn't ever think I'd be back."

"Tell me. How are you?"

She nods, places the napkin across her lap. "I'm fine," she says, smiling.

"And what about your mother? How is she?"

Stella rolls her eyes. "Crazy. But not really. Just the same as ever," she says halfheartedly.

"Were you able to speak with her. About what happened?"

Stella puckers her lips in thought. "Mmm. Hard to say. I mean, I know what happened, but I'm not sure I really understand any more than I did."

"Well, is she still at risk? For this to happen again?" Ushman asks.

Stella shrugs. "I suppose we all are. At any moment it could feel as though the world is crumbling around us. I know I was close to feeling that way last night. When you wouldn't even come to me because of your *friend*." She says the word as if it's an insult.

"Are you angry?"

"I was. Last night." She looks at him with her eyes wide open. "I wanted to do something reckless. Something to make you mad. Or jealous."

Ushman feels his stomach shrinking beneath his skin. He watches her face, tries to anticipate her words.

Stella must see the concern on his face. She lets it linger there for a moment. Then she assures him, "But I didn't." Stella looks down at the table. Ushman is not relieved. He only hears the way she said *reckless,* over and over in his ears.

"I just watched TV. Like some poor sucker."

"I'm sorry," Ushman says instinctively. But he has not heard her.

"I guess she's, like, a major client, right?"

"Who?"

"The woman. Your friend. Hello?"

Ushman finally looks up from the table. He sees her clear, expectant eyes.

"That's right. She is. In fact, yes."

"So there's no reason for me to be jealous?"

"Jealous?" Ushman does not immediately understand how it is she's happened upon this word in relation to Mrs. Roberts.

"You stood me up for her, Ushman. What am I supposed to think?"

Ushman still cannot believe that Stella might even, for a moment, think he would rather be with Mrs. Roberts than with her. "It was an extraordinary circumstance. It was only that. Nothing personal."

"So you're not into her?" She leans forward, her breath landing, warm and bitter, on Ushman's face.

"Into?" He blushes. "No, nothing like that. Not ever. There is no . . . into."

Stella smiles. "Okay." She reaches her hand across the table. As her fingers fold over his, Ushman breathes a sigh of relief. Her cool skin is startling and comforting, both.

They order their dinner and then Stella, letting go of his hand, tells him about her mother.

"I sat with my mother on this little terrace which had a view of the valley. It was like a beautiful painting. Until *I* started talking." Stella chuckles. "I asked her to please tell me what had happened. And she refused and said that it wasn't necessary for me to know, blah, blah, blah. And so we sat there some more in the beautiful painting until I told her that I thought it *was* necessary for me to know. That if I was to ever be successful in love or life, I needed her guidance. Her wisdom. And this worked."

Ushman listens attentively.

"And so she begins to tell me not just about the trip but about this sense of weakness she's had, ever since I left home. She was careful not to blame me, but it's still a major guilt trip." Stella shakes her head.

"What kind of weakness?"

"She said it was as though the cycle of life had become exceedingly clear to her. And the endless living and dying of each generation suddenly seemed meaningless and cruel. Like a cosmic prank, she called it."

"Prank?" Ushman does not know the word.

"Um, joke. But more mean-spirited."

Ushman nods.

"So that's really why they took the trip, I think. To get out of the house where I was born, the house where they will die. But it didn't help. Instead, with the history of Italy, my mom felt even more smothered. The bridge, the one she jumped from, is an open-air bridge from which you can see the Bridge of Sighs, which is a small little bridge connecting some palace to a prison across the canal. An ancient prison that is now a museum or something."

Ushman nods, remembering the picture in the guidebook.

"Anyway, she's standing there on the bridge, the seagulls are flocking because somebody's thrown out a crust of bread, and their squalls are deafening. My father is fiddling with his camera, not even looking, she says, at this devastating little bridge which men had to cross on the way to their persecution. She reaches for his arm, because it's as though she can hear their agony. The sighs which the bridge is named for. She wants him to listen, to try to hear it also. She hopes maybe this is a moment when they can really be with each other. That he will understand something that she hasn't been able to communicate to him. He pushes her hand away and grunts, something about the exposure. He's not very sympathetic to this mind-set she's in. I mean, he thinks it's the result of boredom and calls it the 'belly-button syndrome.' Too much time staring at her own belly button, he said. He actually said that to her. I can't believe it."

"My own mother invented this very syndrome, I believe," Ushman says, grinning.

"But don't you think that's cruel? To say to your wife, who is clearly having some kind of emotional crisis?" Stella looks incredulous.

Ushman nods vigorously. "Yes. But perhaps he's afraid of his own belly button. If he allows himself to really consider her viewpoint, then he, too, may be at risk for this depression."

Stella cocks her head. "Yeah. I hadn't thought of that. He certainly doesn't have all his shit together. Maybe he's afraid, too." She shrugs. "I dunno. Anyway, all of a sudden she's standing there, looking at this little Bridge of Sighs, which is all enclosed except for two windows covered with iron bars, and she thinks she sees their shadows. The prisoners from 1600. Bound in chains and walking slowly, looking out at the small view of the lagoon between the bars. The seagulls are diving now, becoming aggressive. She rubs her eyes and wants a better view. Wants to see more. She thinks that maybe there is some revelation to be had. Without hesitating, she climbs on the cement rail. It is then, she told me, that she felt sure. And until she stood up there, she had not realized that she might jump. My father still has not seen her, because he's trying to load the film or something. And she just decides to do it. To jump toward the sound of the sighing. Because, sooner or later, she, too, will end up there."

Ushman is entranced. Stella's voice is calm, but her eyes are full of tears and when she blinks, they scatter down her cheeks. He moves his hand toward her face. With his thumb, he wipes her tears.

"That's my sad story," she says, smiling and holding her napkin to her nose.

Ushman smiles, then his face turns serious again. "It's heartbreaking. And what now? Is she receiving treatment? Did you see your father?"

"No. It was so weird. My mother is at this beautiful, like, spa. But it's a medical facility. She has a lovely therapist. Literally, lovely. A tall, olive-skinned, green-eyed Italian woman who is encouraging her to confront these feelings and accept them as a part of life's beauty. No meaning without meaninglessness, no beauty without pain. It seems like a great thing for her. But my father, meanwhile, is romping around the Italian countryside with the tour group. As if it's all perfectly normal. It makes no sense. Obviously, if their relationship were more solid, I think he could help her to find a purpose. She told me, reluctantly, that he offers her no solace. That his refusal to accept her feelings is devastating. That she feels isolated and lonely. But what does that mean? Is it anything different than any two people feel after thirty years of marriage?"

Ushman does not know the answer.

Stella shrugs. "Tell me about your parents. Were they sweethearts?"

Ushman smiles. "My father, he loved money. My mother came with a large dowry. And she never let him forget it."

"Yikes," Stella says. "There's a recipe for happiness. Was your marriage arranged also?"

Ushman is surprised by her question. Had she not understood that his marriage had been happy? That he had married for love? But Ushman himself has sometimes wondered if an arranged marriage would not have been more successful.

"Not as formally. Farak was a weaver in one of my father's workshops. He knew that I fancied her. She was not from a wealthy family; she was his employee. But her family had once been quite notable. She was sort of an orphan. Her uncle was her guardian. My father liked her uncle. But it was not until after he died that we married. I think he would have agreed, finally, because he knew I would never be beholden to her as he was to my mother."

Many times since immigrating, Ushman has been grateful that his father did not live to see Farak betray him. Ushman's father thought that marrying a girl who was beneath him would guarantee some stability in Ushman's life. His father never had much patience with Ushman. He probably anticipated that Farak would become tired of him, too.

Ushman wishes his parents could see him sitting here in Lower Manhattan on a date with this American girl. It is the rebellious spirit of his youth, that would like for his mother, a recent devotee of the Ayatollah, to see her son dining with a Westerner. And he would like to show his father that he has become successful—on his own. That he has gotten this date on his own. And that he is having intimacies with a woman who owes his father nothing.

"In high school, whenever we studied cultures that have arranged marriages, all the kids in my class were so relieved that they didn't have to marry a person of their parents' choosing. But I was always curious. Whomever your parents choose must somehow reflect their own unfulfilled desires. What qualities have made their own union strong, or weak."

Ushman nods. "I think this is right. Although they have to be practical, too. Really, it is not a game."

"It could be. The new reality TV show. Arranged Marriage."

He smiles. "I only know about those shows from the newsstand. It's the worst part of America, isn't it?"

"I suppose. But freedom includes the freedom to be stupid."

"But must your freedom be paraded about in such bad taste? Simply because it is permitted?"

"Are you calling us juvenile?"

"Perhaps, a bit."

"Well, compared to you we are. Your country is nearly two thousand years old."

"More than two thousand years old. Unfortunately, age does not necessitate wisdom, or peace."

"No," Stella agrees, "not at all. I saw that this weekend."

Ushman looks at the faint curve of freckles scattered across Stella's nose. "They must love you very much," he says, reaching for her index finger with his own.

Stella watches his hand. "I think so."

Ushman imagines Stella as a young girl, six years old. Her mother, walking behind her on a sunny sidewalk. She is skipping, her long neck holding her head erect and perfectly poised, even as her feet smack the concrete. He doesn't know where this image came from. The freckles, maybe.

"They tried and tried to have a baby. Ten years of living month to month, period to period would take its toll on anyone, right? But especially my mother, who values cheer and optimism above any other qualities. It's exhausting, really, to be cheerful when your own body is constantly betraying you. I think it wore her out."

Ushman can only nod, staring vacantly at his own hand, wrapped around Stella's.

"And then, only after they'd given up—put away the thermometers, the fertility books, and prenatal vitamins, attended so many christenings that the ceremony began to seem punitive and unholy—Boom. Me. A miracle." She smiles a devilish grin.

"And such a relief," Ushman says, unable to think of anything other than Farak. The baby she has finally had. The baby they might have had if only she'd been a little more patient. A little more optimistic. And then he realizes that the image he'd had earlier of the young girl was not Stella. It was this girl. This daughter that Farak has had without him. She, too, is skipping, with her mother behind her. But she does not have freckles strewn across her cheeks. Instead, it is a blotch. Something terrible, its edges jagged and dark. Farak calls for her to slow down. She does not want the girl to get too far away.

"I told my mother about you. She kind of freaked."

Ushman pulls his hand back into his lap. He blinks, keeping his eyes shut for just a moment too long.

The girl with the marked face stops and looks back at her mother. She is not meek or obedient. She does not yet understand her mother's fears. Farak has protected her too well. On she skips, reckless, vulnerable, ugly.

"She thinks that because you're older than I am that you will take advantage of me. Physically and otherwise."

"What did you tell her?" Ushman asks, his voice quiet.

"That I am old enough to take care of myself. That I no longer wear jackets with animal buttons down the front," Stella says, exasperated.

Ushman smiles. "I mean about me. What did you tell her about me?"

"Just your name, really. And occupation."

"After she's already attempted suicide once?"

Stella laughs.

"I'm serious. Why do you add to her stress? It is cruel."

"Is it my job to protect her? She didn't think of me when she stepped off into the water."

"I understand your point, Stella. But she's ill. Do you really think it was the right time?"

"It was on my mind. You were on my mind. A lot." She looks down at her lap. In consolation, he reaches across the table and takes her hand in his.

For the first time, he sees her youth. Not just her smooth skin, slim hips, and sparkly eye shadow. He sees her proximity to childhood. The impulsive, fickle, egocentric nature of a girl. It is seductive and contagious and terrifying.

Since they've met, Ushman has always felt as if he were the one who was inexperienced, foolish. As if his were the only heart at risk. Now he sees the part of Stella that is not yet grown. And he sees the part of her that is devoted to him. And he sees that these two parts are identical. The part of her that is not yet grown is the same part of her that loves him. And this, he senses, is a prescription for the end. As she matures, her esteem for him will wither.

But Ushman is just a man. He cannot predict the future. He cannot know anything for certain except this moment. Her pale face looking up at him with sincerity. The faint pathos of an Italian opera emerging from the restaurant's speakers. His hand covering hers. The dark street punctuated by the steam escaping from subway vents and manholes. It is a moment Ushman chooses to believe in. A moment he wants.

"Ti penso sempre," he whispers, holding her hand more tightly.

She smiles at him and closes her eyes. Then, abruptly, she opens her eyes, smiling.

"The next time I go to Italy, teach me something useful, too, okay? I mean, something like, 'I would like another piece of chocolate cake, please.'"

"Or, 'Does this gondola stop near a bakery?'" Ushman says, unfolding his wallet.

She nods. "Yeah. Something like that would be good."

"I will be a better teacher next time." Ushman winks, taking her hand again as they stand up. He helps her with her new, poofy jacket and they walk the two blocks together to Ushman's van.

"I've never been to a Catholic church before," Ushman says as they wait for a traffic light on Broadway. As soon as he's said it, he realizes his mistake. Anything to do with Mrs. Roberts is an affront to Stella—to their time together.

Stella's shoulders tense up. She has shed her enormous

jacket on the floor between them. Her skin is pale against the black cashmere of her boatneck sweater. "Really?"

Ushman nods, searching for a way to change the subject.

"It's tomorrow? The service?" Stella turns her face toward him.

"Yes. Eleven o'clock." Ushman pulls a stray hair from the side of her face.

"Where?" Her eyes are wide and alert.

"St. Patrick's. On Fifth Avenue."

"The service is at St. Patrick's? That's a huge church. Who was this guy?"

Ushman shrugs. "A businessman."

"Big business, I guess." She turns her face away and looks out the window. Everything has changed. Ushman has reminded her of a feeling she had parted with. A feeling that is tenacious.

"Will you come with me?" Ushman asks her because he cannot bear the silence. He does not want another moment of her doubt lingering between them.

"To the service?"

"Yes. To the service. I just . . . don't want to go alone."

"Is it appropriate? I mean, will your friend mind?"

"She's a client, Stella. A good customer. Not a friend. I don't know why she's invited me to the service."

"But Ushman, you read his obituary to the *New York Times*. I think she thinks you are friends."

"I merely happened to be there."

"You don't want to be her friend?"

"No. Business is business."

Stella lets his words sink in.

"Okay. I'll go. If you promise you'll sing."

"Sing?"

"I love to stand in the pew and sing the hymns as loud as I can. I want you to sing, too."

Ushman smiles. "I don't know these hymns."

"It doesn't matter. Just choose a word. Like clementine. Or backgammon. As long as you follow the tune. Deal?"

Ushman furrows his brow. "These are not religious words. Clementine? Backgammon?"

Stella smiles. "No, they're not. But they're not nearly as sinful as the words my friends and I used to use. And we were singing in the choir."

Ushman shakes his head.

"So, do we have a deal?"

He nods, grateful. "Deal." She has returned to him. Without any doubt. "Will you, would you like to come to Queens?"

"Tonight?"

"Yes."

"You just want me to sing for you, don't you? To sing those words like I did in the choir."

Ushman reaches his hand out and touches a piece of her hair that is hanging by her face.

"Okay. Drive me uptown and I'll get a dress for tomorrow."

For the first time, Ushman follows her through the black iron gates. She lives in the southernmost tall red-brick building. It is one of four. This complex is called the Quad and houses mainly first-year students.

The lobby is bright, with overstuffed chairs and big glass windows. It does not look like student housing. Except for the uniformed security guard who holds the door for them and checks Stella's ID. Then, there is a desk at which Ushman must surrender his own identification in order to have access to the bank of elevators.

"I will wait here," Ushman says to Stella quietly.

"Why? This is where I live. Don't you want to see?" All of a sudden Ushman feels that she is talking too loud for a public space.

"No, thank you. It doesn't seem —"

He doesn't get to finish his sentence because two more girls have entered the doors behind them and, upon seeing Stella, they run up on either side of her and embrace her. Ushman stands awkwardly, with his face so close to the taller girl's hair that he can smell her shampoo. It is the same as Stella's. He steps back, but then he is completely lost, unanchored. He wants to be next to Stella again, so that his presence is explained. He feels as though the desk attendant and the security guard are both distrustful of him. Suspicious of his existence.

These girls, these friends of Stella's, have pretended not to notice Ushman, though certainly he is not easily overlooked. In tandem, they are recalling their encounter with a particularly fierce professor. Finally, Stella reaches out for Ushman's hand and pulls him into their circle.

"This," she says, looking at him only briefly, "is Ushman. Ushman, this is Kate and Whitney."

Ushman nods, unable to find his voice. They are not shy now about looking at him, every inch of him.

"I like your belt," the shorter one says matter-of-factly.

"Thank you," Ushman says, fingering the buckle of his nondescript plain black belt. "Stella," he says, "I will wait here for you."

She shrugs, still holding his hand. "Sure?"

"Yes." He pulls his hand away and sits in one of the arm-chairs near the door. Her two friends return to pretending not to notice him.

"Okay. Black, right?"

"What's that?"

"The dress. It should be black."

"You would know better than I," he says, watching the three girls turn away from him and walk toward the elevators, with their arms casually draped on each other, as though they are each only parts of a whole.

It feels like an eternity that he sits in that chair, watching the comings and goings of the dormitory. Ushman becomes fascinated by the dynamics of this building. The way some girls' insecurities are transparent, while others are so deeply camouflaged that they almost look inhuman. There are small dramas in nearly every interaction he sees. Just like anywhere, people's lives are a struggle. No matter that their collegiate problems may seem inconsequential, Ushman reminds himself. Pain, like joy, is absolute. Their nineteen-year-old American hearts may be breaking over the minutiae of a prohibited pet cat being discovered and confiscated by the administration or the ten pounds they've gained since September or the pink fleece jacket with pastel animal buttons that was their only birthday gift.

But then Ushman realizes that he has become a part of their drama. They are looking at him, wondering about him. He is making some of them uncomfortable, some of them envious. His presence is not natural here. He is a conversation piece, a hurdle, an event.

When Stella comes off the elevator, a dark dress draped over one arm, he marvels at how distant he feels from her. In her own surroundings, he no longer finds her familiar. He is stiff and formal, standing as soon as he sees her, carefully walking two paces behind her.

"What's wrong?" she says as soon as they're out in the night air.

"Nothing. Are you sure you want to do this? I mean, that you want to come with me?"

"To the funeral?"

"That. And to Queens, too."

Stella stops just outside the gates. She looks at him, her eyes wounded. "What's going on here?" she asks, her voice angry and thin.

For a brief moment, Ushman considers being honest. But he knows better. He knows that she cannot assuage the discomfort he feels here on this campus, among other nineteen-year-old girls. She cannot reassure him that it doesn't matter, that he will get over it, that her friends don't mind his age or his accent or his stiff formality. Instead, she will only begin to mind these things herself. To find him difficult and old.

And, really, he tells himself, he is being old and difficult. Because he has become rather accustomed to feeling out of place. This is nothing new to him. It is only because he has spent so much time alone with Stella that he has forgotten what a stranger he is to her world. She has lulled him into believing that he has a place. And, perhaps, with her he does. Perhaps with Stella he can sip tea and lie on the rugs from his home and close his eyes with his hands on her skin and feel content. This comfort, however, will not extend naturally to her world. Had he assumed it would? Perhaps. Perhaps he expected her long fingers and warm smile would Americanize him by association. Perhaps he had thought that if he was with her, he would no longer be burdened with his own identity. He could become a part of hers. And it is the realization that these assumptions of his were wrong that has left him feeling so despondent. Whomever he's with and wherever he is, among college girls or collectors at the Metropolitan or patrons at the Greek diner, Ushman does not belong.

He simply shrugs. This is his response to her demand. When she continues to look at him with her eyebrows furrowed and her mouth agape, he adds, "I guess I'm just a little tired tonight."

This statement hangs in the air between them. He waits, expecting her to leave him there and return to her guarded building. But in a quiet, unassuming moment that may only be recognized much later, Stella also shrugs. Probably because she truly is tired and does not want to engage him in a lengthy and unproductive questioning, nor face the rows of questions that would meet her if she returned to the dorm now, her dress still on her shoulder, unworn, she follows him to the van dutifully, as if he'd already accepted her dowry and made her his wife.

And in this way, they enter the dark night, crossing over the bridge with neither of them bothering to initiate a conversation. Like so many couples, they have carelessly shrugged their relationship from its bright newness into the territory of neglect.

They take less time on the sex, but it is still good. Ushman feels even more tender toward her, having seen the life she lives without him. He feels lucky, and tells her so.

She closes her eyes and smiles, stretching her arms up and arching her back in a feline gesture. Ushman stands up and walks across the dim room. He blows out the candle on his dresser and feels his way back into bed. Stella scoots into him, cradling herself against his body. It feels like a resolution to the evening. They do not speak, though, as they usually do. Almost immediately Stella's breath is rhythmic and deep. It comforts him, a sign, he believes, that she harbors no offense. Ushman breathes deeply the scent from the back of her neck. He closes his eyes and wonders if Mrs. Roberts can remember the way her husband smelled before he became sick. He thinks of her, unable to sleep tonight, looking out at the lights of Manhattan all around her, and Queens in the distance.

Ushman is so grateful for Stella's perfect warm body next to him. It was wise that he did not share with her how foolish he'd felt at her dorm among her friends. He does not want her pity. With his mouth against the angular slope of her shoulder blade, Ushman lifts the hair away from her neck. As if it were a map, he memorizes the shape of it. Even in the dark, he is moved by the beauty of its contour. Ushman is living as he has so often wished he had in Tabriz. Assigning every detail to memory.

Her small, cool feet beneath the sheet. Her hair wrapped behind her head, its ends tickling his forehead. The smell of her armpits, acrid and sweet. Her breasts, perfect in their roundness. Her fingers, callused in places, but relaxed for now, in a nonchalant curve around his forearm. The salty taste of her skin beneath his tongue. The length of her neck, which is nearly melancholy to him, with its arching grace.

These things he deposits, like coins into a bank, before he, too, abandons himself to sleep.

Twenty

Ushman awakens, but does not move. For a moment he is unsure of his surroundings. Blinking, he senses that he is not alone. But he knows it is not Farak in the bed with him. He does not smell her pomegranate shampoo or hear the faint sighing that her breath makes as it passes through her nostrils. He panics, remembering only that he is married and that having another woman in his bed is a terrible mistake. Immediately he worries about shielding Farak, keeping this betrayal from her. In the grogginess of waking, he has forgotten that he is no longer married, no longer in Iran, and no longer responsible for protecting Farak from heartache.

Gradually, as his eyes adjust, and he sees the outline of the furniture, the small TV set, the burned-out candle, he realizes where he is. In his peripheral vision, he sees Stella's blond hair thick and tangled on the pillow.

He does not want to wake her. Instead, he wants this time to himself, without having to be cheerful or sweet or even polite. How is it that this real life, with this beautiful girl in his bed, could leave a hint of disappointment in the back of his throat? He should be relieved that he has not betrayed Farak. He is free to have these pleasures. He has found a body that he seems, inherently, to know as if from another life. This is a great blessing, especially for a man like him.

It is still dark in the room, and he dreads the day that stretches ahead of him. The exhaustion one feels after a period of enforced mourning. The inevitable sadness that spreads across the crowd, from person to person, from downcast eyes to downcast eyes, until the day feels terminally small and black. And how is it, he wonders, that he has invited Stella to join him for this dismal ceremony? And how will he explain her to Mrs. Roberts?

Of course, part of him knows that he will not have to explain anything. And though this will reflect poorly on him as a husband, here, in the dark, Ushman does not care. He is anxious for Mrs. Roberts to understand that he has a life outside of her. That he does not exist simply to find her the most exquisite rugs, to answer her every call, to eat with her and comfort her like a hired attendant.

But as Ushman looks at the outline of Stella's features, her eyelids barely moving to the hidden rhythms of her dream, he realizes that Mrs. Roberts may assume many things about her, but she will never assume that she is Ushman's lover. She is entirely too young, too pretty, and too composed for anyone to assume that she would give herself to him.

Ushman sneaks out of bed, the cold floor waking his feet and the rest of him entirely. He showers and shaves and stands before his closet, naked. As he unzips the thick black suit bag, the smell of the fine wool takes him by surprise. Its scent recalls for him the memory of the day he bought it. A day when he still had hopes that Farak would someday arrive in America on a jet plane and that he would stand in the terminal, looking out at the tarmac, dressed in this expensive blue suit, waiting for her. He remembers the salesman's thin hands marking the fabric with chalk. The heavy rain as he walked back to his shop. His own anxiety as he fingered the receipt in his pocket, its amount breathtaking. The weight of his head as he lay on the cot in his shop, looking at a photograph of himself and Farak, taken just after Farak became pregnant for the first time.

Since that day, the suit has hung in his closet, nearly forgotten. This memory makes Ushman's hands clumsy as he takes the coat and pants from their hanger.

He does not have a necktie. He refused the salesman's suggestion of a red or striped silk tie. Instead, he wears the dark blue suit with a light blue broadcloth shirt, the top button left open. He feels a bit self-conscious in the suit, as it is such quintessentially Western attire. The jacket feels heavy across his shoulders. However, the fabric is so rich and the suit so well made that Ushman also cannot help but feel it has made him more handsome and important.

Stella does not hide her admiration. She, too, has showered without speaking. But she is still rubbing her eyes when she finds him, standing in the kitchen.

"Wow. You look amazing," she says as Ushman spreads a roll with feta for her.

"You like my suit?" he asks, smiling at her wet hair, her bare feet on his kitchen floor. Suddenly he no longer disregards the blessing that she is.

"It's, yes, it's beautiful. Does someone have to die for you to wear it?"

"I want to show respect. But it is not really my style. I am not a banker."

"You are foxy," Stella says, smiling and blushing slightly.

"What is this word?" Ushman thinks she has teased him.

"It means desirable. You're desirable." Stella sets her roll down on the counter. She slides her hand onto Ushman's. For a moment, they each stare at their hands there, together. Then, with the clumsy movements of a novice, Stella eventually unzips Ushman and places her mouth on him.

He stands in the kitchen, just where he had this summer, when his desire had overcome his judgment, and he paid the prostitute to do what it is that Stella does to him now. Her wet hair sticks to his groin and he closes his eyes, once again whispering Allah's name, this time in gratitude. Perhaps, Ushman thinks, there is balance in the universe. Perhaps there will be no more heartache for me. How could there be, he wonders, when he is given this blessing? He believes, in the moment of his joy, that this will protect him from ever feeling pain again.

Stella is quiet, though, as they drive into the city. Ushman senses her staring at his hands on the wheel.

"You are contemplating something?" he asks as they enter Manhattan.

"No, not really."

"Are you changing your mind about today?"

"No. I'm actually just amazed that you want me to go."

"Why?"

"Because this is business. And you seem so serious about your business."

Her words are simple, but there is something about the tone of her voice that is accusatory. As though he should not be so serious about his work or his clients. Or, rather, that he should be more serious about her. He feels he must explain himself. "I am serious about it. This is my life. It is my connection to my home, my past. But it is also my future. It takes hard work to become more than just an immigrant in this country. In any country. I want something of my own."

"So why do you want me to come with you?"

Ushman thinks for a moment. But there is nothing about his invitation that he can explain to her.

"I just would like it," he says quietly.

Stella shrugs. "Okay." She smiles. "You don't have to have a reason."

Ushman reaches over and takes her hand in his.

Stella wears a dark navy wrap dress, with long sleeves and a satin lapel. The dress fits her perfectly. It is a classic cut. And something about the shade of the fabric suddenly makes her gray eyes appear blue. In contrast to the dark fabric, her skin is like porcelain. Ushman stood when he saw her emerge from his bedroom, as if to express his utter approval.

Stella has pinned her hair up on top of her head. They walk briskly, holding hands. When they reach St. Patrick's, her ears and cheeks are bright red with cold. They climb the steps and Ushman opens the heavy door for Stella, abruptly dropping her hand.

Inside, there is an organist playing a woeful tune far too loud to be melancholy. It is oddly celebratory. An usher directs them to a pew. The sanctuary is quite full already. They sit on an aisle about halfway up. Ushman can see Mrs. Roberts in the front pew, a thick choker of pearls punctuating her black suit.

Stella leans into Ushman. "Is that her?" she asks, motioning toward Mrs. Roberts.

Ushman bows his head, suddenly panicked by Stella's presence. What was he thinking, bringing her here? It is so transparent that she is here for the spectacle. That she is here for the benefit of a widow. Yes, Ushman had wanted Mrs. Roberts to see Stella, to be made aware, somehow, of his own humanity. But he now understands the cruel irony of his own desire. Trying to show her that he has a full life by bringing his life here, to her husband's funeral. A petty, foolish decision.

Ushman begins to sweat.

"Yes?" Stella asks again.

Ushman nods. He wishes for the organ to stop. It seems to be mocking him. It is overpowering, making his head ache.

He leans into her ear. "I may have to leave early. There's an appointment I forgot about."

Stella looks at him, her brow furrowed. "No lunch? We're like Mr. And Mrs. Fabulous. We have to do lunch."

Ushman shrugs.

Stella casts her eyes back up the aisle at Mrs. Roberts. Ushman looks down at his shoes. He does not notice the stained glass or the apostles or the height of the ceiling.

Finally, the organ subsides and a quartet of strings begin a much quieter ode. The priest stands at a podium, swinging incense.

The music stops and the mass begins. As the ritual unfolds, Ushman tries to relax. He watches Mrs. Roberts kneel and stand and he imitates her movements. Stella has become solemn and quiet next to him. He assures himself that Mrs. Roberts may not even notice him. Or Stella. Surely her mind is filled with many other things. Ushman continues to mimic the kneeling and standing of the congregation, but Stella does not. She sits quietly, with her hands in her lap and her head bowed.

As he watches Mrs. Roberts and her son take communion, Ushman's mind wanders to the day of his own father's death.

It was a hot day, the air still and dry.

In the garden of their home, his father kept a small pond, stocked with exotic fish. It was a hobby, but also his father's own personal status symbol. He believed that the fountain was not a sufficient display of his wealth. Many houses in the neighborhood had fountains in the garden. But that the fish, with their bright colors and lumbering size, spoke of the true capacity of Mr. Khan's empire. Secretly, Ushman hated the fish. He didn't like the smell of the garden now that the pond housed lilies and algae for the fishes' habitat. When Ushman's father placed his pinky just beneath the surface of the water and allowed the big red fish to suck his fingertip, Ushman shuddered.

In the days leading up to his father's death, there had been a strange bird flying about the neighborhood. It was large and would rest on the tops of walls or roofs, silently watching. Neighbors conjectured that it was a crane, escaped from a nearby zoo. But nobody bothered to call the authorities. Twice, Ushman's father had noticed the bird standing on the wall just adjacent to his fish pond. Promptly, Mr. Khan had retrieved his revolver from the house and shot in the direction of the oversized bird.

The first time, Ushman's mother had been in the bath and she told Ushman and his father later that she'd thought of drowning herself right then, afraid of an Iraqi ambush. Neither of his father's shots had injured the bird. It simply glided, majestically, above Mr. Khan's head, squawking once and disappearing into the blue sky.

The third time, Ushman's father set a trap for the bird. He left a pile of fish innards he'd purchased from the local seafood merchant on the wall above his pond. Then, with his gun at his side, he sat on the garden bench and waited. But the bird did not make an appearance. Mr. Khan persevered. He took his lunch in the garden, determined to kill the bird. As the afternoon heat climbed over the garden wall, Mr. Khan stretched out on the bench, his hands resting on his stomach, cradling the gun. He fell into a deep sleep, undisturbed even by the sweat rolling from his temples to his neck.

But sometime around dusk, the bird silently floated into the garden and stood by the edge of the pond. A proud hunter, he gulped one of Mr. Khan's prized koi, and then let out a squawk of defiance. Ushman later conjectured that it was this squawk that must have so startled Mr. Khan that he fired the gun without sitting up, without aiming, without, probably, being fully awake. He was determined to protect those fish. And so the bullet pierced Mr. Khan's chin and traveled straight through his jaw and up into his brain.

The bird flew away, another koi in his beak, and was never seen again. At the end of the week, Ushman collected the remaining fish in a bucket and went to the bank of the Talkheh. He sat for a long time, watching the fish knock against the side of the bucket, their scales shining in the midday sun. Finally, Ushman tipped the bucket and let the fish struggle on the dirt. Frantically squirming, without any idea that they were less than six inches from the water. He waited until they had stopped moving. He could see their gills hinging slowly, so close to death. Ushman stood, and with the toe of his shoe, kicked each fish into the river.

At the end of the service, Stella nudges Ushman's arm. He is startled back into the present.

Ushman looks at Stella. She stands, as the rest of the mourners do, too. They are beginning to file out, down the center aisle toward the exit. Ushman is suddenly impatient. He should have been ready to go, to push ahead of the crowd that is gathered in the aisle. Now they are stuck, waiting for each row of pews behind them to empty. Stella is standing so close to him that he senses the rhythm of her breath against his shoulders. Again, there is organ music. Again, it is too loud.

In the vestibule of the church, Stella tells Ushman she is going to the restroom. Ushman would like to stop her and tell her no. That she must hold it until they get back to his shop. She can use the facility there. But she is already making her way down the hall, out of his reach. And just as Ushman steps back against the wall in order to be out of the way, he sees Mrs. Roberts, with her son on her arm, coming down the center aisle. She has seen Ushman step away, out of her path.

He is trapped. So he waits. And just as Stella returns down the hallway, so, too, do Mrs. Roberts and her son enter the vestibule.

"Ushman," Mrs. Roberts says, extending her hand and offering Ushman her cheek. He feels obligated, and forces his lips to touch her skin. Never before has she required this greeting. Ushman is shocked by the softness of her skin. It is cool and dry and powdered, so that it is as though he has kissed something other than skin. A ball of dough, risen. Or a dusty porcelain vase. "So good of you to come. This is my son, Charles."

"I'm sorry for your loss," Ushman says. "I only met your father once, but he seemed a . . ." Ushman searches for an appropriate word. "A very strong man." There is an awkward pause as Mrs. Roberts turns her head to Stella. She stares, without restraint. Finally, Ushman adds, "This is Stella."

"Stella. The service was so large, even though it was private. Remind me, I'm not sure where we've met." Mrs. Roberts cocks her head to one side, never moving her eyes from Stella's.

"We have never met. I am a friend of Ushman's. It was a lovely service." For a brief moment, Ushman is grateful that he has brought Stella. Not because she is poised and beautiful, and smiles warmly at Mrs. Roberts and her son, but because, finally, he is not alone.

Mrs. Roberts looks quickly at Ushman. "A friend. How nice," she says grimly, then takes her son's arm again as he dutifully guides her to the exit. Just before he opens the door, she turns back to Ushman and looks at him in a way she never has before. Then, looking only at Stella, she says, "I didn't know you had *other* friends, Ushman." The cold comes at them as the heavy door is opened and she follows her son out.

They stand in his shop together, shivering a little. Ushman starts a kettle for tea. Stella stands in front of the window, looking down at the sidewalks of Madison. She has not spoken to him since the service.

"What about your appointment, Ushman?" Her voice is accusatory.

"It was nothing." Ushman looks down at the calendar on his desk, pretending to check. "No, nothing."

There is a long silence. Stella takes a deep breath. Her voice goes shallow. "Is she your lover, Ushman?"

"What? No. Not at all. Nothing," he says quickly, wanting to be finished with this conversation before it's even started.

"Then why . . . what was that all about? That whole dramatic showdown?"

"I haven't any idea. She has just lost her husband. Grief, perhaps, made her . . ." Ushman does not finish his sentence. He, too, is confused. The way Mrs. Roberts reacted to Stella was as if she believed that Ushman was her own lover. That Stella was an interloper. That he had betrayed her. There, at her husband's funeral, could she really have been threatened by Stella? Could she really believe that Ushman owed her some loyalty? Or was she simply angry on behalf of Farak? On behalf of the wife she still understands him to have?

"How long was he sick?" Stella says to Ushman as she folds her arms across her chest.

"I don't really know. Quite some time, I believe."

"So, maybe, once, you guys, like, got together or something. Like to console her. Just tell me, Ushman. Maybe it was a while ago. Before we met."

Ushman turns to look at the pile of rugs behind him. He remembers that day, that hot summer morning, when they did lie down together. How raw and empty he was. He shakes his head. He knows what Stella wants him to say. That she needs a concrete explanation of his connection to this woman. Something firm to look at and then set aside. A momentary tryst. A long-gone affection.

He moves closer to the window, thinking that perhaps he can explain about the rug, about the man who died, about the chance Ushman took and the misfortune it brought. About Mrs. Roberts's coincidental involvement in that fateful turn of events. This may satisfy Stella's curiosity. But something out the window catches his eye.

"Look," he says, pointing, "it's the watch guy."

The kettle begins softly whining. Stella cranes her neck to see the vendor, setting up his briefcase on the corner.

"What a bully," Ushman says, letting the kettle blow a little louder.

"She didn't want me there today. With you." Stella's voice is flat.

Ushman doesn't answer.

Stella and Ushman both continue to gaze out the window. Watching the vendor down below as he smokes and hawks his wares, the two of them, in their navy blue dress clothes, stand shoulder to shoulder.

"In her mind, you are hers. In some way. Tell me the truth, Ushman."

Ushman looks away from the window at the stack of rugs just beyond Stella. If he concentrates, he can conjure the smell of the wool and dye and dirt of his workshops in Tabriz.

Ushman heaves and shrugs. He must raise his voice, now, over the whistle of the kettle to which neither of them attends. "Probably. She has spent a fortune on the rugs in her collection. All of them from my shop. With each rug, she is also buying an aura—my past, my culture. This gives her some feeling of closeness, maybe, to me." It is true. But it has not satisfied her.

Stella turns away from him and crosses the room, lifting the kettle away from the heat. The room goes quiet.

"Bullshit," she says, then puts the kettle back in its place so it can go on screaming.

Ushman is startled by the finality in her voice.

In a quick, unforgettable motion, she lifts her bag from the floor and swings it over her shoulder. She turns as if to go. Ushman cannot believe she really means to until her hand is on the doorknob.

"Stella, please," he says to her back. He crosses the room with his arms outstretched. "Please. What can I do? Tell me something to do. . . ."

When she turns around, she is crying, her mouth wide open but not making any sound. Her chest and shoulders are quaking unnaturally.

"You should sit down, Stella. This is all wrong. She's just an old woman." Ushman lowers his hands so that he can stand close to her. If he can just stand close enough, he could place his hands on her body to quiet it. To stop her from shaking so.

But Stella backs away from him, so that he cannot. "Don't," she finally says. "Please, don't." And then her tears begin in earnest. Ushman reaches for his handkerchief. She takes it from him.

The kettle is screaming still, like a siren in a burning building. It makes it difficult for Ushman to focus. He turns away from Stella and walks across the room, removing the kettle from the heat. It is immediately quiet.

Ushman realizes what he has forgotten. His promise. He puts his hands in his pockets and shrugs, as though defeated. For a moment, he is ready to give up. Then he remembers the

naughty look in her eyes. The incredible softness of her hair between his fingers.

In a hoarse and unmelodic voice, he sings the word slowly,
three times, as he walks toward her. "Clementine, clementine,
clementine." He does not stop until he is standing as close to her
as he can without touching her. He continues his singing until
his mouth has reached her ear. He holds his final note so that
the vibration is only broken by his breath.

"You didn't even sing with me," Stella says, her voice meager
and forlorn. She then covers her eyes with his handkerchief and
hangs her head.

Ushman thinks of the church. It is true, he failed her. He
was thinking of his father, of his home.

Stella drops the handkerchief from her face. It is soiled by
her makeup. She leans her head against Ushman's face, so that
his mouth is now against her cheek. He senses the relief in her
body as she allows herself to be anchored by his weight.

But it does not last. There is one final sigh, the breath from
her mouth hot and moist and so close to his own. Then she lifts
her head. She wipes her face again and looks at him. Her eyes
are burdened with pain. He starts to touch her face, as though
his fingertips could remove some of it, and she intercepts his
hand with her own.

"Please," she says, replacing his hand by his side and then
letting it go. Without another look at his face and without another word from her mouth, she turns away from him. The door
shudders a little as she pulls it closed. Ushman does not stop her.

His eyes follow her as she walks west, away from him.
When he can no longer see the paleness of her hair, he looks
back at the sidewalk just below.

"Oh, look," Ushman says out loud, forgetting that she cannot hear him. "He's sold one."

The customer is a middle-aged woman with an overcoat and an umbrella. She thumbs through her wallet clumsily, giving herself away as a tourist. The vendor watches her carefully as she counts her fives. He is nodding furiously. Ushman leans his head against the glass, letting his tears fall away from his face onto the windowsill as he watches the exchange of money for goods.

Twenty-One

For two days, Ushman does not leave his apartment. He feels worn out, depleted. Though he knows that Stella thinks it is she who has had her heart broken, Ushman knows the truth. He knows that she will soon be recovered and reembarked on her beautiful young life. While Ushman must accept the crumbled reality of his own. Perhaps he is a little glad that it ended before she could outgrow him. So that in her memory, if nowhere else, Ushman will remain desirable and powerful; full of possibility. He is grateful to her for following her convictions. Grateful that she did not waver, did not shy away from pain and righteousness for the sake of comfort. But this gratitude, this admiration of her, increases his sorrow.

Ushman does not try to call her. Though he would like nothing more than to hear her voice again, he accepts that he will not. This, he knows, is the only ending there ever was between them. The specifics are somewhat irrelevant for him. As much as he would like to clarify the situation between himself and Mrs. Roberts, Ushman cannot take the gamble that Stella will no longer care. That, perhaps, she has reconciled this misunderstanding as only a symptom and not a cause. He cannot chance that she has already seen the error of her ways. That she knows now what Ushman had always: He was not worth her trouble.

For two days, he does not change his clothes. He stays in the blue mourning suit, finding every once in a while a long blond hair on his lapel or cuff. Her half-eaten roll remains on his counter, he finds her socks under his bed. This, he thinks, is how it would have been had I stayed in Tabriz. Farak would have left and I would have been tortured by the things in the house. The food in the refrigerator that she prepared before going. Her soap in the shower that had caressed her body. A covert list in our bedroom of reasons to leave.

As he is stretched out on the bed in his wrinkled suit, Ushman sees ghosts of both women moving through the apartment. Out in the bright light of the living room, it is as though they are preparing to bury him. As if this were the end. Speaking to one another in hushed tones, cleaning and straightening his mess, standing in front of the window, looking out at nothing, wiping their eyes, sitting only briefly to look through a book or organize his albums. They seem natural together, as if they were part of the same family. Their beauty is startling—the one so dark, the other so fair. Their voices mingle, English and Farsi, until all he can hear is the hum; the lovely, meaningless hum of other people nearby. Ushman breathes deeply, afraid to close his eyes, afraid they will disappear if he does. He could watch from here, unable to speak to them or touch them, forever. Just this, he thinks, would be enough.

He awakens to the phone ringing. He picks it up. It is she.

"I'm at the airport." Her voice is clear, determined. This is not a dream.

Yes. I'll be right there. I overslept. I've got on a new suit. I'll make dinner. Your first American dinner.

"I don't know why I called."

All is forgiven. You can bring the baby, too. Don't worry. You do not need to explain.

"Except I'm here and it makes me think of you. I can't help it."

I don't think I'll ever stop thinking of you. My home.

"Ushman? Hello?"

Ushman clears his throat. He sits up, finally awake enough to understand.

"Yes. I'm here. Are you traveling?" he asks foolishly.

"Home. For the holidays. I finished finals yesterday. I need to get out of the city."

"Very good. Time at home. You'll come back? To school, I mean."

"Sure."

There is a long pause. Ushman can hear the announcements of flights departing and arriving. He should say something.

"Stella," is all he can think of. Then silence.

"I just wanted you to know, Ushman. I don't hate you."

"Thank you. There really is nothing at all between, I mean, certainly not—"

She interrupts. "It's not important. I understand that things can get complicated. And I know that I knew there were these things up front. Complications, I mean. They're attractive to me, you know. You told me, the first time we met. Change your taste for sad stories. So, I'm trying, Ushman. I wish, sometimes, that I could be more . . . I don't know, more grown-up about it all. But I'm not. I'm just not as equipped as I thought. Not yet, anyway. I'll have my own complications, won't I?"

Ushman nods, unable to find his voice.

"Sad stories. Complications. It's all in store for me."

"I hope not," Ushman says. "But I believe it's true."

"But there's more, Ushman. Don't forget."

"What do you mean?"

"Don't forget that there is joy, too. You can't leave that out of your sad stories." Here, he recognizes her tone of voice and knows the look that is surely in her eyes. Their triumphant intensity when she's stumbled onto the truth.

"You are correct," he says, "and I'm sure that there is much joy waiting for you, Stella. Along with the complications. There will be much joy."

"*Ti penso sempre.* Merry Christmas, Ushman."

She hangs up and is gone. Ushman replaces the phone, remembering the way her neck looked in the dim light of his bedroom, the way her skin felt next to his. He thinks of the stale roll on the counter and the socks under his bed. Despite the tears running down his cheeks, he smiles.

On the third day, Ushman takes off the suit. He showers and shaves and dresses for work. Midtown Manhattan is congested with holiday shoppers. He hates the crowds, but there is something of a contagious cheer floating out from the glittering, expensive boutiques. Town cars are double-parked nearly as far as he can see on Madison, waiting for their clients to emerge, laden with packages. At his office, Ushman has a phone message from the rug cleaner, reminding him that Mrs. Roberts's carpet is ready. Ushman had forgotten about the stain, forgotten about the rug entirely. Forgotten, too, about her bare floor. But now that he's been reminded of it, he thinks it strange that Mrs. Roberts has not telephoned, using the rugs as an excuse to inquire about Stella. But there are no other messages.

Ushman calls the rug cleaner and arranges to retrieve the rug this afternoon before going home. He is busy for the rest of the day with calls from out-of-town clients and a few browsers who come in and require him to fold back all the rugs in the pile so that they can see every single one. At the end of the day, he is tired.

The rug cleaner operates out of a renovated filling station in Queens. Ushman stands over the rug at one end of the workroom trying to distinguish any discoloration in the wool. The old man gives Ushman some privacy to inspect his work.

"Perfect. Beautiful," Ushman finally calls to the Armenian, who is hunched over another rug, gently working the water through its weave.

"Blood is easy," the old man says, standing up.

Ushman nods, averting his eyes.

There is another rug for Ushman. One of his own. It is a garden carpet that a very wealthy client of his father's had commissioned before he and Farak were married. It is one of the last rugs that she wove. His father bought it back from the client and gave it to Ushman unexpectedly. It was an uncharacteristically thoughtful gift. Typical of a garden carpet, which represents Paradise, it is composed of squares in which there are cypress, Tree of Life, flower, and *boteh* insets. It is woven

from camel hair, silk, and wool. Its colors are muted, with vary-
ing tones of brown, red, and gold. Newly cleaned, it is exquisite. And priceless.

Together, Ushman and the old man fold both rugs and load
them into the van.

Standing outside next to an inoperable gas pump, Ushman
calls Mrs. Roberts on his cell phone. The traffic is noisy, but he
can distinguish a certain surprise in her voice. She agrees that
he can come by tomorrow morning to deliver it.

Ushman tries not to look in the back, tries not to glance at
the rug that he had unfolded and dirtied with Stella. He is anxious to deliver it tomorrow, so that he will no longer feel its pull
from the back of his van, urging him to remember.

At home, Ushman makes rice and lentils. As he and Farak did
when they had many people for dinner, he sits on the rug in the
living room, with his bowl in his lap. There is a soccer match on
TV. The game keeps him company. He accepts his loneliness
with resolve. It is familiar to him. There are no surprises in it.

When he has cleaned his dishes, he wipes his hands on the
kitchen towel, and, for some reason, it reminds him of the scarf
he bought months ago. The scarf that he hid in the back of his
closet. The gray cashmere he bought for Stella before he really
knew her and then forgot about once he did. He goes to his
closet and unwraps it. It is even more beautiful than he had re-
membered. Holding one end between his fingers, he thinks of
sending it to Stella in Alabama. A Christmas present.

He thinks of her phone call. How generous she'd been to
him. What a gift it had been.

He decides he will wrap it and send it. But not to Stella. That is finished. Stella had the grace to finish it properly. Now it is his turn.

He wraps the scarf back up, carefully tucking the tissue paper around it. He tapes the box shut and wraps it in an old issue of a Farsi newspaper. With a red pen, he sketches some long-stemmed flowers over the newsprint.

He sits at his table with a note card and a pen for what seems like half of the night. Finally, he begins.

Dear Farak, I hope you are well. I've heard news of your baby girl. What joy she must give you. I know that we've shared much pain between us. But there was also much happiness. You cannot imagine the life I live here in America. And I cannot imagine the life you've found in Turkey. But, please know this: I do not hate you. My wish is that this knowledge brings you peace and the liberty to go on in search of more happiness without the burden of the past. Please accept this gift on behalf of your baby girl. Yours, Ushman.

Ushman places the card in an envelope. A thing of beauty for an ugly little girl. Perhaps it will mean something to her someday. Like a beautiful rug in a barren room, perhaps it will give her some significance. Carefully, he transcribes the address that Farak sent to him months ago. He places the box and the card into a plastic grocery bag and puts it by the door. He will take it to the post office tomorrow.

The rain starts early in the morning. Its noise against the windowpanes awakens Ushman. He would like to continue sleeping, but as soon as he's awake, he remembers his appointment with Mrs. Roberts this morning, and he feels anxious. He moves to the living room rug, where he lies down on his back, seeing only himself in the window, with darkness outside. Taking deep breaths, he thinks of going to mosque. Of morning prayers. The sound of voices worshipping all around him. The ritual of kneeling, men surrounding him, temporarily all of one spirit. As the faint light of dawn begins to reveal the world outside, Ushman raises himself, faces east, and prays. It seems an eternity since he last recited these words. The familiar rhythms once again comfort him.

When he finally stands, it is still raining. Ushman glances at the package by the door. He will leave in time to stop at the post office before delivering the rug.

The streets are empty as Ushman drives across the bridge. The rain continues, becoming only a mist as the clouds thin and stretch across the sky. When Ushman pulls up in front of the post office on East 50th Street, he sees that the lights are off. He parks the van and tries the door. It is locked. Looking around, Ushman sees nobody on the street except a young boy walking his dog. The boy looks at him, then looks back down at his feet.

It is Thursday. Ushman does not understand. As the boy approaches, Ushman tries the door again.

"They're closed today," the boy says, his voice hitched between childhood and adolescence.

Ushman nods. "Why?"

" 'Cause of Christmas, I guess," the boy says, stopping to wait for the dog, who has found a hot dog wrapper in the gutter.

Ushman is ashamed. "Oh," he says. He had not realized the date. "Of course. Merry Christmas," Ushman says, trying to compensate for his ignorance.

"Yeah, thanks. I'm Jewish, though." The dog has finished licking the trash.

"Oh," Ushman says, "sorry."

" 'S all right. The safe bet is 'Happy Holidays.' Then you got everyone covered. Know what I mean?"

Ushman nods. "Sure."

He tosses the plastic bag back into the van. The boy walks on with his dog. Ushman sits behind the wheel and calls Mrs. Roberts.

"I'm sorry," he says when she answers. "I did not realize that today is Christmas. I will bring the rug on Monday, then."

"Not at all," she says. "I didn't forget Christmas, Ushman. But Charles and his wife aren't coming until four. You know, it's really like any other day to me. I guess for you, too. Come ahead. I want the rug."

She has hung up before Ushman can say another word.

The lights in the trees that line the sidewalk glow brightly because of the overcast day. Ushman parks his van right in front and unloads the rug onto his shoulder. The doorman nods at him. "Working on a holiday?"

"Both of us," Ushman says as he steps into the elevator.

Mrs. Roberts opens the door herself today. She is alone in the apartment. No husband. No maid. Though it is always quiet here, Ushman immediately notices a difference in the quality of the air. There are no other traces of life. This kind of silence is stifling.

"Hello," she says simply, moving out of his way. "Did you get wet?"

"The rain has stopped," Ushman says, placing the rug down and digging in his pocket for a knife.

She does not say anything, but closes the door and watches him work.

Finally, after he has unrolled the rug and stood up, she turns her head away from him and says, "You see what I mean?"

Ushman does not know what she's talking about.

"Today is just another day here. No Santa, no sleigh bells. But I do have a tree. Do you care to see it?"

Ushman points at the rug. "Is it satisfactory?"

She glances down. "I'm sure. You would tell me if it weren't."

There is a long silence between them. Mrs. Roberts is simply looking at Ushman, watching him as he fidgets. He bends down and straightens the fringe along the edge of the rug, then stands again, turning his signet ring around and around, looking everywhere but at her.

She turns and walks away from him, her black mules slapping the parquet floor. He follows.

In the den, in front of the windows, there is an enormous spruce, lit only with white lights and trimmed with white satin bows.

"It smells . . . nice," Ushman says, amused by the smell of sap so far away from any forest.

"I can't stand the fake ones. I'm having a Bloody Mary. It's red. It's festive." She returns to the chair where she must have been sitting before he arrived. On the side table is her drink.

Ushman looks again at the tree, the impeccable furnishings, the bare floor beneath his feet. For once, he is not in a rush. Ushman feels grateful. Never before has he been glad for her delays and elaborations. Her assumptions that he has no other customer, no other life. But today, as Ushman looks carefully at her belongings, he realizes that Mrs. Roberts has overlooked

convention for him. She has always allowed him into her apartment, into the private moments of her life. Previously, he has
wished she would abide by the standard customs of a merchant-
client relationship. That she would not ask about his life, not allow him into hers. That she would not feel so entitled to make
demands upon him. But, Ushman now thinks, as he is surrounded by the rugs that have secured his future, though she
has required much of him, in doing so she has honored him.

He looks again at the bare stretch of floor beneath his feet
and thinks of the rug that is still left in his van. The one from
his private collection. That his father gave him. That was in
his home in Tabriz. That Farak wove and upon which he first
discovered Stella. The one that he truly had never intended to
sell. It would be perfect for this room. Delicate and rare.

After two sips from her glass, Mrs. Roberts props her feet
on an ottoman and says, "You don't drink. You're a soft-spoken
man. I never figured you for a philanderer."

Ushman does not know the word, but understands her
meaning. He is looking out the window at the lights in Central
Park, the handful of skaters making graceful loops on the ice
rink.

He shrugs. He does not care to defend himself.

"She's a pretty girl. Wholesome is sexy again. That's what I
hear," she says, her voice smiling.

"She's a friend," he says quietly.

"Friends are not so pretty," she says, moving the glass to her
lips again.

Ushman shrugs again.

"Come, now, Ushman. Speak openly with me. I'm a widow.
Alone. Give me some bit of your romance."

"It's not a romance. Not anymore."

"Over? So soon?" she says, covering a hint of a smile with her glass.

He nods and walks across the room to sit in the chair adjacent to her own.

"Will you tell Farak?"

Ushman shakes his head. "It would not interest her."

"Really? I would bet that—"

"She has divorced me. There is a new husband. And child. They've emigrated. To Istanbul." Ushman can feel the perspiration forming around his hairline. He does not look at her.

Mrs. Roberts places her drink back on the table. One of her hands fiddles with the beads around her neck. "Good God, Ushman. I didn't think your country allowed things like that."

"If I had protested, they would not have. If her father had been alive, he might have stopped her. Or worse. But I do not believe in enforced marriage. Once she abandoned me in her heart, it mattered little whether we were married or not."

"When did this happen? How long have you known?" She is insulted.

"She had the baby last month. But it was this summer that I found out it was over. She told me it was over."

Mrs. Roberts is quiet for a moment. "That day," she whispers to herself. Then, looking at Ushman she says, in a louder voice, "You didn't tell me. Why didn't you tell me?"

Ushman bows his head. "I was ashamed. That is my only excuse."

There is a long silence while she looks beyond Ushman, toward the window. Then she stands, walking to the tree to rearrange a bow on one of the branches. "You are much more evolved than many American men. To let her go, I mean."

Ushman shakes his head. "I had little choice. I am thousands of miles away. Perhaps if I'd been less evolved, she would have felt obliged to stay with me. And there have been many days I think that would be fine. Having her under obligation versus not having her at all. It is a difficult question."

"For all of us," Mrs. Roberts says under her breath. She rubs the needles of the tree between her fingers and then sits back down. "And Stella, then? She is a rebound girl." It is a statement, not a question.

"I don't know this term," Ushman says. The way she has said it, though, he understands it is not complimentary.

"A girl used to prove a point. Improve the state of your manhood."

Ushman shakes his head. "No. I would not say that. I would not. It was—"

"Don't argue about semantics, Ushman. It's over. I need no explanation. She was nobody special; simply available. It is a common phenomenon. A rebound. For women, as well."

Ushman does not argue. But in his mind, he refutes her. He cites the improbability of his romance with Stella. How utterly unexpected, unrehearsed, unconventional it had been. Perhaps he has had a rebound, as Mrs. Roberts believes. But Ushman is sure the term could only be applied to his neighborhood whore, not to Stella.

"You disagree?" she says, sitting forward. "Tell me I'm wrong. Tell me that you loved her, Ushman."

It is a dare. Ushman cannot help but smile. "Young people, perhaps, believe that love is around every corner. I am not so naïve."

"She loved you, then?"

Ushman is trying to understand. Trying to determine what story she would best like to be told.

"You had a . . . chemistry, I gather?" she raises her eyebrows.

Ushman twirls the signet ring on his pinky finger. "Yes. Unexpectedly, yes. I have not found many American women appealing."

She shifts in her chair.

"Stella was simply open to me, in a way that no other woman has been. The first time I touched her . . ." Ushman looks at Mrs. Roberts to see if he should continue. She is nodding, but looking down at her hands in her lap. Ushman has never spoken words like these aloud. Certainly never shared such intimate, personal details. But by speaking the words, he can almost re-create the joy of it. He continues. "I did not undress her. Though I desired her completely, it was as though I did not immediately need her skin. She was uncovered enough. There on the rug in my living room, with an eclipse overhead, and all her clothes on, it was electric."

Ushman can tell from her silence that he has pleased her. He clears his throat, trying to think of what next to say; how to carry on.

"Continue," she says, her voice soft but demanding.

"She loved to feel good." Ushman smiles at this memory. "There was no shame in her pleasure. When I touched her skin, it was sometimes as if our nervous systems were united and I could feel my own touch on her body. How perfect, how unyielding, how complete another's touch can be."

Mrs. Roberts leans her head back against the chair and closes her eyes. Ushman continues to speak, choosing his words carefully. He tells her everything. He even tells her about that night. The stain. The way his sweet, pale Barnard girl left her virginity in a dark spot of blood on Mrs. Roberts's Bijar. He told her about the way he'd just parked, so brazenly, by the park.

Right near a streetlight. And that it was snowing, their skin like gooseflesh nearly the whole time. And as he tells it, he relives it.

The joy. He can hear Stella's words still. *You can't leave that out of your sad stories.*

But he does not tell Mrs. Roberts the ending. Instead, he lies. Ushman does not want her to know that she achieved her sabotage. That Stella ever doubted Ushman. Instead he tells her this:

"And, finally, when she told me that she loved me, I took her face in my hands. Stroking her cheeks with my thumbs, her gray eyes clear and beautiful, I told her no. 'This is not love,' I said. 'Do not let the desire you feel now become an expectation of love. It would be a terrible thing. Forget these feelings. Someday you could be standing next to love, and if it does not feel like this, you will not recognize it. You will be disappointed. Because love is not desire. Love is sacrifice. It is mathematical, not chemical.' I kissed her one last time. That was all."

Mrs. Roberts is so still, he would think that she was sleeping but for the narrow tracks of tears glistening across her temples. Ushman sees her chest heave, but she makes no sound. For the first time, but perhaps not the last, he has finally given her what she wanted. What she thought she could never have.

Ushman looks around the room for a tissue. On the bar there is a leather dispenser. He stands, removes one, and sits again, waiting for her to open her eyes so that he may hand it to her.

She does not.

He waits, ashamed to be watching. To be sitting so close, to be witness to her pain, to have caused her to lose control. Finally, the tears run down the side of her face, partially along her jawbone, and then drip. Onto her silk blouse.

Ushman kneels, raising the tissue, hoping she senses its presence near her face. She does not. Her eyes remain closed. The tears continue to drip.

Carefully, Ushman places the tissue to her cheek. It absorbs the tears. She does not open her eyes, but she reaches her hand toward the tissue. In doing so, her hand overlaps Ushman's. She holds it tightly, without hesitation or surprise. Slowly, she guides his hand across her cheek, across her temples, across her chin. Ushman does not pull away. He remains in her service. Even as the tissue becomes wet between his fingertips. Even as her hands tremble beneath the weight of his. Even as the day's first glimpse of sunlight breaks through the clouds and casts shadows about the room, Ushman continues to move his hand across the sadness on her face.

Acknowledgments

I am endlessly grateful to my parents, who have trusted me with so much, and to my sister, who has always taken me seriously.

My enormous gratitude to the folks at the Aaron M. Priest Agency, whose professionalism is first-rate, especially Molly Friedrich, my wise, certain, and enthusiastic agent.

And to Molly Stern, my very stellar editor with whom I feel a cosmic connection, I am indebted for her subtlety, her insight, and her friendship.

I enjoyed the early support and encouragement from book clubs in both Albuquerque and Phoenix—thank you.

For their friendship in real life, I am grateful to the following: Sacha Adorno, Arlaina Tibensky, Cynthia Madansky, Julie Raynor, Meg Giles, Marianne Merola, Amy Quintero, Shelly Kennedy, Liz Groth, and Julia Heaphy-Nufer.

Finally, I thank my husband and our children for giving me so many moments of absolute joy.